The Heritage of
Hatcher Ide

BOOKS BY

BOOTH TARKINGTON

ALICE ADAMS

BEASLEY'S CHRISTMAS PARTY · BEAUTY AND THE JACOBIN

CHERRY · CLAIRE AMBLER · CONQUEST OF CANAAN

GENTLE JULIA · GROWTH

HARLEQUIN AND COLUMBINE

HIS OWN PEOPLE · IN THE ARENA

LITTLE ORVIE · LOOKING FORWARD AND OTHERS

MARY'S NECK · MIRTHFUL HAVEN

MONSIEUR BEAUCAIRE · MR. WHITE, THE RED BARN, HELL, AND BRIDEWATER

PENROD · PENROD AND SAM · THE NEW PENROD BOOK—PENROD JASHBER

PENROD: HIS COMPLETE STORY

PRESENTING LILY MARS · RAMSEY MILHOLLAND

RUMBIN GALLERIES · SEVENTEEN

SOME OLD PORTRAITS · THE BEAUTIFUL LADY

THE FASCINATING STRANGER AND OTHER STORIES

THE FLIRT · THE GENTLEMAN FROM INDIANA

THE GUEST OF QUESNAY · THE HERITAGE OF HATCHER IDE

THE LORENZO BUNCH · THE MAGNIFICENT AMBERSONS

THE MAN FROM HOME · THE MIDLANDER

THE PLUTOCRAT · THE TURMOIL

THE TWO VANREVELS · THE WORLD DOES MOVE

WANTON MALLY · WOMEN

YOUNG MRS. GREELEY

BOOTH TARKINGTON

The Heritage
of
Hatcher Ide

Doubleday, Doran and Company, Inc.

NEW YORK 1941

PRINTED AT THE *Country Life Press*, GARDEN CITY, N. Y., U. S. A.

bw

· TL745he

To
Margaret Booth Jameson

The Heritage of
Hatcher Ide

I

SCIENTIFIC DIGGING into buried towns sometimes finds previous foundations, one beneath another,
making it clear that the ancient communities had every
one in turn been overwhelmed by a newer that built
upon the ruins. As he works downward, the excavator
thus reveals clues to the history of the town's dead
periods; but a living city, as it spreads, leaves upon the
surface some vestiges of the previous stages of its life,
relics as eloquent to the interested eye as if the city were
already being dug for, which it must be in the end.

So with this American city of the great central plain,
the very location of the skyscrapers, of the Statehouse
and the Courthouse and the old "New Market Building", betokens the site of the earliest settlement. Where
stood the pioneers' straggling cabins, the store and the

blacksmith shop, here still to-day is the community's middle, and here the price of land has always been highest. Not till the last decade of the Nineteenth Century, though, did that increasing price acquire such momentum as to begin to force upward the skyscrapers and noticeably distend the city's middle, swelling it northward. A few blocks to the south the railroads crossed the town from east to west, making a South Side and a North Side; but the South Siders had to cross the tracks to reach the city's middle, where all the great business was, and they had to cross the tracks again to go home afterward, so the North Side became the affluent side.

Affluence, following broad streets northward for residence, before the Civil War, seemed to be establishing itself permanently just north of the business heart of the city. In the late 'Sixties and early 'Seventies its domain so spread that the outer boundaries of the "best residence section" were more than a mile north of the banks, the shops and the three and four story office buildings. Then were built the big brick houses, imposing and comfortable, that took throngs of workmen more than a year to finish; and the owning families settled down among old trees and new clipped lawns to be imposing and comfortable forever, like their houses.

These families were not "new rich". They were the ablest descendants of the ablest pioneers, and it was their intelligence, energy and sound thrift that had slowly built a prosperous town. They it was who had held the state for the Union throughout the Civil War; had sent forth many who came not home; had sent forth privates

and corporals who came home captains and majors; had
sent forth colonels who came home generals. Ancestrally
almost all of the families were of Revolutionary stock,
British in remote origin, with able, industrious and patri-
otic Germans second to these in number.

Good stock and strong backbones were needed, not
only to win the War but to confront the great business
collapse that came eight years later with the "Panic of
'73". That was what is now called a "Major Depression";
but the country and its citizens were sturdy then; they
knew how to bear adversity, how to meet it manfully
and to survive it by a time-proven process, the tightening of belts.

Some of the brick houses changed owners; but of the
families that moved out, and temporarily down, most
were building again before the end of the 'Seventies.
Independent, every man free to make his own way, and
doing it, they led their town back into prosperous ways,
and, through the 'Eighties and early 'Nineties, in spite
of minor depressions, steadily enlarged it. The big new
houses, like the older, were solid, imposing and comfortable; but the inhabitants of neither were given over
to luxury or to living upon their heritages. They knew
one another well; they intermarried, spread cousinships
and were indeed a caste but never a caste of snobs. As
citizens of the Republic and in their businesses and professions, and in their manners, they were democratic.
To describe them conveniently a phrase was sometimes
used, though seldom by themselves; they were called the
"best people", and, in spite of every human frailty
among them, they were.

They organized charities and built hospitals, founded associations to bring music, painting and sculpture before those of their fellow citizens who could or would enjoy such things. They entered together into literary clubs, into clubs for theatricals and dances; they believed in dignity, in refinement, in tactfulness; they believed in deference to wisdom, learning, achievement, talent, historical greatness, and to the good life. They went to church, took the children with them, willing or no; they asked the minister to dinner and were delighted with his broadmindedness when he told a story with a quoted damn in it.

They read Emerson, Carlyle, Herbert Spencer, Darwin, Matthew Arnold, John Ruskin, Thoreau, Tennyson, Robert Browning, Robert Burns and Owen Meredith; they read Shelley, Keats, Wordsworth, Tom Moore and Byron; they read Lowell, Oliver Wendell Holmes and Thomas Bailey Aldrich; they read Washington Irving, Walter Scott, Victor Hugo, Poe, Bulwer Lytton, Robert Louis Stevenson and Bret Harte; they read George Eliot, Jane Austen, Harriet Beecher Stowe, Joel Chandler Harris, Thomas Nelson Page, Lew Wallace and George W. Cable; they read Shakespeare and Goethe; they read Howells, Henry James, Mark Twain, George Meredith and Thomas Hardy; they read Tolstoi, Alphonse Daudet, Victor Cherbuliez, the elder Dumas, Balzac, Zola, Gautier and Flaubert. They read Thackeray and Dickens; most of all they read Dickens, made his people a part of their daily talk. Many of the girls wanted to be "Jane Eyre" and the children learned "declamations" from Longfellow, Whittier, William

Cullen Bryant, James Whitcomb Riley and Eugene
Field.

The painters they most admired were Raphael, Mu-
rillo, Leonardo da Vinci, Rembrandt, Sir Joshua Reyn-
olds, David, Greuze, Meissonier, Jean François Millet,
Burne-Jones, Alma Tadema and William M. Chase.
They thought Gustave Doré the greatest of all illustra-
tors; they had Landseer engravings on their walls, and
on top of their bookshelves there were usually the head
of Dante in black plaster and a small cream-colored
Venus of Milo. The composers they liked were Verdi,
Balfe, Arthur Sullivan, Schubert, Beethoven, Chopin,
Liszt, Johann Strauss, Wagner, and Stephen Foster. The
actors who filled the "standing room" semicircle were
Edwin Booth, Irving and Terry, Sarah Bernhardt, Mme.
Modjeska, Salvini and Joseph Jefferson. Thus to the arts
the "best people", leaders of the public taste, were even
then by no means indifferent; many were enthusiasts.

These ablest people of the city, the most prosperous
and the most useful in spreading prosperity to others,
were not without assailants. Sometimes it happened that
one or another of them moved into the histrionic intrica-
cies of politics, perhaps going so far as to aspire to the
governorship of the state or a curule chair in Washington; and there were campaigns, too, when the members
of the caste were stirred to favor a mayoralty or con-
gressional candidate for his probity, intelligence or general worth. Such episodes always inspired the obvious
incitements: the "best people" were hotly called "North
Side Silk Stockings!" "North Side Dudes!" "The Idle
Rich!" and later, as a reproach bitterly conveying every-

thing, simply "The Rich!" Those thus accused were seldom more than distantly aware of being made oratorical targets; when they heard that a candidate rousing a South Side meeting called them the "Purse-proud silk-hat element that exploit you" they said it was only the old game, laughed and forgot.

In this period, when still were alive a few of the "early settlers", men and women who in their youth had seen Indians on the city's site, there were already professional and business firms of the third generation, grandfathers the founders, grandsons coming in after college to begin at the beginning. Of these the most notably successful were the Linleys at the law, the Ides in real estate and the Gilpins with their rolling mill. It was Governor Linley who built the thirty-room stone-trimmed brick house on Sheridan Avenue in Eighteen sixty-six. The house was of course called palatial, which may have gratified him; but he was as old as the century and had a short occupancy, though he lived to see his grandson christened there by Bishop Hatcher, a month after the house-warming party.

Other families were as ambitious as the Linleys to have space about them at home. The Ides and the Gilpins, building at about the same time in the next block, were only a little less elaborate than the Linleys. The first and second generations of the Ides had kept their attention upon real estate, acquired a great deal of it for themselves and profitably acted as agents for others; but the third head of the family, Oliver Ide, young and commercially imaginative at the time when the country was recovering from the shock of 'Seventy-three, added a trust and investment business that presently became more important to the firm than real estate. The Ides, a broad-shouldered, strong stock, had qualifications— caution in the handling of money, especially in the handling of other people's money; they were of immaculate probity, had quiet foresightedness and a sense of honor that was a known and quoted standard for their fellow-citizens.

More, they were generous; and, when the Gilpins lost their rolling mill and their fine new house in 'Seventy-three, it was Oliver Ide who risked the better part of his own fortune to get the rolling mill back for them, though neither he nor they could put them again into their house. It had been bought by a newcomer, a jovial adventurous fat young man, Sheffley Lash, who'd built and sold a spur railroad in far west mining country, to his great advantage. Lash settled himself in the Gilpins' house, faced it with flamboyantly carved limestone, and, when he and his partner, Erdvynn, had bought the Gas Works, the Old Jamaica Wholesale Drug Company, the Bragg and Dorcy Distillery Company, and the National House (renamed Hotel Lash), visibly enjoyed being known as "the richest man in town".

The Lashes and the Erdvynns, gay young couples, had a liking for what was known as high living. They gave "champagne suppers" and drove behind docked and jingling horses; Mrs. Lash and Mrs. Erdvynn went to Paris, not to see the Mona Lisa but for clothes. The "best people" never took the Lashes and Erdvynns quite to their hearts. There existed a feeling that there was such a thing as being too fashionable and a little too rich.

The Erdvynns, with an increasing family, built the last of the substantial houses that went up in the affluent neighborhood that had then spread more than a mile north of business. This was in Eighteen ninety-five; and the city, though it grew, was physically almost spotless, for the newer expansion had been accompanied by the discovery of adjacent natural gas. Downtown and Uptown, the sky was blue; trees and foliage, clean green, flourished; snow and white linen stayed white; the air was pure, and autopsies revealed unblackened lungs.

Before the end of the century the great phase of the Growth had begun; unlimited immigration and the doubtful blessing of "industrial progress" were already creating their immensities. The last of natural gas burned blue and went out; soft coal and its heavy dust sputtered oilily into flame, instead—and the smoke began to come. There were an East Side and a West Side now, as well as a South Side; but the old North Side lost that appellation. It wasn't north enough, came to be too near the middle of the city, and year by year business took block after block of its broad streets.

Apartment houses, too, appeared here and there upon these thoroughfares; and established families, their shrubberies, lawns and peace encroached upon, were at first resentful; then, one after another, put their ground upon the market. There began a migration. New houses of stone or brick, roofed with tile or slate, were built a mile and a mile-and-a-half and even two miles north of the old North Side; but that migration didn't go far enough, for, after the turn into the Twentieth Century,

the "automotive age" was swiftly preparing its destruc-
tions.

Downtown, squeezed upward, business clustered the
skyscrapers in the smoke from themselves and from the
tall industrial chimneys that were rising on the city's
rim to the east and west and south. Everybody thought
that the cheaper the coal the better, and from all the
crowding multitudes of dwelling houses, and from the
schools, churches, hospitals, groceries, drug stores,
saloons, north, south, east and west, rolled forth the
brown-black smoke to thicken the clouds that pulsated
from skyscrapers, apartment houses, factories and
freight yards. The migration from the old North Side
continued; migration from the newer houses to the north
began, for the smoke was now upon both.

Almost abruptly the town had become a horseless
city, and, as the automobile made distances inconsequent,
new suburbs appeared. The city first swallowed its old
suburbs, then closed the gaps between itself and the new
ones. Before the Great War the Growth was giganti-
cally at work, and, after the hesitation that followed the
return of the soldiers, it resumed its enormities, uproari-
ously cheering for itself in the noise and dust and smoke
that it was making. Optimism trumpeted unceasingly
through soot-grimed horns of gold: the Growth would
go on illimitably. The National Debt was shrinking; the
people of the city, and all Americans, would be richer
and richer forever.

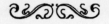

II

As early as Nineteen-hundred and five
the Aldriches, a farming family whose sons "went east
to college", had sold land to smoked-out "North Siders".
Beyond the northernmost suburb of that day, the Aldrich farm lay higher than the plain where spread the
city; and it was found that at the edges of the low
plateau, and between the trunks of old forest trees, there
was such a thing as a View. Sunrises, sunsets and even
horizons could be known again from here; and far to
the southwest in the haze could sometimes be discerned
the faint blue dome of the capitol.

Through the old forest groves ran a rough country
road, called by the Aldriches "Butternut Lane", and
along this irregular sylvan highway, landscaping began
and costly houses in new fashions displaced the thickets.

Family followed family, vacating the sooty brick houses in the region that now began to be called "downtown"; and, though farther from the city there was here and there "real country life" in bankers' farm houses, Butternut Lane finally had most of the elderly survivors of the Nineteenth Century's caste of the ablest and the greater number of their descendants. By the end of the first decade after the Great War, Butternut Lane was, in fact, the successor to the old North Side and the Twentieth Century's home of the "best people". All in all, though more loosely united and with many a newcomer among them, they still were that.

The Ides and the Linleys clung longest to Sheridan Avenue and their old North Side neighborhood. The rumble and jar of the new mechanical traffic shook their windows by day; thundered intermittently by night. Burnt coal and burnt gas were the air they breathed; and they could seldom alight at the old carriage blocks before their houses, where still stood the obsolete black cast-iron hitching posts with horses' heads. Parked cars took all the space, and in Nineteen-sixteen, when a wedding last filled the Linley house with flowers and music, influence and police were needed to let the guests arrive at the awning's entrance.

That was when the stalwart Frederic Ide married Harriet Linley. The wedding was gay, though the gayety imperfectly covered anxieties; the bridegroom and his Best Man, the bride's brother, Victor Linley, were to leave within the same week to be made into soldiers by the training camp at Plattsburg. Young Victor Linley, mild-mannered, studious, and, like all of his tribe, fastidious of mind and delicate in body, had broken the Linley line of lawyers. A Beaux Arts student of architecture in Paris, he'd also acquired expert chauffeuring by driving an ambulance, but came home for the wedding and to join his new brother-in-law in absorbing as much of the military art as they could hastily stuff into themselves.

This, though they were peaceful young men, they did because, like their forebears of 1812, they believed that their country would and should maintain American Rights and the Freedom of the Seas, and that a nation timorously obedient to the commands of a foreign State in matters involving murder has lost its independence. So the two old-fashioned young men went not only to the camp but presently afterward to fight in a war that was to become in no very long time the most misunderstood, mis-propagandized and innocently maligned conflict in the country's history. The Linley house began to brighten again with the return of Frederic Ide, sound and brown; and the tall plate-glass windows were radiant far into the smoky night when Major Victor Linley came home, not sound nor brown but with the four decorations he never wore except upon the days when he received them.

It was a lighthearted household then, with a baby in it of whom the father had caught little more than a glimpse before going to war. Frederic Ide, his happy wife and their first-born, lived with the Linleys until Nineteen-twenty, when Frederic finished the building of his spacious new house among the forest trees of Butternut Lane. After this departure the Linleys still clung to their

house, though people laughed and said their attachment
to it was absurd; asked them why they couldn't see that
the old neighborhood was doomed. Realistic irony, sup-
planting sentiment, had become the fashion, especially
among the youthful; and the Linleys were demonstrably
sentimental.

There were only four of them left. Victor's twin
brother had died at fourteen when the two had diph-
theria together; and the youngest of his three sisters,
Alice, married to an engineer, lived in Oregon. The remaining sister, Nancy, authoritatively called the "most
delightful girl of her time", a delicate slight lovely creature, was frequently sought in marriage but found life
at home too agreeable. She couldn't help comparing
other men with her father and her brother, and she had
something like a passion for the house itself, in spite of
what the Growth was doing to it.

Even after the deaths of their mother and father,
within a month of each other in Nineteen twenty-four,
Nancy and Victor, devotedly congenial, went on living
there. The next year, on a summer day, Nancy was
struck down by a truck and brought home in an ambulance. As they carried her in she made a little gesture
with her hand as though she waved a farewell to the
house. "What a dear place it's been!" she said to Victor,
and spoke never again. After that, Victor Linley went to
live at the Carlyle Club, and it was helpful that pressure
of work upon a rising architect could occupy most of his
daytime thoughts.

He had his share in the rushing expansions of the city
as it over-built itself in those booming years, not so large

a share as that of his brother-in-law, Frederic Ide. The old firm of Ide and Son had become Ide and Aldrich, a partnership of two able young men. Frederic, steady of head and hand, trustworthy in heart and judgment, was called the "brains" of the firm, and jolly big Harry Aldrich the "mixer" and "business getter". This being what is known as an "ideal combination", Ide and Aldrich rode happily atop the great wave that began to sink in bubble and foam in 'Twenty-nine.

Ide and Aldrich sank with it, but didn't drown—Frederic was too careful a swimmer. "We've all got to do what our grandfathers did after 'Seventy-three," he said, in Nineteen thirty-one, to his partner. "The city's been doing what it had done then—over-borrowing, over-buying, over-expanding, and, worst of all, over-building. That's why the building trades went down first, taking the rest of us with 'em. The stock market didn't do it; that was only the pie-crust falling down. Retrenchment, tightening the belt, everybody getting along with less, hard economies—we'll have to do it on a bigger scale than our grandfathers did; but it's the same and only answer. Business is the life of the country and business is sick; but it'll cure itself. That'll take some time and there's already great hardship. I don't doubt that before the sickness of business is over, the city will be feeding fifteen thousand people a day. That means more taxes on top of other drains; but naturally we'll do it."

They did it. The city fed more than fifteen thousand people a day; but business had troubles in addition to its sickness and didn't make a recovery. Relapse and collapse reached depths, and Frederic was mystified when the year Nineteen Thirty-three brought new bafflements instead of an overdue convalescence. His brother-in-law, Victor Linley, gave him the detached opinion of a meditative observer.

"We're all in for it," Victor said. "When business is sick, the rest of us ail, too; and business is about to have the peculiar experience of a doctoring that systematically kicks the patient in his vitals. Of course the physicians will praise themselves for their benignity."

Frederic asked him what on earth he meant.

"Politics," Victor explained. "You business men used to think it didn't much matter when the office-seekers assaulted you from down in the South Side, and it didn't; but now, with distress and bewilderment running epidemic through a population more educated and less intelligent than it used to be when it was smaller, look out for soap-boxers! When the type, politician, first evolved, Fred, merely rudimentary cunning must have made one or two of 'em try to do what their later successors have almost all done, and are still doing mostly, of course. I suspect that even in the stone-age somebody ambitiously climbed up on a rock and made a speech to all of the tribe that were idle enough to listen. 'I'm your only friend,' I think he'd shout. 'See those rascals living in better caves than yours? Hate 'em for it; they're your enemies! You are as worthy to have the good things of life as anybody else is, aren't you? It follows that those swindlers must have got the best caves by oppressing and tricking you. Make me and my brothers your chieftains and we'll drive the scoundrels out for you so that we shall *all* enjoy the best caves!' "

Frederic Ide, as simple in thought as in his honesty, was disturbed yet incredulous. "Nonsense about caves would do for those times," he said. "But business must thrive or nobody can. To make things harder for us now —why, what could be worse for everybody?"

"Everybody except the successful politician, Fred. When was practical politics ever anything but the struggle for power over people and property? The politicians have their great chance at last because they have an audience that's sorry for itself and humanly wants to blame somebody else. It's always a relief. Good politics would be pretty stupid if now it doesn't use the old technique; and of course you're the mark for both the politicians and the uplifters to shoot at. They've both got all this convenient social-and-economic type of verbiage to use, and they will—till the politician has pretty much everything and everybody under his thumb. If you business men complain that he's incompetently making rather a botch of affairs that used to be yours he'll say he's saving you from a bloody revolution. Simultaneously he'll announce to the people that you're the selfish few who want to starve the poor."

"That's a horrible prediction," Frederic Ide said. "You utter it lightly. Are you spending your time these days in becoming a philosophic humorist?"

"What else have I to do with it?" his brother-in-law asked, and wasn't answered.

Frederic couldn't develop a philosophic humor, himself; and, as the hard times didn't soften, found little humor in anything. His buoyant partner, Harry Aldrich, worked undespondently, for he was a sprightly and ever-hopeful soul; but Frederic bent to the burden. Not even his wife knew what miles of floor-pacing he did, what care shortened his sleep as he strove to pay his bills, to continue the expensive education of his three children and to keep the old firm on its feet. Ide and Son, and afterward Ide and Aldrich, had a large establishment. The depleted business couldn't carry so many people, and every dismissal in turn was an anguish to the head of the firm and a shock to his light-hearted but kindly partner.

Business got its head up a little now and then, but complained that "for the public good" it was being so "regulated", harried, drained and bedeviled by squads of new officials and their new rulings that the elevations could never be better than momentary. Nevertheless, there were miracles; the very people who bore the largest burdens contrived to widen the enlightenment of their city. Even in these worst of times, they enlarged the hospitals and the art museum; and they supported a symphony orchestra. Nobody thanked them; but public spirit and the American business man's love of his city die hard.

Youth, thrown upon the world by university and high school commencements, had as bad a time as anybody did, and here and there, following a new fashion, insisted upon something's being done for it—a natural clamor at a time when a great deal was being done for all other people whose mutual needs or desires organized them into "pressure groups" sufficiently multitudinous to interest the politicians. Political assistance for youth didn't reach many of the young people who came home from the universities to fathers formerly prosperous but now trying to pay the interest on notes and mortgages.

In better days, when the young graduate returned to the old North Side, or, later, to Butternut Lane or other well-to-do environs, he usually hadn't a problem to face and wasn't one, himself. He was taken into his father's business or perhaps an uncle's office, or a family friend or a college friend of his own might find place for him; but the Depression had changed all that. Possession of property had become an insecure occupation of it; ownership of a business meant fear and the endless compilation of dangerous reports. To practise a profession was to work for fees that mightn't be collected; but even in these hazards there was no room for the yearly multitude of young graduates. They came "out into the world" to face the long granite wall of opportunity denied. Nobody had even advice to give them, and, baffled, hurt and perplexed, some of them turned fitfully to "fascinating new ideologies"; some walked the streets, some went wild, and some mended the lawnmower and cut the grass at home. Of all the sufferers from the Depression the children of "the Rich" were not the least hard-stricken and sorely bewildered.

III

Outside the city and its denser purlieus the sky was blue and the perspective neatly outlined in the clean air of a chilly bright afternoon in mid-September, Nineteen thirty-nine, the tenth year of the Depression. Down in the old "North Side", however, no one could have been positive that the sun shone; the old "best residence section" lay ruinous in the smoke. The bad ten years had made it horrible and the surviving relics of the once imposing neighborhood grotesque. Its former character had become almost indistinguishable among dusty parking lots, "used car sales lots", vacant automobile salesrooms, half empty apartment buildings, languid filling-stations, outrageously colored dirty billboards and the close ranks of small dim houses that had long since yielded their paint to the acids of the smoke.

Here and there, like degraded old aristocrats dying on their feet among sick proletarians, a few of the big thick-walled houses still stood, and the most massively pathetic of the scattered relics, the largest one left on fallen Sheridan Avenue, loomed dimly through that afternoon's five o'clock stoking-time clouds of grime. Apparently await-ing the mercy-stroke of the wrecker, this big dirty old house, painful to the passer's eye, occasionally to his ear, and, at meal times, to his nose, now made itself so vague in its own down-blown smoke that the fly-specked sign, "Rooms", in one of the large, smeared plate-glass front windows could not be seen from a dis-tance of fifty feet. Nevertheless, a sauntering gentleman on the opposite side of Sheridan Avenue paused to gaze that way.

Something over forty and of a slight and short but symmetrical figure, he had eyes so brightly blue that the color surprised any first glance at him. The white-ness of his collar, the trimness of his black clothes, the dustlessness of his hard hat, and the glisten of the malacca walking-stick in his gray-gloved hand were no more to be expected in this neighborhood than was the clean bright-collared golden spaniel that accompanied him. What caught this rather exquisite gentleman's attention, and brought him and the spaniel to a halt, was a colloquy taking place across the street. In the marble-floored soiled vestibule outside the carved walnut front door of the shamed old house, a tallish young man was being harangued by a soiled fat woman who looked like two stuffed sacks, one upon the other, with a large unclean vegetable atop the upper and a pair of torn slippers under the lower.

The vegetable had a voice, cacklingly verbose, and the longer and louder this tireless voice talked, the more nasally reproachful and uninterruptable it became. It was accompanied by gestures with a dust-pan in the one hand and a bunch of rags in the other;—the soiled fat woman seemed to be injuredly resisting a proposal urged upon her with feeble persistence by the young man. Evidently she dramatized their relation, perhaps not without a dramatist's pleasure in effective "situation"; for the young man's brownish "country gentleman" clothes were fair provocation to evoke, for the benefit of passing traffic, a scene of wealth persecuting poverty.

An accusing phrase, "You rich people", often and loudly repeated, interested some colored women who were idling by, and a group of smutted children stopped sidewalk play to listen. The gentleman across the street leaned restfully upon his serviceable malacca stick, smiled faintly, and the golden-haired spaniel sat down. Sometimes completed sentences from the controversial vestibule reached that far: "You rich people think all the poor's got to do's break their backs night and day to keep you in money. You rich people don't 'preciate the poor's got to eat same's you rich people."

All at once the young man in the vestibule seemed to become discouraged. His shoulders drooped, and, as the fat woman retired with a gratified air behind the closing door, he turned, came gloomily down the broad steps between carved stone balustrades and gave to view a boy's face good-looking and pleasant even in disappointment. His hands were deep in his pockets, and his eyes remained downcast in melancholy till he reached the sidewalk; then he glanced up, stared and murmured, "Well, look who's here!"

He crossed the street to the blue-eyed gentleman with the spaniel, and addressed him. "What on earth are you doing here, Uncle Victor?"

"My afternoon walk for Locksie's health," the uncle replied. "We stopped to see how much you'd accomplish with Mrs. Schapp. We couldn't hope it'd be a great deal."

"No! Mrs. Schapp's the most rancid woman I ever had an argument with. You wouldn't have thought I was trying to collect the rent from her; you'd have thought I was asking her for spending money to loaf on. Told me she had her bills to pay! You've never talked to her, have you, sir?"

"Yes. I used to call there on the same mercenary errand, Hatcher. Your father's given you a job as a rent collector, has he?"

Hatcher Linley Ide, the nephew, looked despairingly at his Uncle Victor Linley. "My second day at it. Zero! Everybody said it would be hell to get out of college in Depression; but I'm just finding out. Dante missed this for his Inferno—sending a lost soul out to listen forever to why people that never paid any rent aren't going to. I'm supposed to get a percentage; but I see that was just having fun with me. I think you're all crazy!"

"Yes, we are," the uncle said placidly. "People usually confirm that discovery at about your age—newly twenty-two, isn't it, Hatcher?"

"Yes, 'newly'." The nephew looked annoyed. "I suppose that means you're going to tell me I haven't any idea how young I am. Aunt Ada Ide's been saying that ever since I bought my first pipe. When does it stop? For instance, Uncle Victor, would somebody twice your age—say somebody round eighty or so—tell you that you don't yet know how young you are?"

"I hope so, Hatcher, and I'd no more know what he meant than you do when your Aunt Ada says it to you. We're all engulfed in our ignorance of our own youngness, which probably means that man never has knowledge of himself but is only a sort of cluster, subject to chemical reactions called instincts and emotions. Let's not go into it. You were saying that all people of my age are insane. What symptom of our lunacy most frets you?"

"Why, owning so-called rental property in a section that's gone to rats and roaches! A few years from now you won't hear a human voice in it; the only sounds'll be the termites chirping to their mates at evensong."

" 'Mates', Hatcher? 'Evensong'? Then love and poetry will still be found among the ruins, you feel?"

Hatcher made an indignant gesture. "This region's an eyesore, and I'd hate to tell you how much of it's my father's own property—his mortgaged very own! He owns whole half blocks of run-down houses, a third of 'em owing rent and the other two-thirds empty."

"Yes, Hatcher. Your Grandfather Ide was a great believer in real estate for income. It's why Ide and Aldrich still have a Real Estate Department."

"Real Estate Department?" the nephew echoed.

"Looks more like a Trash Department to me! If they'd give me some used plumbing and enough fresh paint, though, I'd rent some of Father's vacant houses to a class of tenants that'd pay."

"The smoke hasn't much respect for fresh paint, Hatcher."

"I know, I know!" Hatcher said. "You'd have to keep painting. Fresh every hour. I have an idea, though. There's a color—a kind of grayish putty color I'd use with a gray apple-green trim, and I'll bet I could—" He interrupted himself. "What's the use? Father'd say it'd only be sending good money after bad. I certainly wouldn't waste it, myself, on that house across the street. It's hopeless. It's the last place on the list they gave me for to-day and it's the worst, this old Linley house. They told me it's a stinger and that it still belongs to you, Uncle Victor."

"Yes," Mr. Linley admitted. "It's my only tangible asset—to use a legal word frivolously. I tried to collect the rent myself until I felt that I was familiar with all that Mrs. Schapp could ever tell me about everything. Then I entrusted the property to your father's firm; but don't wear yourself out pleading with Mrs. Schapp, Hatcher. She paid the first month's rent when she moved in, four years ago. Since then—fourteen dollars all in one day in a burst of generosity; but that's already long ago and won't be repeated, I feel."

"What!" Hatcher cried. "Fourteen dollars rent in four years? Why don't you put her out?"

"Mrs. Schapp? I'm only afraid she'll go without being put, Hatcher. If she does, nobody else would come in and the house'd be looted of its sturdy old plumbing, and all the windows broken in a night or two. In the meantime the taxes—"

"Taxes! You really are crazy, Uncle Victor! Why don't you tear it down and make the yard into a parking lot, or at least into just a vacant mud flat? Look how many people have done that. At least it cuts the taxes, doesn't it?"

"Somewhat, no doubt," Victor Linley said. "Your mother and I were born there, Hatcher. So were you and so was—"

"Sentimentality about a thing that looks like that! I certainly don't see it!"

"No?" Mr. Linley gazed thoughtfully across the street at the dismal mass that was his. "You were a child the last time you were inside the house, Hatcher; so perhaps you don't remember the drawing-room with the parquetry floor and the brocade paneling. Your grandmother had her piano there and used to play accompaniments to my father and his 'cello. He was born in that house, too, you know, just after your great-grandfather built it. Your father and mother were married there— a pretty wedding. I never went farther than the vestibule in my own interviews with Mrs. Schapp; I shouldn't care to pass that threshold again. The house must look pretty queer inside, now."

"Outside, too, if you ask me!" Hatcher exclaimed ruthlessly. "Trouble is you still seem to think of it as the 'old Linley house' full of dear old memories and so on, whereas the bald truth is it's only Mrs. Schapp's rooming-house cutting into your income with taxes. Ought to be blown up if that's the only way to get rid of it." He coughed, as a cloud of smoke from the cheapest grade of soft coal blew stranglingly down upon them. "Whoo! What a neighborhood! I'm dirty all over from a day in it. Let's get out of it. Going my way?"

"Yes. Pleasure. I haven't seen enough of you since you got home." Uncle and nephew began to walk north-ward together, and the golden spaniel trotted a little in advance of them. "How long's it been since we've had a walk together, Hatcher?"

"Not since the end of my sophomore year, I suppose." The nephew, a head taller than his uncle, mitigated the quick loose-limbed stride at which he usually walked, and he laughed apologetically. "Don't mind my insults about your sentimentalness, Uncle Victor. I'm in a funny condition. I've been away from home too long. I shouldn't have spent my junior vacation on that Scandi-navian cruise and I ought to've come home last June right after Commencement instead of letting a classmate drag me out to his ranch. Seems to me I've been in a kind of trance or something all through these six years away at school and college and I'm just beginning to wake up. Ever had that feeling of having been a child, or in a dream, up to a sudden change in your life? Then you seem to wake up and begin to really look round you for the first time. Damned uncomfortable; but that's how I feel. I'm just getting my eyes open—right in the middle of things I don't understand—and it seems to me that all I can do is to go after the naked truth about everything and be tough."

"Tough? Why?"

"Because everything else is, Uncle Victor. Life, I mean. Everything's changed and my generation's got to face it. We can't look upon life as a bed of roses the way your generation did. You—"

"Did we?" The inquiry was mild; but Hatcher, glancing downward sidewise at his uncle's somewhat delicately modeled figure, caught the inference. Mr. Linley walked with an almost unnoticeable limp; but the stick he carried was for use, and sometimes he became a little short of breath.

"Oh, I know," Hatcher said. "Your generation had to do the 'Over There' stuff, and of course I know about your being shot and gassed, too, sir; but, after all, that was only a tough episode. When you got back life went on being the same old bed of roses it used to be in the Gay 'Nineties and pretty much always was, in this country, up to now. Now it's turned tough. The whole world's turned tough, and you've got to be tough yourself, to deal with it. I seem to've had that bed of roses idea myself up until just two weeks ago."

"What happened then, Hatcher?"

"Why, that was when I got home. First thing that hit me was right in our house. Used to be three maids, a house-man and a cook; chauffeur in the room over the garage. All gone, except the cook and poor old Berry pretending still to be the gardener and do a little weeding round the yard. Practically a pensioner because he's too decrepit to be turned out. No house-man, no maids, no chauffeur, one car instead of three. Father takes a 'bus to his office and leaves the old rattle-box for Mother to cash-and-carry in. I'm the one and only un-carred young

business man in the whole country and I'm going to stay
that way, I foresee. I ought to've left college two years
ago and gone to work."

"Ought you, Hatcher?"

"Of course I ought! Look where things have got to—
everything run down, and Mother and Father breaking
their necks to keep Janey in Smith and little Frances
as a day pupil at the Garden School here. Me, I'd always
expected to go into Ide and Aldrich, of course; so I asked
Father when he wanted me to begin. Damn! For a while
he couldn't speak at all."

"Yes," Uncle Victor murmured. "We have those embarrassments nowadays."

"Embarrassments! That what you call 'em? Father
finally explained, and I got the picture: Ide and Aldrich!
—Ide and Aldrich, the oldest and best—Ide and Aldrich
so shot to pieces they haven't got room for the son of the
head of the firm to come in as even an office boy. In the
Real Estate Department they've let everybody go except
the two oldest clerks and that old-maid stenographer
that's been with 'em ever since before even Father was
born. Got to keep them for charity. Chance for me?
Not very! Nor anywhere else. There's Father—one of
the most important men in town and not an idea in his
head how to place me or do anything with me. So here
I am, all educated up and home again to be a problem
child on my parents' hands. What do I do?"

"Apparently you solve the problem yourself, like a
little man, Hatcher. Almost instantly you become Ide
and Aldrich's rent collector."

"Oh, I do, do I?" Hatcher laughed ruefully. "They let
one of the withered clerks, old Mr. Barley, collect the

few still partly collectible rents. Father saw that if I didn't do something I'd probably just decay; so he brightened all up and faked this job for me—trying to collect back rents they've completely given up hoping for, only he didn't put it that way. He thinks it kids me into feeling I'm really working because I'm anyhow walking all day, and breathing smoke and getting filthy inside and out. Good of him; but of course it's just a joke. You don't need a janitor down at your own office, Uncle Victor, do you?"

"My own office?" Uncle Victor inquired. "Where's that?"

"What!" Hatcher half-shouted, and, open-mouthed, he looked both alarmed and indignant. "You're supposed to be an architect, aren't you? You don't mean you've given it up?"

"No; it gave me up. Architecture's rather closely connected with building, you know."

"Not even an office any more!" the staring Hatcher exclaimed. "What in hell do you do?"

"Well—in the afternoon I take a walk with Locksie."

"Is that all? My Cripes!"

"No, Hatcher; he's an absorbing dog," Mr. Linley said. "A gentle modern creature; but nothing's more interesting than to see the punctilio with which he observes the inherited etiquette of his ancestors. A civilized dog; yet every day I learn from him something new about primordial life. Given to me as a pup by a lady who'd named him Goldilocks. I didn't wish to seem critical of her; yet I felt I had to help him out of that, so I call him Locksie. She doesn't mind."

"Now isn't that lucky!" The astounded nephew became satirical. "I must say you take things rather calmly, Uncle Victor. Here's the whole other side of the globe gone to war and this whole side of it gone to pot and you've lost your own profession, even your office; but all that worries you is—" He paused, wondering why his uncle had halted beside a gate in a low iron fence. They had come some distance from the painful Linley house and had reached a less completely dilapidated part of the street. Behind the iron fence was a short space of smoky grass cut through by a cement path that led from the gate to the veranda steps of a narrow brick house. The place was dull, sooty and shabby between a red-painted grocery and a filling station. "What interests you here, Uncle Victor?"

"I live here."

"What?"

"Very comfortable," Mr. Linley said. "The landlady lets me bathe Locksie in the cellar twice a week. Food always digestible and by no means always bad. The other boarders interest me warmly—like a good play. They're all richly what we call 'characters' and most likeable. For instance, there's a steam-fitter's assistant who's become a Buddhist and—"

"Well, I'll be damned!" Hatcher said. "I thought you lived at the Carlyle Club."

"Not now," his Uncle Victor informed him gently. "The Club's gone, too, you see."

"I'm damned!"

"Won't you come in?"

"Thanks," Hatcher said. "I've got to keep walking. Good-by, Uncle Victor!"

IV

Young hatcher ide, released from the slower pace of his uncle and swinging forward at his own natural stride, groped among his emotions, supposing them to be thoughts. "Some jolt!" he murmured, alluding to his interior reception of the fall of his elegant Uncle Victor all the way to a second-rate boarding-house. Uncle Victor's sangfroid also disturbed the nephew; the recent exhibition of indifference to calamity went beyond the human. Pleased because he was allowed to wash his dog twice a week in the cellar! Golly!

Were these older people already calloused to the perishing of the order to which they belonged, or was it a fact that after you're thirty it doesn't much matter to you—or to anyone else—what happens to you? Why had they let everything go to pot? Just dumbness? Well, it

was time for the new generation to get tough, take hold
and do something different.

The only question was how to take hold of what.

He walked unanswering miles northward into air that
smelt as much of burned oil as it did of soft coal smoke.
Then, arrived in a residential fringe, he followed an
ascending thoroughfare to the top of a suburban ridge,
and turned into a shrubberied street labeled upon a corner lamp post, Butternut Lane. The "lane" was hard-
surfaced between cement curbstones; but years of skilled
landscaping had produced cloistral privacies for the
elaborate houses on both sides of what was now a suburban avenue. Every prospect that met the eye spoke
of success ensconced in a luxuriously dignified seclusion.
Hatcher Ide, turning into Butternut Lane as sunset
edged with gilt the silver trunks of noble beech trees and
glazed with rose the autumnal lawns and gardens,
thought this look of things so false as to be sardonic.
Judging by all he'd heard in the two weeks he'd been
at home, he'd come to the conclusion that everybody in
the place was just about broke.

Some of the bankrupts evidently didn't realize their
condition. From between the stone pillars of a driveway
gate there rolled forth a darkly glistening automobile
with white-sided wheels. In the driver's seat, exposed to
the weather, sat a proud-eyed colored man in livery, and
behind him, enclosed but visible through clear glass, a
pretty woman all gray fur and gray velvet smiled out
upon a world she seemed to like. She saw Hatcher,
leaned forward, gayly threw him a kiss; and he responded by fumbling at a hat he wasn't accustomed to

wearing but had donned as appropriate to rent-collecting down in the city.

Fifty feet farther on, he stopped and looked over the top of the hedge that bordered the cement sidewalk. At the other end of a green lawn, near a house outwardly inspired by Mount Vernon, a girl in a pale green shirt and bright blue trousers was raking red and yellow leaves into a pile under one of the tall old trees. She had a neat profile and fair hair; her figure looked able, and she used the rake with a sustained vigor.

She saw Hatcher, waved to him with a high-flung hand, dropped the rake, ran lightly over the grass, and showed him across the top of the hedge a face much like that of the comely lady who'd just thrown a kiss to him. "Any luck?" she asked. "How was the job to-day?"

"Same's yesterday," Hatcher said. "Nothing plus nothing. They're all bums. Me, I'm upside down. Just saw your mother slicking out in her big town-car. Doesn't anything ever worry her, Dorcy?"

"No; especially not when she's going after Harry." Dorcy smiled indulgently. She was the only child of the junior partner in the firm of Ide and Aldrich; and, like almost everybody else, she affectionately called him "Harry". He was that sort of father. "When Mother drives down to the office to bring him home, herself, why, for an hour beforehand you'd think she's going to a party. The Romeo and Juliet stuff's lasted so long with them it sometimes makes me think their generation did themselves a good turn tangling escapist romance

with sex. Anything except rent-collecting get you upside down, Hatch?"

"Uncle Victor Linley," Hatcher said. "Ran into him
down in the dirtiest smoke where everybody used to
live—nothing but a slum—and I found out he lives in it
now, himself. Know what he's doing? Handmaid to a
cocker spaniel. Some woman named it Goldilocks and
gave it to him; so he changed its name to Locksie. Helps
the dog, he told me, and's so tactful it didn't offend
the giver. His mind seemed to dwell on things like that.
Is Uncle Victor screwy or am I?"

Dorcy neglected the question. "He's the most fascinating man in town," she said. "Some woman's given
him a spaniel, has she? There are others who'd like to
give him a lot more than that. I simply worship his blue
eyes! There's something so mysterious and gripping
about that type of slight, delicate-looking men with brilliant minds that have so much to offer and—"

"Listen!" Her enthusiasm seemed to stupefy Hatcher.
"You're talking about my uncle, not me! Have you any
idea of his age? At that, though, he doesn't seem to
realize any more than a child what's happened to him.
He didn't, even when I talked to him about the kind
of world his generation's let us in for. You don't seem
to appreciate that, yourself. Likely enough it's because
of the way your family somehow manage to go on living. Of course you can still do it because your father
hasn't got my father's expenses—three children to keep
in school and college at the same time, for instance. Take
me: right up to when I got home I was spending as if
I were on the top of the wave—and there's Aunt Ada.

Your father hasn't any expensive old-maid sister to support, or old servant pensioners. Dorcy, you don't seem to realize—"

"Don't I?" Dorcy said. "Because I only rake leaves when the gardener has too much to do, I haven't got a social conscience? You think because Father and Mother go on having themselves a big time I'm content to be a parasite? Girls aren't like that these days—not any more than you are, yourself."

"Yes, I know." Hatcher was teasingly skeptical. "You all want to be secretaries or Hollywood, or female broadcasting wagsters, or both kinds of models or—"

"We do not! Look at my best friend, Mary Gilpin, downtown and on her feet about ten hours a day. Look at Amy Murray. Amy's been to department stores and everywhere for weeks and weeks trying to land a job, and if she hadn't told me that wherever she went too many girls had been there before her, I'd have been doing the same thing. If it weren't for that, I'd probably be working harder than you do, Hatcher Linley Ide!"

"Dorcy! You really feel that way? I ask your pardon." Hatcher looked at her solemnly over the top of the hedge. "Well, what's it all mean? It means that youth hasn't got anything but its own unrest and that's something that leads to chaos. Well, what do we do about it? That's up to the individual. Well, you and I are individuals, aren't we? So what ought you and I to do?"

"I've been listening to broadcasts like that, too, Hatch; but I haven't any idea."

"I have," Hatcher said, a little irritated. "It's my own, thanks, and I just thought of it. We can't find out what we ought to do till we first find where any openings are. The simple God's truth, Dorcy, is that we ought to take a car and a trailer, and go up and down this country—I mean all over it, east and west and north and south—with a fine-tooth comb and study what's the matter with it and what we can do to remedy it and find ourselves an opening for a better way of living and—"

"Who?" Dorcy interrupted. "Who ought to take a car and a trailer and—"

"You and I," he said absently. "I suppose we could get married first and—"

"Hatcher Ide!" Dorcy's color heightened; but she laughed amiably. "Isn't your head just a bit in the clouds? If you don't mind being reminded, we're not even engaged."

"Oh, well," he said, "we've always expected to be. I'm serious, Dorcy; we ought to get a car and a trailer and—"

"What with?" she asked. "I made Father cut my allowance in half the other day, and what you're earning —I mean what you're *not* earning—"

"No." He sighed. "Of course it's impractical. Every really sensible idea always is impractical. For instance, my father's got any quantity of vacant old brick and frame houses with the plumbing looted out of 'em and all blacked up with smoke; but if he'd let me buy second-hand plumbing and paint the outside a dark putty-color that wouldn't much show smoke smears and with an attractive apple-green trim, and the inside walls painted—" He stopped abruptly; then added, "Impractical again, of course!"

"But why, Hatch? Why'n't you go ahead and do it?"

Hatcher laughed. "I put it up to one of the old re-
tainers at the office, Mr. Barley, and he looked scared.
Told me I'd better not suggest my father's sinking any
more money in those properties. Said there was no use
painting anything down in the heavy smoke and everybody quit doing it long ago. Maybe he's right. Well—
most likely what'll really happen, we'll get into this war
against Hitler, ourselves, or, if we don't, some day I'll
stop letting Father kid me into pretending I'm a rent
collector and thumb my way to Canada and join up with
some regiment there. You'd probably go, yourself, as a
nurse or something."

"Yes, I wouldn't like to be out of it if—"

"No; you wouldn't. You've got unrest too, of course,
Dorcy. Well—" He sighed again; then was annoyed by
a thunderous rumbling upon the street pavement behind
him. He turned his head and saw a procession of four
ponderous closed trucks moving slowly upon Butternut
Lane. "What's all this?" he asked. "Somebody in our
neighborhood selling their furniture and moving out?"

"No; it's furniture moving in," Dorcy informed him.
"It's from Paris."

"Where's it going?"

"Into the Lash place, next door. The woman that
owns the Lash place is coming home from France on account of the war. She was the Miss Sarah Lash that lived
there when we were little; but I don't remember her.
Do you?"

"Me? Not any."

"She's rich," Dorcy said. "The Lashes always were, of

course, and she's the only one left, so she's got it all. She's been married twice; she's a double grass-widow. Her name's Mrs. Florian, Mother told me; but from the way she spoke I don't think she ever liked her much."

Hatcher wasn't interested. "Well—some old grass-widow," he said vaguely. "I've got a dollar. I'll grab the car after dinner, Dorcy, and run you in to see that jungle picture. Right?"

Dorcy stretched an arm across the hedge, gave him a pat on the shoulder. "Right!"

V

SHE RAN BACK to her rake, and he swung into his stride again; but paused as he reached the farther end of the Aldriches' hedge, because the last of the four big trucks entering the broad driveway of the "Lash place" momentarily blocked his way. The traveling warehouse passed between two tall brick pillars capped with carved stone and followed its monstrous fellows toward the long, many-gabled gray stone house that faced a lawn three hundred feet deep and thus stood impressively that far back from the street. A stooping old man had opened the tall wrought-iron gates for the trucks and was turning to follow, but saw Hatcher and stopped.

"Giants, ain't they?" he said, proud of the size of the trucks. "There's French mantelpieces and doorways in

39

'em, too, along with the furniture that's every stick of it from the Old Country. Been a contractor in there ten days now, tearing the place all up, working on plans she sent him. Yes, sir, I been employed on this place for thirty-one years now, Mr. Hatcher, and sole caretaker all the long time it's been empty; but I guess this is the biggest job I've seen yet. I certainly hope Miss Sarah'll like the way I handle things. How you feeling, Mr. Hatcher?"

"Bad," Hatcher said. "How are you, George?"

"Fine!" George laughed. "I used to say I felt bad, too, sometimes at your age, fifty years ago; but I didn't. Well, I hope everybody's well at your house. Guess I better be doing a little overseeing."

Hatcher walked on. The long hedge beside him now was taller than the Aldriches', walling everything on the other side of it in an impenetrable security from the tarnishing glance of the passer-by, and it ended at a haughty brick pillar higher than the hedge. This pillar, marking a corner of the "Lash place", Hatcher had often climbed, in earlier years, to seat himself atop the chilly scrolled stone ball above its square cap; for it marked also a corner of the smaller domain of the Ides. Beyond the pillar was an upward flourish of Lombardy poplars, then a thicket of varied shrubberies and another driveway, one into which the brooding Hatcher turned.

Hearing his name shouted behind him, he turned again, however, and went back to the sidewalk. A sandy-haired friend-since-childhood's-hour, Gilpin Murray, who lived in the house opposite, was coming across the street to greet him. " 'Lo, Hatch! How long you been home?"

"Two weeks," Hatcher said, as they shook hands heartily. "You been away, too, haven't you, Gilp?"

"Yes. Got back yesterday noon. Had a month's job on a stock farm up near Earlsville. It got auctioned off yesterday, house and all; so that's washed up. Spent most the summer job-hunting up and down the town. Pleasant walking, I don't think. Well, anyhow, we had ourselves a time at Commencement, didn't we? Seems a terrible long time ago, doesn't it? I suppose you're already started merrily in with Ide and Aldrich. Got anything for me down there?"

"Murder!" Hatcher said. "Not for me neither. They're just letting me pretend on no pay."

"Not so bad; not so bad!" Young Gilpin Murray laughed plaintively. "I'd take a job pretending for nothing any day. I don't so much mind doing nothing as I do looking like it. Early in July I had one idea. Practically super-colossal. Get the dandelion rights to all the lawns on Butternut Lane, dig 'em up for nothing and sell the greens for food; but they told me that modern spinach is all so cultivated up nobody eats the plain simple wholesome greens of our forefathers any more, so everything collapsed. There's one comfort: most of us promising Butternut Laners are in the same boat. Not all, though. You had a load o' Pinkie Wilson yet?"

"No. What's he doing?"

"Pinkie?" Gilpin spoke satirically. "Doing? Him? When'd pretty-face Pinkie Wilson ever do a damn thing but wear all the clothes, ride horses and eat half the cocktail sandwiches? Still can do on account of all that Erdvynn money; his mother was an Erdvynn. Phooey!

Do you see the change in me, Hatch? Let it be a lesson to you."

"What's your trouble?"

"It's what idleness does to you, Hatch. Up to this one month's job, me walking the streets and then sitting round just talking. You get to listening to your aunts and grandmothers even; you get to telling people whose mother was who. Yes, sir; I'm all full of genealogy and gossip. I can tell you just who had so damn much jack to start with they've still got it—like the Erdvynn money in Pinkie Wilson's family—and what must be the income tax on this Frenchified old female that's fixing to come back and live next door to you. Heard about her, haven't you? By the way, there's a chance you or I might grab, Hatch."

"Chance? What do you mean, chance?"

"My mother tells me the old thing used to be quite a pirate," Gilpin said. "Out on capture all the time—and, look, she's had two divorces, so she must expect to circulate some even yet. Well, here we are, two enterprising young fellers in what they call dire straits; so let the best man win. What would we care how old or froggified the bride just so she'd clothe and car us the way we used to be accustomed to and keep us in—"

Hatcher interrupted. "Oh, hell; talk sense, Gilp!"

"Same old Hatch!" Gilpin laughed. "Same old serious-minded scholar; won't laugh and joke and cut up about anything!" Then he looked at Hatcher with a friendly curiosity. "Going back to Pinkie Wilson, I suppose you've heard how my handsomest cousin pushed him out the gate?"

"Mary Gilpin? Did she? I thought they were all set."

"Not Mary. She got herself a job in the city library last spring, Hatch, and, after she'd made Pinkie comprehend she preferred it to him, he rather turned his affections to another quarter, as the old books used to say. That's why I'm more or less surprised to hear you haven't run across him since you got back."

"What?" Hatcher asked. "You mean the 'other quarter' is Dorcy Aldrich?"

"Yes; quite a lot. I thought you might find Pinkie sitting round in the way a good deal when you're over there, Hatch. Bore for you and Dorcy both, of course. You're supposed to be rather affianced or something, aren't you? So I thought you might object to the encumbrance."

"Me?" Hatcher laughed. "I'd look pretty objecting, wouldn't I? What business would I have being engaged to any girl in the world—with my prospects? So I'm certainly not."

"No; nor worrying about Pinkie, either," Gilpin said, laughing too. "Everybody knows that pretty boy'd be as big a laugh to Dorcy as he was to Mary or would be to anybody else. Well—I'll go back to my tasks now. I was getting Benedictine off my frazzled dinner coat when I saw you from the window. If you hear of anything that pays better, for God's sake let me know!"

"Right, and if you run into a job where there's room for two—"

"Right. Be seein' you, Hatch."

They separated and Hatcher turned back into the driveway. He walked thoughtfully, though he was not disturbed by his friend's information; he didn't need to be conceited in order to feel certain that Dorcy Aldrich would never find the egregious young Wilson anything but a rather easily disposable form of nuisance. There were serious things to worry about, and Gilpin's gossip was already dismissed from Hatcher's mind. The Tudorish brick and half-timbered house now before him, standing among old forest trees so tall that they shaded its roof, had an appearance slightly shabby; the slate of the roof, here and there, obviously needed repair or replacements. Hatcher Ide was home from his day's work, the second in his life, and was again wondering darkly how many such profitless days he could endure.

He opened the unlocked front door, stepped into the broad half-paneled hall, and went into the living-room. Here a wood fire burned hissingly in a carved oak chimney-breast that reached to the falsely beamed long ceiling; and a brown-haired thin little girl, Hatcher's ten-year-old sister Frances, stood staring out into the paled afterglow through the diamond-shaped panes of a bow window.

"This is getting pretty exciting, Hatch," she said, not turning.

"What is, Francine?"

"Please don't call me 'Francine' nor 'Fanny' either," the little girl said, immobile. "I know my rights, and it's 'Frances'. Hatch, from here you can see through a sort of crack in the bushes into the Lash place—and they're doing just more things over there! They've got the boards off the windows and everything's all full of people in overalls. There's a lady named Mrs. Florian com-

ing to live there; but she hasn't got any children and
can't be expected to very soon because now she hasn't
even got any husband. I asked Mother where's Mr.
Florian and she said he's a Frenchman in the French
army but got divorced from her. Mother told me she
used to know this Mrs. Florian when she lived there before she was ever married at all the first time; but I kind
of think she kind of didn't like her much. She hasn't
come yet; but I want to get a good look at her when she
does. Don't you, too, Hatch?"

"Why?" Hatcher asked absently. "Just some fat old
grass-widow. What you—"

"I asked Berry." Frances turned, regarded her brother
with grave eyes, brown like her hair and almost embar-
rassingly worshipful of him. "Berry was our gardener
even then when this Mrs. Florian lived there, and, being
a next-door gardener, he knows all about her. He even
knew her when she wasn't any older than me. Berry
didn't say she was fat then. He said her name was Sarah
and she's peculiar."

"Oh, she's peculiar, is she? How?"

"Berry didn't say. He said she went away after she got
married, before I got born, and's never been back.
Mother looked funny when I asked her about her some
more and said she didn't care to talk about her; but
maybe that time it was because Father came home sick
and she had to be too busy."

"Father came home sick?" Hatcher said. "What are
you talking about?"

"He did. He came home from the office sick about
half-past three, just when I got here from school."

Frances's large eyes, unwinking, seemed to fix themselves upon a far, far distant point, so profound were
her inward calculations. "I bet Father got sick because
this Mrs. Florian's so peculiar and's coming back to live
next door."

"What!" Hatcher laughed. "Has Father gone to bed?
Where's Mother?"

"No." Systematic, Frances took the questions in turn.
"He's kind of walking round in his room. She's upstairs
now, trying to get him to eat something, the way she
always does when anybody's sick and doesn't like food.
He won't. She—" Footsteps were heard upon the oaken
stairway outside the open double doors of the living-
room, and Frances paused; then added, "She's quit.
Father never got sick and came home before. When he
had that cold I heard him tell Mother he couldn't stay
in the house because he has to make money. He's strong
because in college if he wasn't strong how could he have
been captain of— What you want, Mother?"

Mrs. Ide came into the room. Blue-eyed, comely and
slight, like her brother Victor Linley, she lacked his
philosophical serenity and had allowed the shapely contours of her face to be altered by a host of apprehen-
sions. She smiled, however, as she answered Frances's
question. "I want you to get up to your own room and
do your home work. There's more than an hour before
dinner."

Frances gave the bow window a reluctant glance but
obediently went to the door. "Mother," she said musingly, as she went, "why don't you like Mrs. Florian? Is
it because she's coming home made Father sick?"

"You do have ideas!" Mrs. Ide laughed. "Scram, funny child!" Then, as Frances departed, the mother turned to her son. "Poor Hatch! You don't look as if you'd begun to like your new job yet."

"I don't, Mother. What's the matter with Father?"

"I don't know. He keeps insisting he's all right but says he won't come down for dinner; so of course he isn't. Oh, dear me!" Mrs. Ide sank upon the somewhat worn green upholstery of a sofa before the fire. "I've been so afraid he'd have a breakdown I—"

"Breakdown?" Hatcher was annoyed. "What are you talking about? Don't start imagining—"

"But it can't be anything physical," Harriet Ide protested. "Only a few days before you got home he let me have Dr. Loffen go over him, and the only thing wrong was that he was underweight. The long strain of these dreadful times—how many business men we've seen go down under it! I suppose it comes with a crash when it does come—anything mental."

"Mental?" Hatcher was disgusted. "Are you trying to tell me Father's out of his head?"

"No, of course not; but he's not like himself, Hatcher, and it's the first time in my life I ever knew him to come home from business in the middle of the afternoon because he wasn't well."

At this, Hatcher laughed outright. "There has to be a first time for everything, doesn't there? Seems to me you're just a wee bit out of your head, yourself, Mother."

"I hope so!" she sighed. "If you're going upstairs before dinner I wish you'd go in and see if you can't get him at least to take the broth and toast I left in his room for him."

"If he doesn't, I will," Hatcher said cheerily, and marched upstairs. Outside his father's door, with his hand extended to the bronze knob, he was startled by a sound from within. It was a groan, a brief one—but it suggested extreme nausea. Hatcher opened the door quickly. "What's the matter, Father—seasick?"

The kind of groan he'd heard led him to expect physical throes; but, to his astonishment, his father was walking up and down the large room with his hands clenched behind him. Hatcher was used to seeing him look worried; but never before had known him to be anything except self-contained and steady. He didn't seem to be either, now. Frederic Ide was a broad-shouldered tall man, not fifty, too thin of late for the once-modish clothes of Scotch wool it was his habit to wear. He'd begun to stoop, to grow gray, and his intelligent, conscientious face had lost ruddiness with every Depression year—but Hatcher had never seen him so white as now.

"Father! What's wrong? What's—"

"Nothing!" Ide stopped his pacing, unclenched his hands and used them both in the gesture of a man who passionately repels assistance. "Nothing's the matter! I felt a little ill downtown and came home; that's all. Quiet your mother down if you can—so that she'll let me alone! She—"

"But, Father, I heard you groaning!"

"No, you didn't. I tell you I'm all right. Good heavens! Can't a man have a slight indisposition for just once in his life without upsetting the whole household?

For God's sake, tell your mother to stop fretting and not send me any dinner but just let me alone! Tell her I'm not having a nervous breakdown, either."

"No, sir; of course you're not." Hatcher laughed; then had a thought, not a well-inspired one. "Father, being in the Real Estate Department, it seems as if I wouldn't get much chance to talk to you downtown, and I expect you prefer to put Ide and Aldrich's affairs behind you when you're home; but I got an idea to-day —it's a business idea and I think it's a pretty good one— so I might as well take this opportunity to place it before you. Down at the office after lunch I sprung it on that wizened old Mr. Barley because he kind of seems to be the head of my department, and he rather discouraged me and I— Well, of course I've only had two days' experience but—but—"

"What is it? What are you trying to say?"

"Well, it's this, sir. There's a kind of grayish putty-color that wouldn't show smoke much and it goes with a grayish apple-green I'd use for trim."

"What?"

"Yes, sir. I was thinking that if you'd let me get all those vacant rental properties of yours down round Sheridan Avenue painted and brightened up in these two colors—"

Mr. Ide struck his hands together. "Do you want to do it to-night?"

"No, sir."

"Then let me alone!"

Hatcher, a little startled, had another thought.

"Father, did anything at the office send you into a tail-spin? Are you worrying worse over business?"

"No!" Ide shouted, with a vehemence his son had never heard from him. "Yes! I always am. Who isn't? That's not what's the matter with me, I tell you. I just want a little quiet, for God's sake, and to be spared the sight of food." He pointed to a tray of broth and toast upon a table. "Take those things out with you, will you, please!"

"Yes, sir; if you're sure you're all right—"

"Certainly! Please, please!" The gesture toward the door was one of entreaty.

VI

Hatcher took the tray and went out, carrying it with him to his own room, where, being young and not apprehensive about his appetite for dinner, he kept his word. Of course everything was really all right, he thought, finishing the broth and toast. He didn't happen to remember ever hearing his self-contained father say "for God's sake" before, and certainly he'd never seen him use such gestures; but he'd be all right to-morrow, of course.

The son talked soothingly to his mother at dinner, and afterward, forgetting the cares of the day and all other cares, went forth gayly and took Dorcy to the jungle picture. On the way home they talked about how much it would cost them to get to Africa on a freighter, and, when they reached Butternut Lane, Hatcher left the

car in the Aldriches' driveway and went into the house
with Dorcy. As they opened the front door they heard
the sound of an uproarious piano.

"It's Harry," Dorcy said, and laughed. "They had a
cocktail party here and then went out to dinner somewhere, and after that they were going to a meeting to
raise money for the Boys' Club; but now they're back
and he's playing swing at Mother because she pretends
to hate it. They do have the biggest times together!"

Mrs. Aldrich, even more piquantly pretty in a blue
and gold evening dress than she'd been in her gray furs
and velvet in the afternoon, appeared in the double
doorway that led from the room where resounded the
music. She carried a clinking amber glass in her hand,
and, her sweet eyes sparkling, she laughed happily.
"Come in, you children," she said. "Help me to stop
him. I absolutely can't do a thing with him to-night!"

They did as she asked, and Dorcy, running forward,
threw her arms about the big rubicund blond man who
sat thumping the piano. He was improvising, singing in
a hoarse jolly voice as he played, and he tried to go on
despite Dorcy's arms about his neck. "Boops-a-daisy!
I'm half crazy! Take it aisy!" he sang; then protested,
"Stop it, Dorcy. Ouch! You'll spill my grog." He shook
her off, drank sputteringly from a freshly filled glass
that he lifted from beside him on the piano bench; then
swung himself round and greeted Hatcher shoutingly.
"Sit down, Bo! That's right; sit down. How's the collecting for our grand old firm getting on, laddie boy?
Don't tell me; don't tell me! I'd offer you a highball; but
the guid wifie here always says you're still too young,

Hatch." He let Dorcy push him to the end of the bench
so that she could sit beside him; then he slapped her
loudly on the back. "How's tricks, baby?"

Dorcy slapped his shoulder heartily, in return. "How
went the Boys' Club, Harry? Raise any money for it?"

"Bet your neck we did, baby! Why for have I been
carrying a subscription list around everywhere I went
these last two months? Anybody wants to do business
with me, 'All right,' says I, 'but first: What do I put
your name down for to keep poor kids off the streets
nights even if it has to be only a dollar?' Then here's
my only born child asks me if we raised any money?
Shame!"

Dorcy looked at him with fondest pride. "Nobody
but you could have kept the Boys' Club alive through
these tough times. Know what a good guy this guy is,
Hatch? Fourth of July he and Mother took a hundred
of those kids out to a camp on Silver Creek—kept 'em
there a week; yes, and stayed there with 'em, themselves.
Harry played a tin piano to 'em and went on hikes with
'em, all bit up with chiggers and mosquitoes till he
looked like a raspberry patch. Heat of the summer, and
look how fat poor Harry is, too! Hurrah for Harry!"

She slapped his shoulder again, just as he drank, so that
he choked. "Stop it!" he said, stooped and set his glass
upon the floor. "I'm fat; but I've got human shoulders,
haven't I? Whenever you flatter me up a little, you always seem to think you have to hit me, too. You're so
muscular I should think the boys'd hate you."

Uproarious, Dorcy slapped him again. "Hurrah for
you, Harry! You're the cats!"

"Yes!" he shouted, jumped up, jerked her up with him, clasped her about the waist and began to dance with her, singing to an improvised tune, "Hurrah, hurrah for me! I'm the cats; the cat's whiskers, the cat's ankles, the cat's uncles and even her tail! I'm all the cats, by glory; that's why I never fail!"

Mrs. Aldrich, delighted, made burlesque gestures of helplessness. "Such a man!" she cried to Hatcher. "He's been like this for hours!" She affected an arch jealousy. "Oh, I know why you're so excited, Harry Aldrich! It's because that black-haired siren's coming back next door after all these years and you think you can dazzle her into having one of her affairs of passion with you!"

Harry Aldrich dropped upon the piano bench, pulled Dorcy down beside him, lifted his glass, drank hastily; then bellowed with laughter. "Discovered! Little bright eyes knows my secret. That's a honey! Hatch, my wife's on to me. Sarah Lash Florian! Her and me—oh, my soul!"

He protracted his merriment; and Hatcher's thoughts, following involuntarily one of the myriad trails with which memory crosshatches the human mind, returned momentarily to an inconsequential scene of some hours earlier. This was of his solemn little sister Frances in the bow window and of her absurd small voice announcing her infantile conclusion: "I bet Father got sick because this Mrs. Florian's so peculiar and's coming back to live next door." Frances's nonsense was no more significant than Mrs. Aldrich's; the effect upon Hatcher was only to remind him of his father.

"By the way, sir," he said, "Father wouldn't tell us what was the matter with him when he got sick down at the office this afternoon and came home. Before he left did he say anything to you about how he felt or what was wrong with him?" Mrs. Aldrich and Dorcy instantly made outcries of sympathy; but Hatcher assured them that nothing serious was in question and began to repeat his inquiry. "Sir, did Father say whether he'd eaten anything that disagreed with him or—"

"Why—no," Harry Aldrich said. "I don't think so." He seemed to be trying to remember. "No, I don't think your father went into any details, Hatch. I believe I recall he just mentioned that he felt a little under the weather and thought he'd better go home and lie down a while. No, I'm pretty sure he didn't say. Get off this bench, baby; your mother wants me to play Oompta-Zing."

He renewed his performance upon the piano, while his wife and Dorcy, feigning anguish, tried vainly to dislodge him from the bench. Hatcher was only vaguely aware of this fond scuffle and of the resounding wires. Harry Aldrich's tone had been casual and reassuring; but for no clear reason it evoked imaginings that had slowly been forming themselves under the surface of Hatcher's mind ever since his odd talk with his father before dinner. Harry was one of the friendliest, most sympathetic souls in the world: Was his apparent lack of anxiety assumed out of consideration for his partner's son and with the wish not to alarm him? After all, it must have needed some ailment beyond the ordinary to take that partner home in the middle of the afternoon for the first time in his life; and surely Harry realized this. All at once a feeling that something might be pretty wrong at home came upon Hatcher; he rose to go, and, in spite of reproaches from Dorcy, and Harry Aldrich's protest that the evening was just beginning, got himself out rather abruptly.

At home, after he'd put the shabby car in the empty-looking big garage behind the house, his mother met him at the front door. "Be very quiet, dear," she said. "He hasn't eaten anything; but finally he consented to try those insomnia pills Dr. Loffen gave me after my operation, and took two. For quite a while I could hear his bed creaking with his tossing about; but now it doesn't any more, so I do hope he's asleep."

Hatcher looked at her earnestly. "Did you get him to tell you what was wrong?"

"No, not a thing. He's never had anything but colds before and I don't know how to handle him. When he'd look at me, insisting he only needed to be let alone, his face was just pitiful. It's so strange! Go up quietly, dear."

Hatcher, increasingly disturbed, went upstairs on tip-toe and, as noiselessly, into his own room. He undressed, turned out the light, and, in his pajamas, stepped to his door, opened it and listened. From his father's room, across the hall, he heard no sound and the whole place was still; but to his ears there came from the distance a faintish clatter of busy thumpings. Somewhere in the night, apparently, a lot of idiots had suddenly decided to build a house. He closed the door softly, went to the open window near his bed and heard the hammering more distinctly.

Outside, the big old trees had already shed leaves profusely in high winds and premature frosts, and, between angular half-bare black branches, he saw rows of gleaming oblongs, the windows of the long stone house next door all alight. The noise of the hammers came from there. Mrs. Florian would be home so soon, then, that night-shifts of workmen were needed. Lighted windows in that house were as unprecedented as his father's untimely coming home from business—perhaps because of some mental shock. Two thoughts now seemed to collide in young Hatcher Ide's mind almost as spontaneously as, hours earlier, the still younger fancies of his little sister Frances had put together the two unexpected things that had happened.

Hatcher remembered the strange groan. Was it fantastic to wonder if his father had gagged with nausea—nausea not physical—because Mrs. Florian was coming home? For heaven's sake, then, who and what was this Mrs. Florian—this twice-married Sarah Lash? Hatcher couldn't remember her at all; a boy's mind easily erases an adult absentee. His mother, next-door neighbor to this Sarah Lash, hadn't liked her; and Mrs. Aldrich, next-door neighbor on the other side, laughed about her, alluded derisively to "affairs of passion". Gilpin Murray's mother, just across the street, had used the unpleasantly suggestive term "pirate". Mrs. Florian had been married twice and was now, for the second time, a divorcée. "One of her affairs of passion," Mrs. Aldrich had said. Evidently Mrs. Florian'd had quite a number of such affairs.

The blue darkness outside the window, patched in the middle distance with the rows of lemon-colored oblongs, seemed to become ominous. Night, for youth especially, is incentive to fancies that may be charming— or may be dreadful. Hatcher felt a secret somewhere. Could it be possible that one of this Sarah Lash's affairs of passion—a hidden one—when his father was younger— Hatcher almost gagged, himself; but his imaginings continued. Was this gross old grass-widow coming home to plaster the former object of one of her affairs of passion with reminders and—and some hideous form of blackmail—or what?

"That'd be a hot one for me!" he thought. "Just the finishing touch for little old Hatcher Linley Ide, B. A.!" His was a generous nature, devotedly loyal; nevertheless, it can't be denied that at twenty-two our first misgivings in the face of catastrophe—especially imagined catastrophe—are usually for ourselves. Hatcher's mental picture was of himself returned to a depleted household and no job—and, as "the finishing touch", to bear the conspicuous odium of being the son of a man held up to the city's derision by the clamorous echoes of some sexy old scandal. "Sweet!" he thought. "Wherever I go, everybody looking at me sidewise, wondering if I can take it. Grand!"

Then Hatcher thought of the face of his father—a fine face and a strong, good face, lined with the years of struggle to uphold an old business and a growing family— and a muffled laugh whispered in the darkened bedroom.

"It's a crazy world; but I must be the craziest damnfool in it!" Hatcher said.

He got into bed, and went to sleep thinking about pretty Dorcy Aldrich and about dirty old mortgaged houses freshened up with grayish putty-colored paint and a green trim.

VII

F ATHER'S all right to-day," little Frances
informed him when he came down in the morning and
found her alone at the breakfast table. "Anyhow, Hatch,
he said so and wouldn't say anything else. You're late,
Hatch. Mother said he looked terrible and she wouldn't
let him go downtown in the 'bus. She took him in the
car. Aunt Ada's quit visiting Aunt Alice Upham out
west and's getting home this morning. She sent a tele-
gram and Mother's going to meet her at the station
and told me to tell you please be sure to come home for
lunch to show Aunt Ada you're glad she's back, whether
we are or not. Mother's going to get Uncle Victor to
come to lunch, too. Mother just loves Uncle Victor. So
do I. Mother had a letter from Janey that says she's
crazy over trickonometry and old Berry's got such a

cold he can't rake up the leaves and we mustn't any of us go near him or we'll catch it; but he told me before I came indoors to breakfast that Mrs. Florian's got two Great Danes. They came in boxes big as street-cars and old George's got 'em locked up in the garage over there. There's fifty cents under your plate. Mother left it so you'd have 'bus fare and be sure and come home to lunch. G'by!"

She danced out of the brown-paneled room, emitted slender trillings in the hall, as she set forth for school; and her brother, having somewhat grimly taken the silver coin from under his plate, thanked the elderly, rather infirm colored cook for bringing him sustenance, ate it hurriedly and departed to business.

Neither his father nor the jovial Harry was in the offices of Ide and Aldrich when he arrived. Mr. Barley, withered clerk, gave him a fresh list of delinquent tenants, explaining apologetically that most of them were colored and skilled in the art of postponement. Hatcher found them so indeed, as he tramped the smoke-fogged streets and alleys; but he had one success. Just before noon he collected three dollars and fifty cents on an account totaling eighty-five dollars. Thus he had something to show for his work when he reached home for lunch. He exhibited the money to a brightly blue-eyed handsome slight gentleman of forty or so and a tall, elegant melancholy lady of similar age, whom he found in the living-room. The tall lady was his Aunt Ada, his father's sister, who'd unfortunately had to live with the Ides ever since the financial collapse of Nineteen thirty-three obliterated two-thirds of her income. Hatcher kissed her jaw dutifully, inquired after his Aunt Alice whom she'd been visiting; then brought forth three unappetizing dollar bills, four dimes and two nickels.

"Beginning to pour in on me!" he said. "Ide and Aldrich get three dollars and fifteen cents and I duly receive my ten per cent commission—thirty-five cents for two days and a half's work as a bad-rent collector. Nothing like beginning the good old career in a big way. Did Mother say if Father's coming home for lunch, Aunt Ada?"

"No; she said he told her he had too much to do to-day. I suppose it's a good sign, his being so busy."

"I wonder!" Hatcher said, and sat down sprawlingly. "For instance, if anybody saw me downtown, tearing from hovel to hovel, they'd think I was as busy as a flea on a strip-tease gal; but neither would be a good sign."

"Hatcher!" Miss Ide seemed to flinch.

"Well, there *are* such things," her nephew said stubbornly. "I know your generation didn't mention 'em, of course. More or less hypocritical of you, wasn't it?" He turned to the blue-eyed gentleman. "You're willing to admit that now, aren't you, Uncle Victor?"

"No; I'm afraid we mentioned everything." Mr. Linley looked vaguely reminiscent. "Your Aunt Ada and I were of the post-war 'wild young people', you see, Hatcher. I fear we were even wilder and 'franker' than your own outfit; we had more money to run wild with and it was more of a novelty then to be shocking. One of the discoveries you'll make as you grow older, Nephew, is that every new generation evolves out of its own inexperience a theory that all generations before it were 'frustrated' by the false dignity of their manners. Youth is always rather self-congratulatory about its own wildness and its consequent freedom from previous interfering hypocrisies; but don't take this thought to heart, Hatcher—your Aunt Ada and I are in no position to reprove you. Twenty years ago you mightn't have recognized either of us."

Hatcher laughed. "I would you, if you talked as much like a book then as you do now, Uncle Victor. Did you?"

"I don't know, Hatcher. I suppose years of idleness in one's profession, with consequently increased reading and meditation, might foster pedantry of speech; but whether or not my friends and family suffered from this impediment of mine when I was at your age might depend upon the type of book of which my stiltedness reminds you."

Mr. Linley spoke, not with an air of superiority but as if Hatcher had suggested a subject upon which it might be rather interesting to hold an amiably informal session of inquiry; and the nephew was piqued. He often found himself somewhat irritated by his uncle and tempted to "get fresh" with him. Hatcher felt that he didn't comprehend what manner of man Victor Linley actually was, and wondered if anybody at any age could be so calmly detached from the "terrible realities of life" as Victor appeared to be. There was perceptible upon him, and in his manner, the kind of distinction that suggested (in Hatcher's phrase) a man with a whale of a past. Hatcher admired this; but his youngness and the contrasted skimpiness of his own past naturally aroused a slight resentment in him without his being aware of its cause. Above all, he was annoyed by Mr. Linley's placidity in the face of the crisis in public affairs at home and abroad, and the serenity with which he seemed merely to observe his own troubles as well as those of his nearest relatives.

"Type of book?" Hatcher responded tartly, the more so as he affected to feel an amused indifference. "Oh, any of those old books of the Gay 'Nineties. Did you talk that way then, sir?"

Aunt Ada crushed him. "Your uncle was born, I believe, in the year Eighteen ninety-six. Lord Macaulay is supposed to have written Latin at the age of three, and your uncle was thought a bright boy; but not that precocious." She turned to Victor. "I suppose the very young always feel that nothing much ever really happened in the world before they arrived in it, themselves."

"May I speak for you, Hatcher?" the uncle asked. "Isn't this where you should use the expression 'Oh, yeah?'—or am I wrong?"

"You am," Hatcher replied. "We don't do that any more—badly dated. Don't try to keep up with us; just be yourself." Then, feeling that after all he'd rather more than held his own against these natural antagonists, he remembered something he'd planned to ask them if he got the chance. "By the way, speaking of wildness, I hear we used to have a neighbor that belonged to your generation and made quite a name for herself in that line. Have you heard this big old place next door's been getting all opened up again while you were away, Aunt Ada?"

"I have," she replied, and her intentionally visible expression of dislike helped to make it significant that she said no more.

Hatcher knew by experience that when Aunt Ada looked like this he wouldn't get any satisfaction from her. He addressed his uncle. "What about it?" he asked. "I suppose of course you used to know this Mrs. What's-her-name when she was a Miss Lash, didn't you, Uncle Victor? From all I hear, her female contemporaries still have it in for her. How'd she go down with the boys? For instance, what do you say she's like, sir?"

At that, there took place an occurrence unexampled in Hatcher's recollections of the most imperturbable person known to him. The fact that the question about Mrs. Florian gave Mr. Linley an emotion was made plain by an involuntary physical effect. His complexion, which was evenly of an agreeable slight pallor, changed its hue so distinctly that Hatcher himself felt suddenly embarrassed.

"Oh—I beg your pardon, Uncle Victor—I—" he stammered. "I didn't know she—I mean—"

"I'm afraid I can't say what she's like," Mr. Linley said coolly. "She's not been here for some time, and people change. Locksie's followed your mother out to the kitchen; but he's supposed to have only one meal a day, in the evening. Notoriously she loves to feed everybody, and your cook, too, being colored, would be generous. If you have any influence with either of them would you mind trying to save Locksie from an indigestion?"

"I'll put him in my room while he's here," Hatcher said, and went upon the errand.

After lunch, when Uncle Victor had strolled away with the golden spaniel flickering about him, the puzzled nephew applied himself to his Aunt Ada before he returned to his unprofitable chores downtown. She'd stepped out of the front door with him and was speaking severely of old Berry's little care of the lawn. "What was the matter with Uncle Victor?" Hatcher asked, interrupting. "I mean when he got so red all over his face because I wanted to know what this Mrs. Florian's like. Look; did he get himself snarled up in one of those affairs of passion she was supposed to be always having with different men?"

"Affairs of passion?" Miss Ide was incredulous chillingly. "Victor Linley? In an affair of passion? Can you imagine it! He's a gentleman, and you might well respect him more than to think such a thing. A woman who married a Spaniard and then—"

"Spaniard, Aunt Ada? I thought he was a—"

"Her first husband was a Spaniard. Came here singing tenor in an opera troupe," Miss Ide said. "She married him almost overnight. Then she went abroad and got rid of him and married a Frenchman and—"

"You're sure Uncle Victor never was in love with her?"

"Never!" Miss Ide said sharply. "He certainly was not; but you don't have to know everything, do you? I don't wish to be critical; but hadn't you better put your mind on your work, Hatcher, and see if you can't help your poor father save this family from abject poverty? You've been home long enough to know that these are bad times, haven't you?"

"Yes; they look that way to me, thanks," Hatcher said absently, and went on his way, frowning.

He'd got at least one thing out of Aunt Ada. With younger people she was always one of these you-don't-have-to-know-everything-do-you old gals—probably because she knew so darned little herself she wanted to make it seem a treasure—but anyhow he'd wormed her into admitting that Uncle Victor hadn't blushed about Mrs. Florian because *he'd* ever had any affair of passion with her. So what? Had Uncle Victor markedly changed color in his capacity as a brother-in-law, resentful because of some old delinquency on the part of his sister's husband? Afraid that Mrs. Florian's return might bring into the light something that had lain long in darkness—something that Uncle Victor knew and probably that Harry Aldrich knew but that Hatcher's mother plainly didn't know?

Uncle Victor was one of these men who know pretty much everything about people but keep it to themselves, just on principle; and when such a man turns red there's something important in the wind. Hatcher's father was in a spot, a bad one; no doubt at all about that. He'd abruptly come home yesterday possessed by some kind of horror—a seasick kind of horror was exactly what his overheard groan had expressed. Hatcher'd finally laughed at himself last night for suspecting that Mrs. Florian's imminent return had caused the groan. Now, with his imaginings accumulatively stirred, he was almost sure that it had.

When he went to the offices of Ide and Aldrich, late in the afternoon, to turn in the day's takings, still three dollars and a half, his father again wasn't there. Both partners had been out all day—"mostly at the banks, I suppose," old Mr. Barley said tiredly, but not as if he spoke of anything unusual. Hatcher walked all the way home because he'd renewed his intention to be tough and meant to squeeze every penny; and when he arrived he found his father reading the evening paper in the small library behind the living-room. Mr. Ide replied with some impatience to the son's inquiries: yesterday's upset amounted to nothing whatever, he said; he was in his customary state of good health and would be greatly obliged if his family'd stop treating him as an invalid. He looked like one, though, Hatcher thought. Within a day and a night his father seemed what people call "changed".

. . . This was Hatcher's word for it, and Harriet Ide's word, too. "Changed!" she lamented, coming to sit with her son at the breakfast table on another morning when he'd descended late. "I never saw anything like it. All through the Depression he's at least had his appetite; but now that's gone. He didn't eat a bite this morning—just black coffee—and then running to the 'bus as if demons were after him. And can I get a word out of him about what's the matter? 'Nothing,' he keeps telling me. 'Nothing at all,' he says—as if I had no eyes. Business has been killing him all these years and now it's come to a head; I know it! Either Ide and Al-

drich are in some dreadful crisis right now or else he
sees one coming and's in despair of holding it off. I
can't understand Harry Aldrich—living the way they
do and whenever you see Harry he's as laughing and
confident and gay as ever. How does he do it?"

"Like a lot of others," Hatcher suggested. "Partners
ought to be opposite in temperament, one always up
and one mostly down. Lots of firms are like that."

"Yes, I know, Hatcher; but nobody ought to be so
'down' as your poor father is. You see what a strain he's
under, don't you, Hatcher?"

Hatcher did. He thought, too, that he himself was
under a rather sharp strain—coming home after six years
of unindustrious carefree living to find his family facing
penury and threatened by worse. Yet how could there
be a public scandal unless this passionate old Mrs. Florian
was the kind of woman to make one? She had plenty of
money: What would she gain by stirring up mud she'd
surely be messed in, herself? It looked crazy; but certainly his father was frightened and this tough world
was getting tougher. The only way to meet that was to
get tougher, yourself. Hatcher went his rounds among
the delinquent tenants, doing his best to be every day
tougher and tougher; but week after week of this endeavor didn't seem to make him tough enough. Being
tough with most of these tenants, indeed, was a waste
of histrionics, they were in such hopeless difficulties;
others were unbelievably adept in the art of promising,
some were openly seductive, and all of them out-talked
him.

One day he did get almost tough, for a few stern moments, in the marble vestibule of the ghastly old Linley house down in the thickest smoke. He'd grown to hate Mrs. Schapp, the landlady; she changed her tactics every time he called, which was, toughly, every third day. He didn't have to be told that his Uncle Victor needed the money for the four years' unpaid rent; Hatcher was determined to get it for him, and his own percentage as well. Mrs. Schapp wept touchingly. The drama ended with the collector's lending her a half-dollar (another his mother'd left under his breakfast plate) and then correctly calling himself a gypped sucker before he reached the sidewalk.

Beginning to doubt the value of toughness, and perceiving that he didn't do it well, he presently discovered that his doorstep conversations were making him sympathetically intimate with a number of the delinquents. Among them was a former house-painter who'd lost his right hand in an accident but spoke boastfully to Hatcher, one day, of what he could do with his left if anybody'd give him a chance.

"See here," the collector said instantly, "I want to get a special shade of grayish putty-color and one of grayish apple-green that won't show smoke much. Can you mix colors?"

"Can I mix colors!"

Hatcher had almost six dollars that day, immediately bought pigments and had the one-handed expert paint the front doorway and the window frames, not of his own dwelling but of the vacant one next door. The effect was beyond the best expectations.

Having returned to see it improved by a second coat

of putty-color and apple-green on the Saturday afternoon of that week, he congratulated the painter and himself, paid his last cent for labor well done; then set forth to tell Dorcy all about it. Exuberant, he gave Uncle Victor's narrow-fronted boarding-house a jocularly condescending grunt when he passed it on his northward way, and strode on buoyantly through the miles of thinning smoke to Butternut Lane.

When he came to the Aldriches' hedge he moved more slowly, for it was Dorcy's seemingly casual habit to be somewhere about the front lawn at this hour; but to-day he walked half the length of the hedge before he saw her—and then he saw her disappointedly. She came round a corner of the house, disheveled, swinging a tennis racquet and chatteringly accompanied by another girl and two boys; they'd been playing on Dorcy's court behind her mother's garden. The four young people, Butternut Lane intimates since earliest childhood, walked familiarly, and the boy beside Dorcy had his arm about her.

Hatcher didn't like that, especially because he didn't like the boy, Erdvynn Wilson. More than one unfavorable discussion of this person had taken place of late between Hatcher and his still jobless friend, Gilpin Murray, and the two were as one in finding Pinkie Wilson increasingly an incentive to left-wing radicalism. They agreed that there must be something fundamentally wrong with the capitalistic system since the bird-brained, showy Wilsons were almost the only Butternut Lane family that hadn't been at least half-shattered by the Depression. It was pretty tough, the friends thought, that the bird-brainedest of all the Wilsons, Pinkie, who'd had to leave college prematurely but not surprisingly, was allowed by our lax form of government to display himself upon the polo field while his obvious intellectual betters walked the streets unsalaried. Polo and all of Pinkie's other light activities were criminally inappropriate to the times, Hatcher and Gilpin often told each other earnestly. Moreover, girls had a habit of saying that Pinkie was "too good-looking for his own good"; and only a night or two ago Hatcher'd used almost his worst profanity when Dorcy innocently expressed this theory. Now she was cheerfully wearing Pinkie's arm round her!

She saw the hat and head bobbing along above the hedge, waved her racquet, called "Hatch! Hatch!" and ran forward. She had to run fast. "Wait! What's the matter? Wait!" she cried, and contrived to stop him just at the end of the hedge. "What's the news? How's the house-painting coming on? How'd things go to-day, Hatch?"

"All right," he said. "Better than usual. Pretty good. I'm feeling fine. Well, cherish your health, gal!"

"But, Hatch—" she called, as he moved on. "What's your hurry?"

"Me?" He laughed genially back at her over his shoulder. "Busy business man. Cherish your health, gal; cherish your health. G'by!"

VIII

He knew that she was looking hurtly after him, not understanding; and that pleased him. Then he was bitter again. Fine world, this was! Most impressive old firm in the city gone plumb stagnant— and one partner singing and laughing, and the other shot to pieces because the ghost of some long-buried wanton idiocy threatened to come to life and plaster him and his family with infamy! Then, just when there was something interesting to tell her about putty-color and green paint, here was the best girl in the world using the arm of a gilded wart like Pinkie Wilson for a sash! "What next?" Hatcher asked aloud, addressing the inquiry to sadistic destiny. "What next?"

The unpleasing answer delayed not longer than the following day.

In the morning his father and mother went to church; they returned late from Communion Service, looking gravely somewhat emotional, Hatcher thought. He spent the afternoon playing a two-ball foursome on a public course with three companions who, like himself, had to make the best of things since the lapse of family memberships in the decimated Butternut Lane Country Club. The three were congenial to Hatcher—Gilpin Murray, Gilpin's cheerful, commonsense sister Amy, and their comely tall cousin Mary Gilpin, a "grand gal" by Hatcher's definition, because she'd done her last two years of college "under her own steam", because she was now earning a salary, and most of all because she'd turned a denying back upon Pinkie Wilson. She was Dorcy Aldrich's most intimate friend, a relation of which Hatcher strongly approved; but he didn't talk of Dorcy to Mary Gilpin this afternoon, though she was his partner in the match. Glumly, he spoke only of golf.

Saving even gasoline, the four had walked all the way to the links; they returned as economically. Toward the end of their homeward trudge in the sunset, they passed the Butternut Lane Country Club gates and were just in time to see a laughing Dorcy Aldrich shooting forth beside young Mr. Wilson in his open yellow car. All of the pedestrians responded enthusiastically to Dorcy's waving hand; then Hatcher and Gilpin, walking behind the two girls, again told each other, with helpless repetitions, what they thought of Pinkie Wilson. To Hatcher it seemed that his "What next?" had been answered in full.

He was mistaken. When he reached home he found his little sister Frances on the darkening front lawn waiting for him.

"Something bad's happened," she said. "I want to tell you about it because you're my friend and the only one I can, because if I try to tell Aunt Ada anything she always says 'That'll *do!*' She isn't here anyways; she's at Vespers. Hatch, I bet it's terrible!"

"What is?" he asked crossly. "Vespers?"

"No. Hatch, Father went in Mother's room over two hours ago, and I happened to go upstairs and I could hear him talking and talking to her; but I don't know what he said because I'm too honorable to try and listen. So then after a while I went back; but the door's pretty thick and I was just walking by; but I did hear Mother sort of scream. She said, 'No, no, no, no!' She said it like she was begging him not to say something she didn't want him to. Then, when I came by the next time I heard her crying out loud, Hatch; but I couldn't tell what about. I bet somebody's dead. You don't expect it's Janey, do you, Hatch?"

"Janey? No! There was a letter from her yesterday. Are they still up there in Mother's room?"

"No. Father's in his own room and you can't hear a sound. I bet he's fixing to commit suicide! I bet—"

Hatcher shouted at her. "Shut up! You ought to be ashamed of being so silly!"

"Well, then," Frances said, "I bet he's anyways reading the Bible or something. Mother came downstairs and wouldn't let me ask her any questions and went in the lib'ary. She's there now."

Hatcher strode into the house, down the hall and into the library. Harriet Ide sat at a desk, writing names upon a long sheet of paper, and the lighted lamp beside the desk showed new tears upon her cheeks. She didn't look up, but moved so as to avert her face from her son and spoke in a low controlled voice. "If there's something you want, Hatch, I can't talk to you just now; I'm busy."

He came near her. "What are you crying about, Mother?"

"Nothing. I'm not."

"I saw you," he said. "What's worse, I know a good deal more about why you're crying than you think I do."

"What?" At this, she turned and looked at him, startled. "You say—"

"Yes, Mother; I do. I admit I don't know the details; but I'd be pretty dumb if I didn't see what's happened. Father's in a spot and it's got so bad that at last he's had to tell you because you'd find out anyhow—and pretty soon, too—if he didn't. He told you this afternoon. Well, I'm your son; I'm grown up and I've got my eyes open. I haven't accomplished much yet; but I'm going to, one way or another, and it's time a little confidence was placed in me. Mother, will you just kindly tell me what's the matter?"

"Please, Hatch!" Mrs. Ide wiped her eyes. "Frances is playing outdoors somewhere. Will you please get her in and see if she's done her home work for Monday? If she hasn't, will you—"

"No, I won't! Mother, I can see you're going to

4

stand by Father, no matter what, and I honor you for it; I think it's the goods. Well, I like Father as much as you do. I want to be loyal to him, too. I can see now what sacrifices he's made for me, to put me through school and col—"

"Hatcher!" Mrs. Ide's voice became imploring. "Will you please, please let me get on with what I'm doing? Can't you see I'm busy?"

"What at?" he asked imperiously.

"This list. I stopped the Blue Book years ago and I've got to make a list of people that must be invited to a Tea we're giving next—"

"A Tea?" Hatcher cried, aghast. "A Tea? Everything's on the way to hell and you're giving a Tea? What for?"

"For Mrs. Florian," his mother said.

"What? For whom? What? Why—"

"For Mrs. Florian. I'm trying not to leave out any old friends of the Lash family; but she's been away so long and there've been so many changes—"

"Listen!" Hatcher said. "Mother, if you're making this sacrifice—"

"Hatcher! Don't you suppose I know we can't afford it? But it has to be done and I've got to send the cards out to-morrow morning. It's for Thursday, so I haven't any time to—"

"When's she coming?"

"She came yesterday, Hatcher."

"Yesterday? She's already here!" Hatcher's voice was solemn. "Mother, I'm your son and Father's son. I want you to talk to me freely and I have the right to ask it. Are you going to or aren't you?"

"There's nothing I can tell you," she said, and looked at him piteously. "Please just let me get ahead with my list, dear."

"All right!" Hatcher drew in his breath emotionally, turned on his heel and marched out of the room. In the hall he encountered his Aunt Ada, who'd just come in. "Aunt Ada," he said dramatically, because he felt that way, "did you know that my mother is giving a Tea for Mrs. Florian on Thursday?"

"Why, no." Aunt Ada looked reflective. "I suppose we'd have to, though. After so many years somebody'd have to show her some attention; get her started again, so to speak. Naturally, it'd be we or the Aldriches."

To Hatcher, Aunt Ada seemed pretty obtuse. He went outdoors, walked vaguely about the lawn in the early dark, thinking painfully. His father's silence was at last broken; he'd thrown himself on his wife's mercy. Hatcher thought of little Frances's hearing the tragic outcry of that afternoon: "No, no, no, no!" But his mother was game; she could take it all right, for now she was going to face the world, let it file by and see her openly standing up to it with Mrs. Florian beside her. Was the Tea to be a challenge to the public or to Mrs. Florian—or to try to placate her? Mrs. Florian! Just how horrible was that woman?

He went round the corner of the house, then bore to his right, pressed among shrubberies and stood looking at a long stone mass in its great space of darkness. A few windows were lighted, and, as he looked, a varicolored illumination appeared suddenly upon the face of the night—blackly outlined scarlets, greens, yellows, blues and vermilions—a slim pointed window of stained glass in the end wall of the nearer wing. She was there. A change had come upon that house;—for the first time in his memory it seemed to be living. It contained not people but a presence, and the house itself was a part of that impending presence. Hatcher looked at the slim patch of lighted colors and had impulses as various as its glowing hues.

. . . Babies, having more in common than the rest of us, show more resemblance to one another. Later, as we pass through the "seven ages", we increasingly diverge, becoming more and more markedly individual. Thus, at twenty-two, Hatcher Ide was in some things older than his age; but in others he was younger. If need arose he could utter discourse upon Aristotle or Beowulf, or even upon what a physicist defines as Forbidden; yet because of various inexperiences personal to himself he was at times capable of ideas no more mature than those of his little sister Frances.

Where others of his age might be worldly-wise, snappy and precocious, Hatcher Ide could be infantile. He could also be acute, and, in his renewed alarm for his father, he was suddenly able to take a new view of him. In childhood carefully trained to be respectful, and afterward returning but briefly from school and college, Hatcher had never once thought of Frederic Ide as a person; he'd always viewed him as a valued sample of the class labeled "Fathers"—a sample of course excelling others in wisdom, liberality and appropriate

reticence. Now suddenly inspired, Hatcher comprehended that Frederic Ide was a man and in this capacity
had led a life of his own before a son arrived and failed
to make his acquaintance. Hatcher was at least worldly-
wise enough to be aware that nobody of much experience or reading is surprised by any revelation of follies
committed with ladies by able-minded men of better
reputation than Solomon.

Standing in the shrubberies, Frederic Ide's son then
had an interesting vision of himself in action. He'd go
decisively and immediately to his father, stand before
him and say, "Father, you've done the sporting thing in
spilling this sickening old mush of yours to Mother;
but don't let's let her in for *too* much. She oughtn't to
have to stand up in a receiving line at a Tea with that
woman; there's a better way of doing this thing. You
can see I know practically all about the whole business;
but I haven't any reproaches for you—I only want the
slate wiped clean. I'm here to help you. Father, get
out of that chair and walk right straight over to the
Lash place with me! I'm your son, and you and I'll go
in there with our heads up and show that woman whatever she thinks she's got up her sleeve, your family's
standing by you. We'll have it out with her right here
and now!"

"*Hatch! Hatcher Ide!* Hatchie!" A childish voice
called him urgently. "Where are you, Hatch? Uncle
Victor and everybody's here and everything's on the
table and Mother says if you don't come in right now
it'll all get cold. You come in, Hatcher Ide!"

"I'm coming, Frances."

He went indoors and found his mother, his father, his Aunt Ada and his Uncle Victor half through the evening meal. Both Mr. and Mrs. Ide, pallid but self-contained, proved able to discuss foreign affairs with Mr. Linley; and Hatcher, observing his father surreptitiously, felt that it would be wiser not to make any offer to join him in an out-facing call upon Mrs. Florian. The son perceived, in fact, that his parents intended to keep their trouble to themselves and that the best thing he could do was to be tactful about it. Tactful seemed to mean silent.

IX

THIS WEEK he began to have better luck with his collections and in three days brought almost a hundred dollars into the office. Old Mr. Barley said that such progress was unbelievable; and, faintly brightening, he remarked that business seemed to be picking up quite a little all over town, and indeed—maybe because of the war in Europe—improving a bit elsewhere in the country, so he heard. Moreover, he'd been to see the one-armed house-painter's doorway and window frames. Mr. Barley thought there might be something in Hatcher's idea, after all—people liked new paint and freshened up houses—and he was going to recommend to Mr. Ide that Mr. Hatcher be allowed to go just a trifle further with the experiment if it could be done very, very economically.

"Economically!" Hatcher laughed aloud. "For practically nothing I've got Mr. Floatus, the one-armed man —he's a genius—and I've been talking about it to two out-and-down tenants who can do anything when they're sober. Then I know two active widows, both of 'em colored; they're high-spirited because they want to get off Relief, and for a mere song I can put them at cleaning up and painting the insides of our houses. I've got a friend, Gilp Murray, who wants the job of scraping all the old wallpaper off the walls and patching the plaster before it's painted. He'll work for no pay whatever unless and until the houses he works on get rented. One trouble with those empty houses is you've always had 'em papered. In the smoke you need walls that'll wash."

"You're certainly very persuasive," Mr. Barley said. "If I can gain Mr. Ide's attention, I hope I can convince him we should go ahead—on a minute scale, of course, and always remembering that it's only an experiment."

Hatcher, a little chesty in spite of himself, began dreamily to foresee a day when he'd be able to purchase a pair of low-priced but workable "used cars", one for his father and one for himself; and a brief conversation overheard at home, from the large pantry between the dining-room and the kitchen, increased his pleasure. His appetite, in spite of his troubles, often reverted to what it had been during his adolescence and even earlier; he'd quietly gone to the pantry for cookies when he heard his name mentioned in the kitchen by Lora, the elderly colored cook. "Mist' Hatcher, he a hard worker, I tell you. Yes, ma'am! I hear the Boss tellin' the Madam

how Mist' Hatcher doin' fine. Yes, ma'am, now the
Boss lookin' so peakid, I prophesy Mist' Hatcher he go'
be the man of the family."

"The man of the family?" This was the voice of old
Berry, the gardener. "No, no, Lora! Mr. Hatcher's a
good boy; but so long as his father's alive the man of
the family won't be anybody else."

Little Frances spoke then, though not distinctly because she was eating. "I think Uncle Victor's the man
of the family."

"No'm," Lora said. "He nice man; but if somebody
walk over him he ain't go' make a fuss about it. No'm,
Mist' Berry, you watch what I say: Mist' Hatcher go' be
the man of the family."

Hatcher retired softly, with a handful of cookies and
a good opinion of himself. Unexpected tributes, even
from the lowly, are the most heartening.

On the next afternoon, nevertheless, it was with a
sluggish step that the young collector came home to
Butternut Lane. This had been the most successful day
of his business life, thus far; but it was the Thursday of
his mother's strange Tea for Mrs. Florian, and he approached the festival reluctantly. In the distance the
sight of lines of automobiles waiting at the curb on both
sides of the street daunted him, and, as he came nearer,
their feeble glistenings where thin last sunshine reached
them seemed lights of ill omen. He walked more and
more slowly.

Old Berry, grandiosely directing traffic along the Ides'
driveway, saw him coming and spared for him the wave
of a conspicuous, unfamiliar white glove; then called

genially, "Better hurry if you expect to get any chicken salad; this crowd's like old times!" Hatcher went round the house to the back door, passed through a tumultuous kitchen, ascended the dark rear stairway, and, with a beating heart, was in his own room.

He removed the grime of the city, and, preoccupied with troubled imaginings, refurbished himself completely. He had to turn on the light before he donned the long coat he'd last worn at a classmate's wedding in June, and after that he became aware that for some time he'd been hearing music. He listened more attentively. "Great grief!" he muttered. "Lansor's orchestra! House full of caterer's waiters and Lansor's orchestra. Well, the good old Ide family's blowing up with a bang!"

From the top of the front stairway he looked down and saw the broad hall below him almost jostlingly crowded with people more or less well known to him and of all ages over seventeen. The house must be packed, he thought. Blended smells came up to him— odors of coffee, rum-spiced punch, warm foods, clustered flowers and the synthetic scents with which many women had powdered or sprayed themselves. Thronging noises pressed upward into his ears, making one conglomerate sound of fiddlings, flutings, the shoutings of women, interspersing soprano laughter, and the animal-like fanfares of saxophones as the orchestra, previously dulcet, edged into "swing". Hatcher came down the stairs slowly, troubled and antagonistic, nevertheless not unpleasingly aware of himself as a figure of drama. The sense of crisis was strong upon him. He felt that he was at a turning point in his life, and he prepared to meet it sternly: he intended to look Mrs. Florian straight in the eye. Maybe it'd be a good idea to put his hand on his mother's shoulder first and then look Mrs. Florian straight in the eye—or would it be better to look Mrs. Florian straight in the eye first and then put his hand on his mother's shoulder?

He was looked straight in the eye, himself, before he reached the foot of the stairway. Dorcy Aldrich, pretty and in pretty clothes, and with her pretty mother, was one of a Tea-clamorous group there. Laughing with Mary Gilpin and Amy Murray, she turned her head, glanced up over her shoulder and saw Hatcher. She ascended three steps of the stairway, stopped him, grasped his elbow roughly and looked him straight in the eye. "Why so late?" she said. "You oaf, what's been eating you? Do you think I'm going to wear my blue pants out forever raking leaves and weeding from four-thirty to six every afternoon waiting for you to come by and tell me what's happened to your idea about painting those vacant houses? Show me much more of this pouting and you'll have to get somebody else to plan trailer trips with and stowing away on a freighter with and life in the African jungle with. There are a few other wishful-thinking glamor boys in this town, you know!"

"Not for you, Dorcy!" he said, making an effort to laugh tauntingly. "Go try the others, just to show me how sore you are!"

He moved down a step, meaning to leave her; but she held his arm strongly. "What have you stopped coming by for? You tell me!"

He liked this; but used a pleading tone. "I've got to go, Dorcy. Honestly. It's just been an accident. I'm working pretty hard these days, and walking all the way home it's almost a block shorter to come into Butternut Lane from town at the other end. That's why—"

"You little liar!" Dorcy said. "You're more frenzied about me than ever and you're acting up merely because Pinkie Wilson—" She stopped, seeing that she had lost his attention. "Will you listen to me! Who you looking at?"

As they stood thus upon the stairway the music came from the living-room at their left, where upon the cleared floor there was a crowded dancing. To their right were the open double doors of Mrs. Ide's large "reception-room", which likewise was crowded; Hatcher stared over moving heads and through this doorway at a face he didn't know—that of a dark-eyed, black-haired woman who was talking to his Uncle Victor Linley. She was slender, tall, had to bend her graceful head a little to look into Mr. Linley's eyes—which she seemed to be doing—and Hatcher's instant impression was of someone unusual, a person distinguishable from all others anywhere.

"Who's that?" he asked.

"It's my Ideal!" Dorcy mocked him. "Your fascinating uncle. You'd never be jealous of poor Pinkie Wilson again if you knew how my heart flutters whenever I see Mr. Victor Linley. He could have me for just a glance —and about every other gal in the house, too, darn it! I wish you'd get the dear sweet mysterious man to talk to me seriously, just for once. He's the grandest—"

"I don't mean my uncle," Hatcher said, and, as he spoke, the gaze of the dark lady beyond the doorway moved from his uncle's face, swept slightly upward and came to rest for an appreciable moment upon himself. He had a new experience. The deeply lustrous dark eyes seemed to envelop him in an intensely personal comprehension of him, and to speak to him invitingly, in a mystic language, the silent words best translatable as "You—and I." The deep and brilliant glance passed on, came back to him again, lingered briefly again, and returned to his uncle's face. "I don't mean my uncle," Hatcher repeated slowly. "Who's that girl?"

"Girl?" Dorcy asked. "What girl?"

"The one Uncle Victor's talking to."

"Girl?" Dorcy couldn't believe her ears. "Girl!"

"Who is she, Dorcy?"

"It's Mrs. Florian!"

"Why, no. I mean the one my uncle—"

"Certainly," Dorcy said. "Mr. Linley's talking to her; but don't you see she hasn't any hat and she's standing between your mother and your Aunt Ada, receiving? Idiot, it's Mrs. Florian!"

"Why, no; that can't be," he insisted. "Mrs. Florian's a—"

"Yes; so she is, Hatch. Double grass-widow and all that, though I don't deny she doesn't look it. But calling her a 'girl'— Murder! Come back to my question. If it isn't Pinkie Wilson that's the matter with you, what is it?"

"Nothing," the dazed Hatcher said. "Nothing at all."

Dorcy was left upon the stairway calling after him

hotly. "Well, darn you!" Hatcher, with a blank mind, fumblingly passed through groups in the hall, through the wide doorway, and stood staring before his mother.

He looked at her; but was only faintly aware of her and so didn't observe that she'd used rouge to-day or that her smile was a brief convulsion of the lips. She turned toward Mrs. Florian. "This is our Hatcher—the little boy next door you once wanted spanked for chasing your Siamese cat."

Hatcher might have thought the manner of this introduction outrageously ill-chosen; but only his ears, not his mind, heard it. Sarah Florian had turned her head and was looking at him for the third time.

X

HER warm dark eyes, now at close range, avowed an already increased knowledge of him and a prescience of more. "Yes. Here you are," the look implied. "Well, here am I! How much would you care to have that mean?"

There exist constitutionally flirtatious men and boys whose eyes habitually invite the ladies to adventure; but the thing is more successfully feminine. Men and boys, even to-day, are of the more gullible sex and readily fail to perceive that the ocular invitations they receive would be extended to all others of their kind within eye-reach. Hatcher's field of vision lost area, excluding everything but Mrs. Florian's lustrous eyes, the smooth shapeliness of her ageless face, and the green sparklings of emeralds clipped to her small ears. The exquisitely dressed black hair had never been cropped; she had it all, and, if her lips were touched with color not theirs, Hatcher didn't know it. She spoke, and the very quality of her slightly hushed contralto voice seemed to say the same thing that her eyes did, no matter what the words.

"Yes," Mrs. Florian said in this lovely voice, "you're Hatcher Linley Ide. Your uncle pointed you out to me as you stood on the stairway a moment ago." She gave him a warm hand with long fingers that closed about his firmly. "I think you look rather like him. Are you?"

"Me? I—" Hatcher was confused; had really nothing to say. "Do you mean am I like Uncle Victor?"

She withdrew her hand slowly and smiled. "Is he, Victor?" She didn't await an answer. "I've been at home for almost a week. When are you coming to see me, Victor? To-night?"

"Unfortunately—" Mr. Linley began; but his reply consisted of only the one word, for she stopped him.

"Oh, very!" she said sharply; then her voice was hushedly rich again. "Mr. Ide, will you be a Moses and find water for me in this wilderness?"

Making his way perforce slowly, though people were beginning to leave, Hatcher had to go to the dining-room upon the errand. When he returned he found his uncle in the act of moving away from Mrs. Florian, whose fine complexion showed a heightened color.

"Do! Do go!" Hatcher heard her say, though she spoke under her breath. "You and your excuses!" Mr. Linley, mildly preoccupied, bowed submissively and continued upon his way. She took the glass from

Hatcher and drank. "Thank you. I much prefer you to
your uncle!" Then, as she gave back the glass, she delighted and astonished him. "Don't you go away, too,"
she said hurriedly. "A lot of these people are coming
back to swarm about; but it won't be long. They're
going, and then we—"

She was interrupted and Hatcher politely pushed
aside by a group of ladies and a man or two, all insisting
that they must tell her once more how delighted they
were that she'd returned to her native habitat. Holding
the half-empty glass, Hatcher stood just outside the fluc-
tuant semicircle of backs. "And then we—" remained
excitingly with him. What fascinating promise was implied? "And then we—" what?

The exclamative people about Mrs. Florian were succeeded by others. He heard most of them calling her
"Sarah"; but "Sally" came from a few of the older
ones; and they were all noisily polite, congratulating
Butternut Lane upon having her again. He caught
glimpses of her through the orifices between bobbing
heads; once had another look from her through such an
aperture. "Good!" the look seemed to say. "You understand, you're waiting. This'll soon be over and then
we—"

Dorcy's father and mother took an almost boister-
ously hospitable leave of the returned neighbor. "Sarah!
As wonderful-looking as ever!" Hatcher heard Mrs.
Aldrich exclaiming. "Harry and I are planning a wel-
come home dinner for you, Sarah, if you'll let us."

The laughter of the rubicund Harry, always hearty,
was loud. "Yes, I'm going to make it splendiferous; but

my wife'll keep it as formal as she can—to stop me from sitting in a corner with you, Sally!" he explained. "Eleanor'll do anything to keep us apart because she's jealous of you. Been jealous of you all these years—and right she is, at that! Didn't I tell you yesterday you're a marvel? Not a line—younger than ever—handsomer than ever—I swear it!—not a pound too much, still the young Diana!" He finished by shouting "Ouch!" and roaring jovially as Mrs. Aldrich pushed him along to make way for others.

A cloud of confusion drifted out of Hatcher's mind, vanished as he stood there; and he was aware of neither its vanishing nor of its having oppressed his recent imaginings. In youth's field of imagination hobgoblin herds may graze night after night, only to be swept away in an instant by a breath, leaving but buttercups and daisies waving in the sunshine. Hatcher'd already forgotten his strange wonderings about his father and Mrs. Florian, his picturings of her as an impending presence. All of his previous thoughts about her were so magically erased by the sight of her that they didn't even seem to him preposterous; they didn't seem anything at all because they no longer had any existence. Mrs. Florian's first upward glance at him as he paused upon the stairway had annihilated everything he'd heard about her; and now he forgot everything he'd thought about her, himself.

He was unaware, too, that he still stood holding the glass from which she'd drunk and that his attentive posture could suggest to certain minds a cup-bearer to royalty or an anxious bedside nurse bearing a precious medicament. Thus his realization that several of his contemporaries were laughing at him was slow. Across the room, Dorcy Aldrich stood clutching the shoulder of an almost too good-looking blond boy, and both were in a high state of merriment, Dorcy's young cheeks being flushed with it. In the wide doorway, just behind this pair and halted in the act of leaving, Gilpin Murray, his sister Amy and his cousin Mary, had heard the laughter and perceived the cause of it. They, too, laughed freely.

Over the noise of other voices, Hatcher heard Dorcy gurglingly shouting his name, and he looked at her and young Mr. Wilson with the disapproving wonder of one who beholds the causeless jocosities of strangers. Dorcy, clinging more helplessly to Pinkie Wilson, pointed to the glass in Hatcher's hand; and Hatcher, after seeming surprised to find it there, set it down inappropriately upon the brown velvet seat of an upholstered chair beside him.

This increased the enjoyment of the young people who were watching him; in particular it seemed to carry the mirth of Dorcy and her clutched friend to an ecstasy. Hatcher stood staring inquiringly—upon which the laughter was even louder—and then Gilpin Murray, wiping his eyes, departed with his sister and his cousin. Dorcy's father and mother joined her and her handsome blond companion; and the party of four moved out into the hall. Hearty Harry Aldrich had his arm about Dorcy's mirthful friend's shoulders, and Mrs. Aldrich, too, appeared to be delighted with this young man. Somewhere in the back of Hatcher's mind was the impression that the Aldriches were rather fondly taking Pinkie Wilson home to dinner with them; that Dorcy's parents were making much of him. This seemed rather silly and in questionable taste, Hatcher thought; but he felt no strong objection. It seemed to him that poor Dorcy wasn't looking her best to-day; he'd never noticed before that her face was almost just the least bit unformed. Somehow, she seemed to look rather too pink, a little awkward—and too young.

For some time the gabble of hurried high voices had become less voluminous. Cars rolled away in steady procession from the porte-cochère beside the house, and the front door was constantly opened for the departure of unchauffeured guests, who gladly began resting their throats the instant they got them outdoors. The musicians had gone, a final group in the hall fluttered away; and all at once the scented still air of the bright quiet rooms seemed filled with the vacuous languor that comes upon a house just emptied of a throng. Hatcher perceived that Mrs. Florian was taking her leave of his father and his mother and his Aunt Ada; that she was thanking them and that his father and mother, though tired, were still valiantly hospitable.

"And then we—" Hatcher thought. He stepped forward and Mrs. Florian took his arm.

"I'm going to steal you," she said. "Your mother's told me I may. Will you mind taking me home?"

"No; not at all," he replied. "I'd rather. I mean I—I'll be delighted."

He walked with her into the hall, would have turned toward the front door but a pressure upon his arm guided him the other way. "I think my car will be under the porte-cochère, Mr. Ide. That's at the side door, isn't it?"

"Oh!" he said. "Oh, I beg your pardon!" Then he felt that this was a silly thing to have said, and began to say it again. "I beg your— I mean, is it? I mean, yes, of course the porte-cochère's outside the side door. Yes—I—" His voice seemed to run out of power; an overwhelming self-consciousness possessed him and he didn't know how to be rid of it.

Just inside the door that led to the porte-cochère a mulatto chauffeur stood holding a long cloak of dark fur. He didn't offer it to Mrs. Florian; but, after a quick side-glance at the approaching pair, handed it to Hatcher. Hatcher held it for her, put it deferentially upon her; they stepped into the lighted car and a moment later rolled in darkness out of the driveway.

"I want to show you my house," Mrs. Florian said. "It's been done over for me in a terrific hurry; but I think you'll see that it's agreeably changed."

"I wouldn't know," Hatcher said. "Maybe I was in it once or twice years ago; but I don't remember."

"It's just as well that you don't. What a dreary place it was then!—all early Twentieth Century American, largely over-stuffed satin sofas and lamps six feet high with enormous fringed shades. It always oppressed me horribly. I took the first desperate chance of escape."

Hatcher had a qualm. Hadn't Aunt Ada or somebody told him that Sarah Lash had married a Spanish tenor "almost overnight"? Already the thought hurt him. Did the "first desperate chance of escape" mean that Spaniard?

"You—" he began; then finished inadequately, "you did?"

They were in the light again, for the swift car had already brought them to her door, or at least to the foot of a flight of stone steps that led up to one of her doors. It opened, apparently of itself, as Hatcher and Mrs. Florian reached the top step; but, when they'd passed into a high and wide dim hall, he perceived that the person who had opened the door, and now closed it with care that it should make no noise, was a Philippine Islander in white. Mrs. Florian made a gesture toward a doorway at the left.

"Give me fifteen minutes," she said, and walked quickly down the hall toward a stairway.

Hatcher went into the room at the left, and, although the light was there as faint as in the hall, found himself reminded of Eighteenth Century French prints that he'd seen somewhere. A dark reflection of himself approached him in a long mirror over a narrow marble mantelpiece upon which stood a pair of two-pronged crystal candelabra wherein wax candles burned. From the high long ceiling, like floating crystalline ghosts, hung aligned three unlighted glass chandeliers; but other candles in sconces upon the walls gave the room a spotty illumination. He saw delicate needlepoint sofas, palely brocaded chairs with curved slim legs, fragile-looking tables with gilt little boxes and porcelain figurines upon them. He'd seen rooms done in the French style before —usually called "Louie Cans" by sturdy Americans—but this one, he thought, had something different about it, a finer validity. A harmonizing fadedness everywhere made him feel himself in the presence of "genuine antiques", daunting because he knew nothing about them.

Mrs. Florian naturally would have just such things as part of her background; so he was thinking when the Filipino who had admitted them came in, bringing cocktails and cigarettes. Hatcher took a cocktail and a cigarette, sat down and tried to prepare something effective to say when Mrs. Florian should return. A little gold and porcelain clock upon a marquetry and ormulu commode struck seven in a tiny silver voice. This was the dinner hour at home, and the clock didn't help him to prepare a witty word or two with which to greet her entrance. "I'm sunk because I've got to hop," was the best he thought he could do, and it didn't seem to be in the right key. He said nothing at all when she came.

Not because of men's alleged preference for black velvet did she wear this fabric; she knew that her eyes and hair suggested it, and thus she appeared to Hatcher as a woman all of finely shaped black velvet and an ineffable pearliness—this latter quality being put into his mind, without his knowing it, by the pearls with which she'd supplanted the emeralds clipped to her ears in the afternoon. Hatcher had seen handsome women in black velvet and pearls before; but, like the reproductions of French furniture he'd beheld elsewhere, they now seemed to him imitations and spurious.

An effulgence seemed to come into the room, glowing about Sarah Florian. This was a hypnotic phosphorescence produced in Hatcher's mind by the stirring grace with which she came into view and moved toward him. She did nothing, not even the crossing of a threshold, without somehow making what she did dramatic, and to

Hatcher she seemed to advance not only into the room
but into a fate predestined to march with his. He'd
planned to be tough in a tough-grown world; but he was
young, and, in a changing universe, some things don't
change.

"I should have consulted you as well as your mother,"
she said, once more enriching his hearing with the lovely
voice. "I'm keeping you to dinner with me unless you—
In America do people still say they have 'a date'?"

"I haven't." This was beyond his hoping. "If I had I'd
—I'd skip it. I wouldn't mind standing anybody up. I'd
rather."

"I think I won't take you over the house," she said.
"There's too much of it and we'll just talk, instead; but
we have time now before dinner for me to show you
just one thing. Perhaps it won't interest you much. I'd
like to see if it does." She crossed the room to an inner
door. "Will you follow me?"

"Why, certainly!" he responded, and was at once sorry
he'd said it. For some reason "Why, certainly" hadn't
sounded just right.

Keeping a little in advance of him, she led him through
a corridor, and he wished that the soles of his shoes didn't
make such a noise upon its marble floor; but unless he
went on tiptoe, which would be ridiculous, there didn't
seem to be any help for it. At the end of the corridor
was an old brown, worm-holed closed door under a
pointed stone arch. "What I'm going to show you," she
said, "I had before I escaped from this town and this
house that the foolish war's driven me back to. It's just
the same as it was before I left. I haven't changed it, be-

cause it means a part of my girlhood that can still stir wings within me."

She opened the door and they stepped into what seemed to Hatcher a small stone-walled Gothic chapel. Opposite him was the stained-glass window he'd seen flash into color one night, and before it stood something like an altar, a priedieu between lighted big candles spiked upon tall candlesticks of ancient wrought iron. Hatcher was puzzled but reverent.

"This was my oratory when I was a young girl," Mrs. Florian said. "At fifteen I became a Romanist and offered up long, long prayers here. Of course I'm a pagan now. Every sensible person is; don't you think?"

"Yes," Hatcher replied, and just stopped himself from saying "Why, certainly!" again.

"I'm a pagan," she repeated, facing the priedieu. "Only pagans can find any reality in this brief flight of a swallow's wing across the light, this little flicker of consciousness we call life." She turned her eyes to him gravely. "Being a pagan, I'm never false to myself; I'm never cowardly enough to resist my impulses. You understand that I had one the first moment I saw you, don't you?"

"An impulse about—about me? You mean you had an impulse to bring me home with you?"

"Yes—even to bring you here, to my oratory, with me. I wondered."

"You did? You wondered—"

"I wondered if you were somebody with whom I could be utterly myself."

"Well, I certainly hope so," Hatcher said. "I'm sure I—"

"We'll see," she interrupted, speaking softly. "I'm a pagan but—isn't it strange?—I'm still religious. I've never once in my life come into this place without saying a prayer. I don't know to whom or to what I pray; but I always do it. I'm afraid you'll have to let me."

Hatcher felt alarmingly clumsy. "You mean—right now?"

"Yes, I do." She smiled at him; then was grave again. Turning away from him suddenly, she advanced a long, sweeping step toward the priedieu, sank with disarming grace upon one knee before it, raised both arms high, widely apart; then slowly brought the palms of her hands together, and closed her eyes. Her shapely lips moved, and the uplifted hands, pearly in the thin still candlelight, remained poised for moments; there were rhythmic faint gleamings in the trimly waved thick black hair, and Hatcher knew that never before had he seen so beautiful a kneeling figure. He was startled but touched, too, by so much faith in his sympathetic understanding; and she was quickly upon her feet again, as gracefully as she'd sunk down.

"There!" she said, and smiled wistfully. "Does that prove what I wondered about you?"

"I certainly—I do hope so."

"No," she interrupted. "You're only thinking you've just found out how theatrical I can be!"

"I'm not," he assured her. "Indeed I'm not! I wouldn't have any such idea."

"You're sure? Then perhaps I'll tell you what I prayed." Again she seemed doubtful of him. "Americans nowadays use an expression, I believe—'putting on an act'. You're sure you don't think that's what I've just been doing for you?"

"No, no! Never! I wouldn't—"

She smiled again, and nodded, satisfied. "No, I see you don't. You do understand. You're very different from your uncle. He used to tell me that my little oratory was —was near-silk!" Her smile departed.

"Uncle Victor?" Hatcher said. "No, I'm really not a bit like him; you never can tell what he's going to say."

"No, you cannot. I found that out long ago. He doesn't seem to have changed a great deal."

"Well—" Hatcher didn't care to put in much time, just now, talking about his uncle. "You said perhaps you'd tell me what you prayed."

"Perhaps I shall. You're taller than your uncle, more an Ide than a Linley, and yet there's something about you that's like him. I thought I noticed he limps a little more than he used to."

"Yes," Hatcher said. "He got smashed up a bit in the other World War, you know."

"Yes, I know. I suppose that's still found a part of his fascination for the girls?"

" 'Girls'?" Hatcher was puzzled. "Of course they like him and make the sort of fuss over him they do over older people; but if you mean do they get gaga about him, why, of course they wouldn't on account of his age."

"I see," Mrs. Florian said. "No, of course they wouldn't—on account of his age. I suppose, though, in older circles—among faded widows and married women—"

"Oh, yes; everybody likes him."

"Naturally." She gave Hatcher a side glance and smiled again. "We won't waste any more words on him. We're more interesting, ourselves, aren't we? Do you like my little oratory?"

"I think it's great."

She looked down, then up; and laughed charmingly. "And me?"

This took his breath. "I think—I think you're the goods!" he said, and, again feeling off key, he tried to do better. "I think you're rather glorious."

"Nonsense!"

"I do!"

"Then—" She stopped laughing. "Then I'll tell you what I prayed. I prayed that I might find a new friend. Since I came home I've heard another American expression. See if I use it correctly. I prayed that I might find a new friend. 'So what?' "

"Do you mean—" he began.

"Yes, I do!"

"Oh!" Hatcher said.

They stood looking at each other then in a silence that seemed spontaneous between them and was understood by Hatcher as a ceremonial hush following the completion of an emotional compact—one that was to be effective his whole life long. This look, full of earnest promises on his part and mysteries on hers, was slowly being severed when another Philippine Islander, not he who had opened the front door, spoke from the entrance to the corridor.

"Madam serve'."

XI

Mrs. FLORIAN explained that her dining-room was a vast and lonely place still occupied by scaffolding and step-ladders; they dined in a small but rosy bower, lighted by candles and a brisk little fire. The guest, no expert, suspected that he partook of subtle foods and distinguished wines; but he wasn't able to give them much attention. He was not himself—at least not as he'd heretofore known himself. He wished to talk brilliantly, but could barely talk at all; and, when he did, he heard himself with misgiving. He couldn't remember ever listening to himself before when he spoke; he wished he'd formed the habit, for even his pronunciation of certain simple words seemed execrable. He heard himself burring his R's and nasally shortening his A's, and, when once or twice he tried to improve his utterance, he blushed in shame of the affectation. He felt fluttery under the breastbone; his head seemed to be filled with light—rosy amber light, a little foggy. Sometimes he didn't know what the lady across the table was saying to him; he was too preoccupied with just the sound of her voice and the sight of her face above the bowl of yellow-hearted pink small chrysanthemums in the center of the lacy table.

Fortunately he wasn't expected to say much. She told him of her life in France, now and then speaking of it intimately. "How quickly a whole phase of one's existence can become dreamlike!" she said, finishing this subject. "Already it seems a mere vapor of my imagination that I ever lived in that villa at Vesinet. Sometimes I wonder how on earth it's happened that here I am again in this American Midland town that I was born in; but of course I had to come somewhere—and here was this house of mine. I couldn't stay in France, and naturally I had to become an American citizen again, with a man as grasping as Colonel Florian trying to seize upon everything—oh, yes; even after the decree of divorce! I suppose one learns to live through almost anything, even through scenes of unspeakable sordidness. One mustn't go into the details of a disillusionment, though, not even with a—friend."

"Please do," Hatcher said. "I'd like to hear 'em. I mean —I don't mean—I mean—"

"No, no." She smiled, and rose from the table. "We'll talk of lovelier things. If you've finished your coffee we'll just sit by the fire and pretend we've known each other ever since we were born. Could you?"

Hatcher could; and, upon a gesture from her, the two

Islanders who had begun to clear the table moved a delicate little sofa from the wall and placed it before the fire. Hatcher and Mrs. Florian sat down, side by side. She waved her cigarette toward his and the two thin streams of smoke were joined for a moment before disappearing upward in the firelight.

"People's lives are like that sometimes, aren't they?" she said. "They float to each other—mingle a while—then separate like that—and go up the chimney! Are our two lives like that, perhaps?"

"Our two lives?" Hatcher spoke in a low voice. "Yours and mine? I certainly hope—"

"Help me," she said, and leaned back. "Almost all the faces at your mother's this afternoon were familiar to me; but I've forgotten so much—the names and who people are and what they are. I must begin to know about them again of course, since I'm to live with them. You'll tell me?"

"Sure. I mean—"

"I tried," Mrs. Florian went on. "This morning, for instance, I took the telephone book and began to pick out the names I remembered and bring to mind the faces that belonged to them. Curiously, I recall quite a number of names that aren't in the telephone book any more. By the way, your uncle's was one of them." She laughed absently. "Does he feel himself to be so terrifically important nowadays that he won't have his name in the telephone book?"

"Uncle Victor?"

"Yes, Victor Linley. Is he so besieged by telephone calls that he—"

"Good Lord, no!" Hatcher said. "I mean, certainly not business calls. He hasn't even got an office any more."

"He's retired?"

"Retired? No. Plumb flopped!" Hatcher said. "The Depression—"

"Really?" Mrs. Florian spoke quickly. "But he always—"

"Uncle Victor's an architect, you know, and for years there hasn't been any building going on, to speak of."

"I see." She was meditative for a moment. "I'm glad he didn't come to-night. I suppose you heard me asking him? If he'd come it would have prevented—this!" With light fingers she just touched the back of Hatcher's hand. "I suppose when ladies want to get hold of him—if they still do—they call him at his club. I think it used to be the Carlyle Club; but to-day, in the telephone book, I couldn't find—"

"No, it's out," Hatcher said. "It's gone and he doesn't belong to any nowadays. I'm afraid you'll have to get used to a lot of things being different; I've had to do that, myself. For instance, most of those people you met this afternoon at my mother's, old Butternut Lane and Company, of course they're still putting up a front all right; but a lot of it must be just window-dressing—certainly with those who depend on real estate for their incomes. Speaking of that, there's something I'd like your advice about."

"My advice?" A somewhat dry amusement might have been detected in Mrs. Florian's expression. "My advice—about real estate?"

"Yes. You see my father owns a lot of vacant houses

that we couldn't even give away because they eat their heads off in taxes and interest on mortgages; but I have a theory that even in a dirty neighborhood if you keep a house all freshened up in new paint you can always rent it. Don't you think so?"

Her response was not elaborate. "Very likely."

"What I want to ask you," Hatcher went on eagerly, "it's that there's a certain shade of grayish putty-color I'd use on the main body of the house, with a grayish apple-green for trim; and I never saw more taste in color than you've got in this house, so do you think—"

"Your uncle's an architect." Mrs. Florian showed more animation. "Why don't you ask him?"

Hatcher felt a little let down. "I did; but I don't think I got him to put his mind on it much. As I was saying, real estate in this town's gone blooey complete. I hope you don't own any."

"No; except this house," Mrs. Florian said. "My grand-father never believed in real property for investment. I suppose your uncle's gone out in the country?" Then, as Hatcher looked blank, she laughed as if slightly amused by an inconsequent recollection. "I seem to recall that he used to talk about building a house on some ground he owned along a pretty creek, miles out of town. He al-ways loved the country, and now, since his club's gone, I just wondered if perhaps he'd built that house he planned."

"Lord, no!" Hatcher laughed ruefully. "He doesn't own any land in the country nowadays, or anything worth anything that I know of. All he seems to have left is the old Linley house 'way down on Sheridan Avenue;

and I happen to know the gross income from that's amounted to exactly fourteen dollars in four years. I don't know what the poor old bird does live on; but he seems to get along somehow in his own way."

"Where?" Mrs. Florian again spoke quickly. "At your house? Does he live with—"

"No. He lives down on Sheridan Avenue, a few blocks from the terrible old Linley place. I suppose as boarding-houses in that part of town go, it's not so bad; but—"

"A boarding-house?" The idea seemed to startle Mrs. Florian. "Victor Linley! Why, Sheridan Avenue was beginning to be a wreck even before I left here!"

"Oh, good old Uncle Victor takes it all right," Hatcher said. "Got a dog they let him wash in the cellar and you'd never know from him he's not perfectly contented."

"No," she assented. "I'm sure you wouldn't—from him."

"Me, I don't get him," Hatcher said, and for a troubled moment wondered if it could be possible that Mrs. Florian had brought him home with her less on his own account than his uncle's. Then, feeling the strongly personal glow of her eyes upon him, he dismissed the suspicion; nevertheless, he changed the subject. "I mean Uncle Victor's like a lot of these other people that seem to be just taking it lying down and still smiling. Why did they ever let the country get into this condition? Of course I'm just beginning to be a miserable kind of rent collector down in that very section. I try to collect rents all up and down Sheridan Avenue every day, and is it a bum job! I'm trying to learn my father's business from somewhere below the bottom; but I—" He paused, and the firelight

upon his earnest young face made clear his expression of
conscientious modesty. "I don't suppose I ought to talk
so much about myself; but—well, you've made me feel—
Well, if I could, I'd like to tell you—"

"Yes." She leaned forward, resting her elbow upon
her knee and her cheek upon her hand, with her eyes in
warm shadow. "You must tell me all about yourself.
Everything. I want to know everything. Didn't I say we
were going to talk as if we'd known each other all our
lives?"

"Yes." Hatcher's moved voice was almost a whisper.
"Yes, somehow I feel as if we had."

"Yes," she said. "When did this happen to him—to
Victor Linley? How long has he been living in a
boarding-house on Sheridan Avenue?"

"Oh, quite a while, I gather. You see, I've been mostly
away a long time, myself—wasting my energy in college
while the whole world was going to pot. I—I'd like to tell
you how I feel about that. I—"

"Yes, you must. Everything," Mrs. Florian said, and
rose. "First I want to play to you."

"On a piano?" Hatcher asked, and wondered why on
earth he'd thought of such a question. "Yes, I see; of
course it would be. Yes, certainly I—" Then he finished
by adding, "That'll be definitely wonderful!" and rightly
feeling that he couldn't have been more banal.

He followed her through another corridor and into a
big square room so dark that for a moment or two the
furniture was indistinguishable. The only light was that
of a blue-shaded small lamp upon a distant table, and near
this lamp a great black wing seemed to rise, poised for

flight—the lifted lid of a concert piano. Mrs. Florian touched his arm. "Sit here," she said, and, as he took the chair she indicated, he discovered with a groping hand that part of it was metal. Then his eyes, accommodating themselves to the interior twilight, began to perceive that the room and its furniture were "modernistic", the dim forms were "starkly functional", and here was another vivid token of the rich variety of the owner's esthetic nature. She went to the piano, sank upon the bench before the keyboard, was a faintly seen still shape there for moments; then her hands slowly rose and she began to play.

XII

WHAT she first played completely mystified Hatcher. There seemed to be no harmonies at all; certainly there was never the hint of a melody and nowhere could he hear any resemblance to even what he was accustomed to think of as modern music. There were thunderous passages that ended indecisively; then there were patterings from the upper reaches of the keyboard; then there were both but without any cohesion, or, so far as he could perceive, any meaning.

"That's Bretsch," she said, stopping abruptly. "He hasn't been heard much in America. Do you see any resemblance to me?"

"To you?" Hatcher asked. "Well, I—"

"Bretsch calls it 'One Woman'." Mrs. Florian laughed.

"He dedicated it to me. It's his impression of me, he insists. Well, my friend, does it teach you to know me a little?"

"I wish it could!" Hatcher spoke out so earnestly and so loudly that the sound of his voice in the big quiet room horrified him, and the directness of what he said struck him as almost vulgar. He felt that he ought to say only subtle implying things to Mrs. Florian, especially in this spacious darkness and after such advanced music. "I mean I don't get it," he went on, trying to improve his effect. "That is, I get it and I don't get it. There's kind of a something—it's a something—"

"Yes," Mrs. Florian said. "Everybody knows Bretsch is a great man; but I'm not there. He and I were too brutally different; so how could he? We were always quarreling. I'm glad you didn't find me in it. Tell me: Do you get much music here?"

"I? Well, you see, I haven't been back here long enough to—"

"I used to starve in this town," she said. "For music—among other things. Your uncle gave a few dinners one winter, with a Russian string quartet to play afterward—nothing but classics! I told him I couldn't bear it. I understand the place is trying to be more civilized nowadays and has something like a real symphony orchestra; but I reserve my opinion till I've heard it. I went into the art museum they seem to rather brag about now; and a young man there told me that they were at last hoping to acquire a Picasso. About time! I found they didn't even know anything at all about Mördling and how far he's gone beyond Picasso. Mördling told me at Biarritz last year that only two museums and one collector in America had pictures of his! What do you think of that?"

"Well, I—I suppose it's pretty grim; but I—I ought to say that I myself—I don't—"

She didn't listen; she shrugged her shoulders. "If I starve again it's my own fault for coming back here when I ought to have known how it would be, of course. Well, that's enough repining. Now we'll be sentimental."

With that, she began to play, expertly and with exquisite feeling, fragments familiar to Hatcher, though he couldn't have named them except as probably bits from Chopin and Liszt most likely. When she stopped he was panicky, afraid he'd say the wrong thing; therefore he only murmured "Great!" in a voice so low that he didn't know whether she heard him or not. She rose, came toward him and stood before him. He got out of his chair.

"Do you know the most frequently repeated line in Shakespeare's plays?" she asked. "I think it is, 'Give me your hand.' "

"Is—is it? You mean you—" He took the hand she extended.

"I mustn't keep you any later to-night, my new old friend," she said. "Men tire easily if they're quickly given —much. To-morrow?"

"To-morrow?" Uplifted, Hatcher was breathless. "You'll make it a date? I mean—"

"Yes," she said. "Could you come about four o'clock? I'd like to take you driving with me. Would you?"

"I would!" Hatcher said, with an emphasis that again seemed to be almost vulgar; but he was reassured by the

fact that her hand remained firmly in his for the moment
of silence that followed and was their parting.

Out of Mrs. Florian's house, he couldn't go home at
once. His head and chest were both tumultuous, and the
autumnal night air was delicious upon cheeks that tingled
from within. He walked the whole length of Butternut
Lane, then back again to where it debouched from the
boulevard that came out from the city, and, as he passed
along a familiar hedge, near this upper end of the Lane,
he heard faint sounds of a jazzing piano and hints of singing voices. The windows of the Aldriches' house were a
merrymaking illumination in the night, and he felt an
easy condescension toward what was going on there—
Harry Aldrich at the piano, with his doting wife and
Dorcy, and Pinkie Wilson, and probably some more of
"the crowd" whooping and "swinging", having themselves a big time. To Hatcher their pleasures seemed
childish, even ignoble, and yet befitting. Why shouldn't
little people have their little enjoyment of the kind of
things they enjoy?

Nothing about himself could have seemed more ridiculous than that he'd lately been rather jealous of Pinkie
Wilson. Lately? Yes, lately by the calendar—but already
that feeling appeared to have been an experience in another life, a dull small life from which he'd suddenly and
marvelously emerged. There wasn't anything really to
object to about Pinkie Wilson. A perfectly decent fellow in his pretty-faced dumb little way. Dorcy Aldrich
was a good girl, and Hatcher liked her; but if she wanted

to grope about with Pinkie Wilson, why shouldn't she? Hatcher felt nothing but benevolence for all those obscure good creatures at the Aldriches' to-night.

He felt something else, at least temporarily, when he finally entered his father's house. His mother sat alone in the living-room, with a book face down upon her lap, and, though she smiled when he spoke to her, there was a wan anxiety in her face; it reached him even through the exaltation of his mood. "What's the matter, Mother?" he asked. "I'm afraid you must be tired to death after standing up through all that party this afternoon."

"No, I'm not tired, Hatcher."

"Then what's the—" He paused. Disturbing recent events, for some hours forgotten, recalled themselves to his mind. "See here, Father's in some kind of jam and you know what it is and it's eating you up. Well, I ought to be helping; but how can I if you don't tell me? I wouldn't dare ask Father again, and down at the offices of Ide and Aldrich I practically never see him. I'm only there about fifteen minutes twice a day, and, though Harry Aldrich says 'Hi, boy!' to me when he's going in or out, the only person I ever get to talk to's old Mr. Barley, and he's in his second childhood and never knew anything anyhow. Yet I'm supposed to be learning the business! Well, if this is a business trouble, oughtn't you to tell me?" He put his hand upon his mother's shoulder. "Why won't you come clean with me? What is it that's griping you like this?"

"Nothing," she said, in a voice so frail that it was almost unheard; then she looked up, smiled again and tried to speak casually. "Did you have a pleasant evening? Did

Sarah Florian seem pleased with our having had the Tea
for her?"

"Pleased, Mother? Why, naturally. I'm sure she was."

"Did she say so, Hatcher?"

"Well, I don't exactly—" He was vague.

"Did she—" Mrs. Ide paused, looked down at her hands,
which were folded rather tightly above the book upon
her lap. "Did Sarah— Do you think she's pleased to be
back among the old friends of her family? Did she happen to speak of any of us—the Aldriches, for instance, or
your Aunt Ada—or your Uncle Victor—or anybody?"

"Aunt Ada? No, I don't think so, Mother; but it seems
to me we did talk a little about Uncle Victor. Yes, I
remember. I happened to mention that he's living in a
boarding-house down on Sheridan Avenue and she
seemed surprised to hear it."

"Was that all—just surprised?"

"Why, yes. What—"

"Nothing," Mrs. Ide said. "We all used to know her
pretty well, you see, and I just wondered if she still takes
some interest in us. Was your Uncle Victor the only one
of us she spoke of?"

"Yes, I believe so, Mother. You see, with a woman like
that you find so many things to talk about because she's—"
Hatcher, with sudden caution, denied his desire to continue warmly upon this theme. He yearned to talk to his
mother of Sarah Florian, to ask a thousand questions
about her and to learn everything of her that he could;
but something within him warned him to shy away from
the subject. He had an impression that it wouldn't be
loyal to ask questions that mightn't be answered sympa-

thetically; intuition strongly suggested that he'd be happier if he didn't talk about Mrs. Florian to anyone at all —or listen, either. Somebody'd be certain to tell him about that Spaniard again. "Yes, I believe Uncle Victor was the only one of the family we mentioned," he said, and added quickly, "You really ought to be in bed by this time, Mother."

"Yes, I suppose so." Mrs. Ide set her book upon a table beside her, rose and in a troubled way looked as if something had pleased her. She kissed her son. "Goodnight, dear. Walk lightly as you pass your father's room. I'm afraid so many people this afternoon tired him, and then of course there's the dreadful expense. Goodnight, dear."

. . . Hatcher, in bed, didn't fall asleep so quickly as was his custom; but he was glad to remain awake. Ethereal, he seemed to float through Mrs. Florian's great house, following a stirringly graceful black velvet figure and a white neck with dully glistening black hair above it—following through corridors into candle-lighted rooms, one of them with an altar and a stained-glass window, another with rosy firelight that played upon crystal and silver and white lace and pink chrysanthemums, and flashed twinkling little highlights into a pair of softly inscrutable dark eyes that looked at him long and mysteriously. Mysteriously? Yes, mysterious with unfathomable prophecies. Prophecies that were all almost promises?

He remembered lightheaded pretty little Mrs. Aldrich's jocose allusion to Sarah Florian's "affairs of passion" and again he recalled his Aunt Ada's sniffy reference to Sarah Florian's marrying a Spaniard "almost overnight"; but he thought himself already above being indignant with either of these traducers. People dislike what they don't understand, he thought, and how could these commonplace neighborhood ladies understand a magnificent, dark, glowing woman like Mrs. Florian, a brilliant woman of the world who dwelt deeply and richly in exotic life and not in their provincial corners. They were mere petty local extroverts; whereas she was really of a hardboiled paganism, bold and frank—yet at the same time she was touchingly religious and so wrapped in darkest velvet that she'd never be revealed except to the eyes she herself selected.

Now, so long as he lived, he'd never forget her answered prayer for a new friend—nor what Shakespeare most often wrote: "Give me your hand". Again and again he felt that hand, strong within his own, heard the lovely voice hushed in the almost complete darkness of the music-room. "Give me your hand"! Then, as he came nearer to his sleep, another literary allusion drifted into his charmed mind—a recollection of one of those old Nineteenth Century books that had been required reading during a long-ago phase of his education, "Henry Esmond". Yes, Henry Esmond had married a woman quite a little older than Henry Esmond was, and it had been a happy marriage.

With this last somewhat coherent thought, young Hatcher Ide passed into a state of slumber.

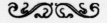

XIII

HE MIGHT almost as well have remained in that slumber throughout the next day. As he went his rounds he presented to view, if anybody had understood, a fine sample of dual personality. One of his selves, mainly body, performed the functions of a struggling young business man while the other, gone poet, floated among mirages of pink chrysanthemums, Gothic glass and kneeling beauty, to the accompaniment of an ethereal grand piano. Toward noon he drifted into a gloomy smoke-colored small house on a side street off Sheridan Avenue, downtown, and found Gilpin Murray and Gilpin's cousin, Mary, scraping off dampened wallpaper in a dismaying little parlor.

Mary, looking tall in a green smock, and with her

sleeves rolled high, didn't stop work when Hatcher appeared; but Gilpin willingly paused to explain her and for conversation. "Don't worry; she isn't in on my contract with you, Hatch," he said. "She's only helping me out because of cousinly admiration for me and love of my new art. She has a day's vacation from the Library on account of it's the County Chairman's funeral or something. Tried to get Amy too; but Mother stuck her to sew." With the air of a collector displaying a masterpiece, he stepped backward and waved a hand toward the horrible wall. "Well, how does it look to you?"

"To me?" Hatcher asked. "Look?"

Gilpin gave him a puzzled scrutiny. "See here, is what was the matter with you at your mother's Tea yesterday afternoon still going on?"

Hatcher frowned vaguely. "What's on your mind?"

"What's on *mine?* Haven't you come out of it? I mean when you were holding that goblet and so choked with your wing collar or something you didn't know that Dorcy and all of us were laughing at you. You didn't know it even after you put the water down on a velvet chair for somebody to sit on."

"I didn't," Hatcher said. "I don't know what you're talking about. I didn't."

"Did! Mary saw it, too. Didn't you, Mary?"

Mary Gilpin, not turning her head, went on industriously with her scraping. "Yes, I did."

"There!" Gilpin said. "Want any more proof? You didn't look human. You looked—"

Hatcher interrupted him. "Well, I think this work's getting on very satisfactorily here. Mr. Floatus is going to begin the putty color on the outside Monday. I've got to go see him. Good-bye."

Mary stopped scraping and turned her head. "Amy can't get away; but Dorcy said she'd make a four with us this afternoon. We thought we'd have time for nine holes before dinner. Meet us there at five?"

"Meet you?" Hatcher asked. "There? Where?"

"At the municipal links in the Park, Hatcher."

"Oh, no," he said absently. "Thanks, I'd like to—but I can't. I'm sure you'll enjoy it; but I have to see Mr. Floatus now before twelve o'clock, so good-bye."

He wandered away as driftingly as he'd come in. The cousins were left staring at each other, Gilpin wonderingly but with some humor, Mary without any humor at all.

Mrs. Florian met Hatcher almost at the door when he arrived for their afternoon drive, and, though he'd but lately been enough of a radical to censure Pinkie Wilson for playing polo during the Depression, he felt no disapproval of this lady for her need of two spruce maids to aid her final preparation for the outdoors—one to bring her a muff and the other to hand her a bag of enmeshed gold and platinum links. On the spot, and without internal argument, Hatcher revised his view of economics. He perceived that not the rich but those who work for them benefit most by luxurious expenditures; the worker gets his living, the spender only superfluous finery. The costly meshed bag had made employment for many people, beginning with the miners who brought forth its metals; and in his generous new mood Hatcher could

easily have forgiven Pinkie the polo ponies that kept
stablemen off relief rolls. So swift, sometimes, is the
emotional swing from left wing to right.

Mrs. Florian murmured to her handmaidens in French,
a Filipino opened the door, and another Islander, new to
Hatcher, preceded her down the steps and opened the
door of the glossy black car. In the front seat, excluded
from the interior by glass, sat not the mulatto chauffeur
of last evening but a white man in black livery.

Hatcher, having disposed of his previous economics,
felt that a magnificent woman had the right to surround
herself magnificently; luxury had an artistic propriety as
the background for Mrs. Florian and was a perfect part,
so to speak, of her picture. Of that picture, the fore-
ground, holding and compelling the center of his gaze, or
anyone's, was of course the miraculous face, which he
now for the first time saw in the light of day. Something
of mystery was retained, however. The sable collar of
Mrs. Florian's coat was high and close, and a dotted mesh
veil descended half way to her chin.

Old George stood beaming at the gates, and, as the car
passed between them, he removed his cap and bowed enthusiastically. Hatcher waved to him through the closed
window. "Until last night everything about your
gorgeous house has always seemed to be closed off and
locked up, except old George," he said. "Old George is
a lifelong friend of mine."

"Is he?" Mrs. Florian's tone was thoughtful. "I understand the workmen found the place in a state of neglect.
I don't care especially for this English lodge-keeper

effect, bobbing at the gates. I suppose he thinks he has to do it to keep up the pretense of being of use."

"Yes, the poor old fellow," Hatcher said, and thought appreciatively of the kindness that had kept the half-decrepit retainer on pay during so many years. "Poor old George, he's been delighted a lot over your coming home. Have you told your driver where you want to go? Out Silver Creek way, perhaps?"

"No, not to-day," she answered, as the car turned southward from Butternut Lane. "I told him to drive into the city. I think last night you said that down in the grimy old part is where you work so hard day after day. I want to see it."

"You—you want—" Hatcher had to begin again. "You want to see where I—"

"Yes." From behind the wide-meshed veil there came a glance that dazed him. "I want to see where you spend your days working in the smoke. Shouldn't I care to? We had a little ceremony of friendship last night, didn't we?" Then she spoke more briskly. "Besides, I want to go all over the old part of town and have you tell me about the changes. I suppose very few people that I used to know live down in the smoke nowadays."

"Why, no; not any of 'em."

"My sentimentalism may shock you," she said. "I want to see where you work—yes, and I want to see the old dead street where I played as a child. I was born down there, and, though I was only a little girl when my grand-father built the house on Butternut Lane, to-day I feel I'd like to see what's left of poor old Sheridan Avenue. Do you mind?"

"Do I mind!" This brought him another dazing glance from her.

On Sheridan Avenue she had her chauffeur stop twice, once before a sooty "used car" sales lot, the site of the house where she'd been born, and once before the old Linley house. Here she made the delay a little longer. "Unbelievable!" she said, and shivered as she peered intently at the big repellent relic. "The house had been vacated before I went away; but it wasn't like this. There were some trees left and a number of the people one knew still lived in the neighborhood. When I was little we children met for our dancing class in the ballroom on the top floor. Your mother and your Aunt Alice and your uncle were older, of course, and not in the class; but their sister, Nancy, the one killed in an accident, was much younger, so she was a member. Alice married a man out West, didn't she?—and, by the way, I think you said your uncle lives somewhere in this horrid stretch. Where?"

"It's a boarding-house," Hatcher said. "We passed it coming down; it's a few blocks back. Just over on West Eighth Street I've had a doorway and window-trim painted those colors I was telling you about. I'd like to get your ideas about that, and if you like we could look in on a couple of working-people I've got scraping off wallpaper inside a house near there. They—"

"You want me to meet them?" Mrs. Florian was indulgently amused.

"You already know them. Anyhow, you met 'em yesterday at my mother's, and their families are old neighbors of yours. It's Gilp Murray that lives just across Butternut Lane from our house and his cousin Mary Gilpin from

next door beyond. I've got Gilp on my regular staff—
without pay for the present—and Gilp's got Mary on his,
at least for to-day and without pay any time; so you see
what a head for business I have, after all! If they're still
there we could give 'em a look-in. You—you were so
awfully kind as to say you—you felt some interest in
where I work, and I really would like to get your opinion
on what colors we ought to use for the interiors. Besides
that, just below here there are one or two more of the
old big houses left. If you'd like, we'll—"

"No; it's too harrowing!" She tapped upon the glass
before them; signalled the driver to turn about. He did
so and they went northward. For a moment Hatcher felt
a little disappointed by the sketchiness of her survey of
his field of endeavor; but she smiled and her shoulder
touched his. "Sights as sordid as this always half-suffocate
me," she said. "I can't stand much of them; but at least
I've seen enough to know what splendid determination
must be a part of your character—to keep you doggedly
spending your days in such an environment. At my first
sight of you I had the feeling that you care for fine and
beautiful things as much as I do; so now I know what
your hours and hours down here must cost you. You
mentioned that Victor Linley lives somewhere about
here. If we happen to pass the place—"

"It's yonder," Hatcher said. "Up ahead. Now you can
see it. There. It's the house just beyond the filling-station
and—"

"*That?*" She leaned partly across Hatcher, staring from
the window. "That scrawny brick house with the red
grocery on the other side of it?"

"Yes; that's it."

"Victor Linley!" Mrs. Florian spoke the name in a sort of gasp; then she leaned back and laughed briefly and oddly. "Victor Linley!"

Hatcher had a thought inspired by the tone of her laughter. "You don't really like him? Uncle Victor's generally supposed to've always been pretty popular. Did he ever do something you didn't—"

"Oh, dear me, no!" she said quickly. "It was only the contrast that struck me. You see, when I came out he was one of the 'older men' of course and immensely looked up to as always the glass of fashion and the mould of form. That ugly cramped boarding-house down here in this dinginess, it seems just a—a bit inconceivable! Do you know somewhere out of the smoke where we could go for a cup of tea?"

"Ye—es." Hatcher had a qualm; then hastily recalled that there was as much as four dollars, of his own, in his pocket. "Yes, there's a place called The Green Heron about two miles north of Butternut Lane. I don't know how good the tea is."

Mrs. Florian said it didn't matter, just so the place was quiet and they could talk; but after they'd been given a red lacquered table in a rather crowded room at The Green Heron she was by no means talkative. As for Hatcher, he wasn't aware of how silently he sat and looked at her; nor of the proof she gave him that her preference for candle-lighted dim rooms in her own house was an esthetic choice rather than the defensive precaution of a woman who knows she can no longer be beautiful except in shadow. Late sunshine came copiously through the large western windows of the tea-room; Mrs. Florian pushed her veil above her eyes, widely opened the fur collar from her throat and glanced at Hatcher as if she asked gravely, "Did you think I didn't dare?"

He'd had no such doubts and therefore didn't perceive her challenge.

"You're not drinking your tea," she said.

"I'm not?" Hatcher drank seriously, and again occupied himself with gazing at her.

Mrs. Florian's silence gave consent to all his looking, and so did her eyes, now and then; but after a time she asked, "Who are your amused little friends?"

"Where?"

"In the doorway, just going out."

Hatcher turned a blank face slowly to look over his shoulder. Passing out through the doorway were several girls and a boy or two, all of them in a mirthful slight commotion. The last of the girls, flushed with her gayety, looked back at Hatcher, met his stare of vacant inquiry and uttered a giggling squeak. She flicked him the wave of a gloved hand that for an unknown reason seemed mocking, and then was gone.

"That?" Hatcher said. "Oh, that's only some of the Butternut Lane crowd of canaries. The one that waved to me was Lennie Aldrich, Dorcy's cousin—I mean, she's related to Mr. and Mrs. Aldrich next door to you on the other side from our house. They're always whooping; they don't count." Then, as Mrs. Florian smiled upon him, he had a shortness of breath, and added impulsively, "Nothing counts but— I mean nothing counts except— except—" His voice faded out; though not because he suspected that what he was saying hadn't much novelty.

"No, nothing else does," she said satisfactorily; and he felt that another almost unbearably dear and far-reaching ceremony had taken place between them.

When he left her at her own door, at the end of a succeeding almost talkless half hour together, he was again unable to go directly home. Just before the door closed upon her, she'd looked over her shoulder to ask: "You'd like my playing to you again?"

"Like it? Would I *like* it?"

"Then to-night—about nine?"

"Oh!" Hatcher said. "Oh, thank you!"

With long, exultant steps he strode through the twilight. To-night, upon her own initiative, he'd again be with her in a companionship of two alone. Three times she'd asked him—and all in the space of the one day of twenty-four hours! Such a thing couldn't happen without a dizzying significance; no one could be so humbleminded as not to perceive that. Her three invitations were assuredly the promise that this new companionship—a finer, loftier and yet more warmly enticing one than any he'd ever known before—would continue and grow closer. How close who could say? Already it was an intimacy when most was expressed in looks and silences, not words. He'd be content, nay exhilarated, to keep it just as it was; and, radiantly foreseeing that he was to be with her in following days as often as during this first one, he felt that he was entering the door of an exquisite new life in which he could be happy so long as he and she could share moments that seemed complete comprehen-

XIV

YOUTH, even in a Depression, even in "real-istic" hardship—alas! even in war—must still dwell in il-lusion; but when the illusion is sweet the hours of delight are keener than they can be again. So, naturally, the breaking up of fond absorptions in the unreal startle the young into sharp agitations and despondencies. Hatcher Ide so lost himself in the excluding new life he thought he lived with Sarah Florian, through the few fleet weeks between their first hours together and the evening of the dinner Harry Aldrich and his wife gave for her, that the very drawing-room preliminaries to the dinner brought him the sensations of a person summarily banished from home by the authorities. He had only a word from her —and no look at all. Her head was turned another way to speak to somebody else as he reached her; and a regardless

group of people he defined as "old marrieds" immediately
intervened. He felt himself thrust aside as too young and
consequently too unimportant; and the arrangements in
the dining-room, when the company went thither, exas-
peratingly confirmed this impression.

In the movement to the feast he was but an unnoticed
item in a clamorous rabble of young at the tail of a parade
distantly headed, not without some effect of jovial stateli-
ness, by the host with the honored lady upon his arm.
Hatcher, searching for his own proper place at table,
went from disappointment to disappointment before he
discovered the card marked with his name; and, when he
did find it and was seated, he thought he might as well
have been sent to eat outdoors, he was that far from Sarah
Florian.

She was upon the beaming Harry's right at the head
of the long central table; and some thirty middle-aged and
older people sat honored there. Plainly they were thought
more her peers than were the chattering young groups
at the smaller tables that encircled the large one like
inferior sparklings clustered about the light of a great
gem in the setting of a ring. Only at intervals could
Hatcher catch, between heads and through elaborate pat-
terns of flowers, niggard glimpses of the dark lady who
absorbed him—just bits of her face, a gleam of white forehead under rhythmic black hair, a highlight upon a
lustrous eye, a corner of a mouth, pale rose, and a pro-
vocative contour of rounded chin. He had the impression
that most of the time she was talking busily to his Uncle
Victor, who sat upon her right with only the top of his
head visible to Hatcher.

The nephew felt his exile to be an exclusion founded upon his merely numerical age, and his sense of the injustice was acute. The wise laws of his country permitted him to vote: Wasn't that enough to let him be thought fit to associate with adults? His feeling was a little like that of a bright boy who's been encouraged to shine in grown-up company, and, while doing so, is abruptly sent up to the nursery to join the other children. He was the one person present who'd been exalted to bright intimacy with the guest of honor. Amid the throng he was the only one who really knew her, daily sharing a hundred unspoken thoughts with her—yet here he was on the outer fringes, and with obscurity almost conspicuously thrust upon him! Harry Aldrich had promised to make this dinner "splendiferous" and had kept his word; the splendor was an additional annoyance to Hatcher, and so was the mechanized excitement of the many voices.

The more he looked about him, the more mortifyingly his sequestration stressed itself. He wasn't even at Dorcy's table—apparently was thought to be of so little weight in the world that he wasn't asked to sit at the same table with the daughter of the family giving the party! Would Mrs. Florian perhaps observe this genuine slight and deduce that he was held to be of no consequence, not only by his host and hostess but by his own contemporaries? Dorcy's table, placed near the head of the great central one, was noisy with laughter and importance. Dorcy seemed to be making a rosy whoop-te-do over everything, especially over Pinkie Wilson who sat next to her—and, what was inexplicably outrageous, she had Gilp Murray, Hatcher's own mere employee, at that table; and the mere employee was seen and heard to join Dorcy in approving convulsions caused by something Pinkie Wilson said. Gilp was acting like a dirty hypocrite, Hatcher thought.

True, Dorcy's best friend, Mary Gilpin, was placed next to the self-defined outcast, upon his right; but that didn't assuage his feeling of being snubbed. Gloomy and not caring who knew it, he talked disjointedly to Mary, who'd lately spent another holiday helping her cousin to remove wallpaper. "Gilp says he's on the top of the wave," she told Hatcher. "He says these houses he's helping you do over are going to put him on pay before long because they're sure to rent. He thinks you and he ought to patent that contraption for steaming the wallpaper before it's scraped. The color you're going to use on the interiors is good, too—really quite lovely. Your friends ought to congratulate you on the whole idea, Hatch."

"Ought they?" he asked. "I don't seem to hear 'em doing it. Where are they all?"

"Where—" Mary began, laughed, and then, after a glance down the room to where the hilarity at Dorcy's table was increasing, looked serious and changed the subject. She talked for a time about college psychology courses and had such absent responses that she thought it better to let him brood; she began to speak to the boy on the other side of her. Hatcher was granted a seclusion that lasted until the girl at his left, Dorcy's cousin, Lennie, startled him by a sudden dig of her elbow into his ribs.

"Right you are, darling!" she said. "Don't try to eat or talk or anything. Just sit in that same old trance."

"What old trance?" Hatcher looked at her unamiably. "Don't jab that spike into me again; I'm not one of your darlings. What old trance?"

"The same one a lot of us saw you in that day at The Green Heron, darling, when you didn't have the faintest idea who your lifelong friends were or what a lovey-dove sight you were making of yourself. I hear it goes on all the time."

"You mean now, for instance?" Struck suddenly in almost a vital part, Hatcher instinctively did his poor best to be offensive. "You mean I'm making a lovey-dove sight of myself with you right now, beautiful? Trying to look deep in your marvelous eyes and everything?"

"No, presh!" Lennie laughed in a manner that convinced him he'd been right in never thinking much of her. "My worst enemy couldn't accuse me of being that old."

"That old?" he repeated slowly; then caught her meaning, and was speechless.

"Me, I'm just a squablet," Lennie explained. "*I* couldn't *hope* to make you the talk of the town! You could pursue me foaming with passion in public and nobody'd start chattering about you every time as many as two people get together, the way they do now. How do you *like* all of a sudden living in the great white glare of the spotlight, Hatch old son?"

"See here," Hatcher began, indeed helpless. A choking apprehension of what she'd say next was upon him. "If you enjoy talking gibberish—"

"Gibberish!" Lennie exclaimed gayly. "Can it be I'm the *first* to tell you that you've become practically Butternut Lane's star celebrity? Driving with her every afternoon, closeted with her every night in the dark recesses of the palace, groveling under tables in tea-rooms to find her gloves when she drops 'em—"

"See here—" Hatcher floundered, all the more impotent because of fury. Strange fears, too—fears of hearing incredible defamations—had risen within him. "I always knew this was the worst hell-hole of gossip on earth! I only wish I *did* drive with her 'every afternoon'; unfortunately for me I don't, and I've never been in any tea-room with her oftener than—"

"Wipe the red off your face, pal!" Lennie was in a minor ecstasy. "What a shame all these old spite-cats are starting to say you're on the road to turning into a rich, rich lady's gigolo! So soon after college, too, poor child!" She affected a confidential and compassionate manner. "It's a *crime* a person can't go out driving afternoons reg'lar with another person and not be seen all over everywhere looking all gaspy! Part of it, I bet you, it's nothing but the vulgar prattle of servants—all this about your being there every single night—because one of those Filipino boys is crazy about Aunt Eleanor Aldrich's maid, Ella, and loves to run and tell her—"

"What!" Hatcher exclaimed. "You admit yourself that servants—"

"Sure, Hatch! Maybe that's how Dorcy's the first person to hear the news fresh every morning. Think it might be the reason you're not sitting at her table tonight? Do listen to 'em! Ain't it a shame she's having herself such a big time with the Wilson pulchritude? Me, I say it was a hellish cruelty not to put you at the big

table with the old folks, where that marvelous Mrs.
Florian is. Of course it's perfectly natural for you to go
goofy over her, Hatcher, because it runs in your family,
I hear."

"What?"

"Oh, yes," Lennie said. "My mother told me yesterday
that just before the giddy Sarah started in marrying
around everywhere she was supposed to be engaged to
one of your relatives."

"One of my rel—" The recollection of wild imaginings
of his own rushed upon the staggered Hatcher. "You're
crazy! My father—my father never—"

"Your *father?*" Lennie was first astounded, then uproarious. "Why, you poor babe, you must be afraid she's
even older than she *is!* How long since your father was a
bachelor and in a position to be engaged to anybody?
About twenty-five years?" Her laughter was louder and
louder. "*No,* little Rollo, it wasn't your father everybody
thought she was going to marry; it was your uncle. Just
only your *uncle*, that's all!"

"You—" Hatcher began; but his self-possession was
gone. In a quavering voice, "You're—just crazy!" was all
that he was able to say.

"No, dearie!" Lennie returned, smiling upon him
cruelly. "It was my mother told me. Look at her. She's
sitting at the big mature table next to your own poor
father that you've been traducing. Doesn't she look fairly
sane? She told me it was never announced but everybody
was sure Mr. Victor Linley and the giddy Sarah were
just about to put up the banns when, bingo! the gal
turned a handspring, grabbed a passing Mexican and—"

"Mexican! She never—"

"Never in her life married a Mexican?" Lennie leaped at the chance he gave her. "Never in her whole *life?* Not *once?* Not one single Mexican? Just stuck to French and Span—"

"You're a marvel!" Hatcher contrived to interrupt, and, horribly aware that he was trembling all over, steadied his hands by resting them upon the edge of the table. "Just to think that all this noise could come from such a little chest and throat!"

"Sweet of you!" Lennie squealed. "I wish you could see your face! Goggy-eyed over sacrilege, what? Here's a cute one for you, adorable: it's by special request that your Uncle Victor's sitting next to the guest of honor. *Whose* special request, presh? Why, *hers!* Aunt Eleanor couldn't help telling. Piquant, what, under the circumstances? Wouldn't it be *rapturous* if the dear dead past should come to life again and maybe some day you'll be calling her 'Aunt Sarah'?"

"What a cut-up you are!" Hatcher had strength enough to say savagely, as he turned his shoulder upon her. Cackling voices blasphemed in sacred hidden grottoes where he was an acolyte. His nerves seemed to rock; he was bewildered, insulted, thrown down, stamped upon and scarified. With Lennie's laughter stinging into his reddened left ear, he swung to Mary Gilpin, a movement that was in reality a flight for shelter. Behind this always cool, high-minded girl he hoped to collect himself and be at least a little ready if Lennie struck again. "I suppose you've heard some of the tripe I've been talking with that pinwheel on the other side of me?" he asked.

"Yes," Mary Gilpin said. "If you're really worried about Mrs. Florian's age, Hatcher, I think you can calculate it with some accuracy. I hadn't happened to hear that she was once engaged to Mr. Linley; though of course it's legendary what flutters he caused for years after he came home from the last war. I believe, though, Mrs. Florian wasn't much over twenty-two or twenty-three the first time she was married and left here, and she's been away only a dozen years or so. You see that comes fairly close; she could easily be no more than thirty-five—or even as young as thirty-four."

"I'm not interested! I'm not interested in people's ages!"

"No, Hatcher? Of course everybody's been talking about her these weeks she's been home, though I understand they always did—even when she was quite a young girl. She's the sort of person who creates that."

"Creates what?"

"Talk," Mary said. "She emanates something; everybody's got to look at her. It's as if she herself so intensely feels that she's the star of the play that her emotional conviction of her starship spreads a thought contagion. Everybody here to-night may not be talking of her just at the moment; but they're all conscious of her all the time—and she could hardly bear it if they weren't. You see that inevitably makes anybody who's much seen with her talked about, too. Don't be angry with Lennie, though; she's only being loyal."

"Loyal! What a ridiculous—"

"No," Mary Gilpin said. "She's not the only one who could feel hurt on Dorcy's account, Hatcher."

"What?" He stared at her hotly. "On Dorcy's account? Why, Dorcy— Why, weeks ago she practically dropped me for—" He laughed roughly. "Oh, what's it matter?"

Mary gave him a steady look. "Are you going to let Dorcy go?"

"Let her go? What do you mean? I haven't got her. Never did have. She's—"

"Are you?" Mary Gilpin asked. "Are you going to let her go?"

"Oh, for Cripe's sake!" Hatcher felt he had enough to bear without having these two girls try to make him feel guilty—guilty of what? Hadn't he a right to his own life? What was everybody trying to do to him? "See here," he began. "I've always been Dorcy's friend and always will be; but I certainly—"

Into his leftward ribs little Lennie Aldrich spiked her elbow again. "Listen! Can't you listen even to the *music?*"

"What music?"

From a corridor outside the dining-room there came the strains of a harp, a flute, a violin and a 'cello playing an old Irish air to which famous words had been set by Thomas Moore. Led by their hearty host, the guests at the center table applauded, the young followed; and many of the diners went so far as to lift their voices in the old song.

"Get it, Hatch?" Lennie squeaked. " 'Oh, believe me if all those endearing *young* charms'—my gosh, who thought of *that?* It's in honor of *her*. Under the circumstances, what a boner, huh? Listen, Hatch, here's the best part!"

She joined her shrill voice to the others. " 'And around the dear ruin each wish of my heart'—"

Hatcher listened to the accursed music as long as he could; then shouted brutally, his face almost touching Lennie's. "Will you close that trap, or can't you? I've got some ear and you're flat. You're *flat*, I tell you! For Cripe's sake—"

The music stopped; so did Lennie, and Mary Gilpin touched Hatcher's arm. "*Sh*, Hatch!" she said. "Mr. Aldrich is going to make a speech."

Harry Aldrich, big and smiling, a glass of champagne in his hand, had risen; and, after subduing the greeting shouts of "Yay, good old Harry!" and "Yay, Uncle Harry!" obtained silence. "Just a quick one," he said. "After that the tables'll be cleared away for dancing in this room by all ages, and bridge outfits are set in the living-room for addicts. The library is reserved for fiancées and fiancés, and the breakfast-room for really interested drinkers . . . Who let out that cheer? . . . But first, let's be serious for just one moment. A dear old friend has lately returned among us. More than that, she's a dear old family friend; her family were for three generations the friends of the families of nearly every person here, and she herself spent her bright girlhood with us. Now she returns to us more beautiful and more alluring than ever. May her life among us be as much happier for herself as her presence will make our own lives for us! Neighbors, old friends, young and old comrades in the life of our city, I give you the health of our old new friend, Sarah Lash that was, Sarah Florian that is!" Here the speaker seemed affected by emotion; his voice trembled. "God bless you, Sarah!"

He lifted his glass, drank, and all the company, except Mrs. Florian, stood to honor the toast. Then she, rising, said, "I thank you!" in a clear voice, and sank almost to the floor in a sweeping curtsey. When the prolonged approving collegiate shouting of "*Ya-a-ay!*" had died away, the exodus from the room began, with Harry Aldrich leading and Sarah Florian upon his arm.

Hatcher had looked at her when she rose and stood, before sinking in her exquisitely supple curtsey; then he'd turned his face away. For him she was a worshiped white statue splotched by insulting hands—hands that also strove to daub soilingly something fine, pure and, as he'd vainly thought, untouchable, within himself. Until the resultant turbulence in his breast was quieted he felt that he could not go near her. Among the crowd pressing toward the door, he found himself beside Gilpin Murray who, in high spirits, was unusually tactless.

"Grand party, Hatch, what? Like old times! Who'd think there was any Depression? Had us a big time at our table. One thing I've got to hand Pinkie Wilson, he's there when it comes to wise-cracking! He can certainly be funny, that bird, when he wants to, and so can Dorcy."

"At whose expense?" Hatcher, hot in the head, lost all discretion. "Mine?"

"Yours?" Gilpin Murray was taken aback by his friend's intensity. "Well, everybody's, Hatch. Sort of a riot over pretty much the whole field; can't deny you might have been mentioned."

" 'Mentioned'!" Hatcher said. "Ah, yes—'mentioned'!"

"Why so jumpy, Boss? Don't get sore and fire me."

"I won't!" Hatcher said bitterly, swung away from him and was seized upon by his Aunt Ada.

"Of all the balderdash!" She projected a rapid fire of under-cover indignation. "I never dreamed Harry Aldrich could make such a goose of himself—throwing money around like this! As if the Tea your mother gave for her wasn't enough! Now, look at that!" She made a gesture toward the end of the room where musicians had grouped their chairs and begun to tune their instruments. "Lansor's full orchestra and four or five extra pieces! I should think Eleanor Aldrich would give Harry fits for slopping over in that toast the way he did. Everybody here knows what piffle it was; at least all the grown-up people do. Almost shedding tears over what a dear third-generation family friend she is, when everybody knows that at heart she's always been exactly like that old parvenu barbarian of a grandfather of hers! Did you notice your father during dinner?"

"What?" Hatcher tried to move away. "No, I—"

Aunt Ada detained him; she caught his sleeve. "He looked perfectly ghastly, and even Eleanor saw it and asked me what on earth's the matter with him. He told me before we came he wanted to get away the first instant he could. Now I've lost him, and your mother too, in this shuffle. See if you can't find them for me and tell them I'm going home with them."

Hatcher left his Aunt Ada; but he didn't go to look for his father and mother. He wished to be alone and in the dark; yet, even though he couldn't bear to go near her, he hadn't the will to leave a house that contained Sarah

Florian—his feet wouldn't take him. After a desultory wandering without speaking to anybody, he stood in a corridor and stared through a doorway that gave him a view of her back as she sat at a card-table. Harry Aldrich was her partner and they played against two sleek white-haired gentlemen known to Hatcher as golfing and bridging old widowers. More *old* people! Didn't the Aldriches have *any* sense?

Two nineteen-year-old girls, unaware of Hatcher behind them, were also staring through the doorway. "They say she's a wolf at bridge," one of them said. "Golly, what wicked shoulders! Look, if a woman keeps her figure at least till she's getting towards forty—"

"Righto!" the other murmured covertly, but Hatcher heard her too well. "That's another disgusting advantage a woman her age has over us. We fledglings never seem to know what to do with our shoulders; we keep flopping 'em around. They look meager and minus self-confidence compared to the chastely voluptuous sculpture *she* has to offer. These shapely divorcées! No wonder poor little Hatchie Ide—"

Hatcher heard no more. Quivering, he moved down the hall.

Was everybody in the world talking smearingly about him—and about people's ages? Hateful voices tormented his mind's ear with phrases—"easily be no more than thirty-five" . . . "the first time she was married" . . . "been away only a dozen years or so." A dozen years ago Hatcher had been ten years old; and, at twenty-two, not twice twelve, "a dozen years or so" means a vastness in time. To be twelve years older than twenty-two, maybe "even as young as thirty-four", is imaginable but unthinkable.

These echoings upon the problem of age were not the worst. "A rich, rich lady's gigolo"! Lennie'd raked him with that and then her malice had gone to the utmost limit of hideous comedy: "Maybe some day you'll be calling her 'Aunt Sarah'!"

A sudden recollection came smitingly upon him—of Uncle Victor's turning red when asked a simple question about Mrs. Florian—and Hatcher remembered how often she had talked to him of his uncle, how many questions about him she asked. He remembered, too, the faint suspicions he'd had, sometimes, that maybe she was more interested in him in his capacity as a nephew than—than as a man! Was that what he was to her—a *nephew?* Had he been too happy in his believing, of late, that he "completely understood" her? In reality had he come no nearer to that, nor to her, than on his first evening with her when she'd seemed to him a beautiful mystery—unbelievably kind, inexpressibly lovely, but a mystery?

Aunt Ada'd told him sharply that his Uncle Victor Linley had never been in love with Sarah Lash; but did Aunt Ada know? Did even his mother know? He doubted it. But there were two people here to-night who knew the truth—Uncle Victor and Sarah herself; and Hatcher had to know, couldn't sleep until he knew. If Uncle Victor was still in the house he could find him and have the truth from him.

XV

HE HAD no difficulty in finding his Uncle Victor. Attracted by a sound of ivory clickings as he went down the corridor, Hatcher entered Harry Aldrich's billiard-room and beheld Mr. Linley, who was there alone. He was chalking a cue before resuming a meditative practise with two gleaming white spheres and a red upon a strongly illuminated green cloth, the rest of the room being in shadow. "Good evening, Nephew," he said. "I believe you don't play this—"

"No, I don't. The fact is I—"

"Looking for somebody?" Uncle Victor asked. "If I'm not too intrusive I think that a few minutes ago I saw her dancing with the scion of the still affluent Wilson dynasty and looking—well, almost as pretty as her mother. Eleanor's the sky for prettiness, isn't she? Perhaps I should

146

retract the expression 'Wilson dynasty'. Since the Wilsons derive from the Erdvynns, perhaps 'dynasty' isn't just the proper word; but—"

"Never mind proper words, please!" Hatcher said. "I'm not exactly in a mood to care about proper words."

"No? It's just as well to have a thought to 'em, though." Mr. Linley, leaning across the bright table, planned a shot deliberately, made it with precision. That habitual calmness of his fine profile, as he thus occupied himself, had a baffling effect upon his nephew.

"I don't know if you'll be willing to listen," Hatcher said. "But I came here to—to—"

"Willing to listen?" Mr. Linley again chalked his cue. "Indeed yes. Something to tell me?"

"No; to ask you." Hatcher felt that the only way to ask was to ask. He tried to blurt it out. "I want to know— Well, the fact is, I came here to ask you a question, Uncle Victor."

"Why not?" The uncle planned another shot, sighting carefully. "By all means ask it. I know really so little about anything that I can't guarantee a correct answer."

"You can to this," Hatcher informed him, and was dismayed by a doubt of his voice's steadiness. "You—you're one of the only two persons that can answer the question I came here to—to ask you."

"Two?" Mr. Linley changed his plan and aimed his shot from another angle. "There are only two authorities on your subject, then, and I'm one of them? Who is my colleague?"

"It's—" Hatcher paused. "That doesn't matter. I want to ask you— Perhaps you'll tell me it's not my affair; per-

haps you'll tell me to get the hell out of here; perhaps
you'll—"

"No, I won't, Hatcher; not at all. What is it?"

The uncle made his shot, again with success; then stood
upright, cue in hand, and looked at the nephew. Hatcher,
in shadow himself, saw the quiet blue inquiry of the eyes,
likewise in shadow, on the other side of the table, and
found this mild gaze intolerably embarrassing. "It's a
question I've got to ask. I wouldn't if I didn't. I wouldn't
be intrusive any more than you would, yourself; but—
but some things are important."

"So they are, Hatcher. In fact, I think almost everything is. I don't know of anything at all that wouldn't
be important if we could get at the whole truth of it. If
we'd habitually examine what we pass over as negligible
trifles we might improve our conceptions of the universe
and consequently our conduct and contentment." Uncle
Victor had begun to speak with a brightened interest,
even with eagerness. "Of course the thought isn't new;
but, for instance, by observing the behavior of my friend
and dog, the small Locksie, every morning just after he
wakes up in his easy chair across the room from my bed,
I—"

"Please listen!" Hatcher said. "I don't want to talk
about that. I simply want to ask you—"

"Yes?" Mr. Linley said encouragingly, as his nephew
once more paused. "I've been able to gather that you
have on your mind a question. It seems to distress you,
rather; and you've told me that only one other person
knows the answer. The other, presumably, isn't within
reach at the moment; so you intend to put the question to

me but find a difficulty in so doing. Perhaps I can help
you. Your mother's informed me of the pressure you've
kindly been bringing to collect the rents on the old
Linley house. Possibly your problem concerns it. Would
I be right in guessing that the only other person who
could solve it is my self-centered delinquent tenant, Mrs.
Schapp?"

"Damn!" Hatcher said. "No, you wouldn't!"

"Then I'm all at sea." Mr. Linley again applied himself
to the billiard table. "If you could somehow bring yourself to put your question into spoken words—"

"I will, by God!" Hatcher said, and, staring fiercely at
the serene face once more bent down to the shining
levelled cue, knew that he couldn't. Uncle Victor's placidly detached impersonalness was too much for the
nephew, who now helplessly felt that he was appearing
to be just a boy. "Damn that noise!" he said, referring to
clamors from the not distant dining-room where the
orchestra seemed to be growing "hot". Hatcher wiped his
forehead. "How can anybody think? The fact is, I came
here to ask you—to ask you—"

"Yes, Hatcher?"

Groping for almost any plausible question to substitute
for the one he couldn't put, Hatcher caught at a straw.
"Well, you're supposed by all the family to do a lot of
thinking about everything. I'd like to hear—to hear what
you think about the state of business in this country."

"Dear me!" Mr. Linley was puzzled. "I shouldn't call
that an intrusive question. There must be something behind it, Hatcher. I can't believe you sincere in this flattery
—that I'm one of the only two persons who can answer

you. Would the other perhaps be Mr. Morgan, or the President of the United States, or—"

"All right!" Hatcher said. "Go ahead! Rib me all you care to; I'm just a young fool you wouldn't talk seriously to, of course!"

"I wouldn't? At the slightest prompting I'd talk seriously to anybody, Hatcher, and by the barrel. You tempt me to answer your question by explaining the idea that man progresses only through adapting himself to nature, learning and obeying natural law. In a Depression produced by the natural law of supply and demand, experimenters declared that they would overcome the law by disregarding it. They would do that and they would do this in spite of the law of supply and demand—which is now actively avenging the insult, so business doesn't recover. It may grow worse through two causes, one being the fact that politicians, like most people, love power. Seeking it, they cunningly belittle liberty, knowing that free people, temporarily hungry, will enslave their future for bread in the present. The other cause may be that in countries where the love of liberty has never grown, the politicians, already having complete power over their own people, naturally wish to extend it over all the rest of us and have made this war to which, so far, we seem to be paying too little attention, since presently we, too, may become—"

"Damn!" Hatcher cried again. "Can't you stop? Now I *will* ask you what I came here to ask you!" To the nephew it seemed unbelievable that any intelligent woman could ever have been in love with so discursive a man as this uncle of his. "I will! I—I—"

"Ah, then after all I've failed to catch your purport, Hatcher?"

"Some*what!*" Hatcher said savagely. "Do you think the matter with me is I need a lecture on What's-Behind-The-News? I came here to ask you a question, a personal question, I tell you, and I want an answer! I—"

"Yes?" his uncle said. "As personal as you like, Hatcher. What is it?"

"It's this. It's simply this." Once more Hatcher failed; he couldn't do it. Facing the indomitably cool detachment of his uncle, he couldn't—and again he caught at any straw. "Well, it's this. I didn't mean business in general; I meant— Well, you're one of the family and I meant I'd like to hear—to hear what you know about the state of my father's business."

"You would?" Mr. Linley put his cue in the rack and dusted the chalk from his fingers with a fine white handkerchief. "I see. You meant that your father's the other person who knows the answer but you feel a hesitancy about asking him? I'm sorry not to have the knowledge you've imagined that I have. Aren't you in a position to know rather more about the matter than I?"

"No, I'm not." At the moment Hatcher's interest in this subject was indeed slight; but he felt he'd have to continue to show some or appear completely ridiculous. "I don't know any more about the business now than I did the first day. I thought— I just thought maybe you—"

"No." Mr. Linley had become serious. "Something's occurred that worries you about it, Hatcher?"

"Well— Father's been looking harried and sick, and one day, you know, he came home and seemed to have had some sort of shock not exactly physical—"

"Yes; so your mother told me at the time. Ah—I've noticed that she's seemed distressed, of late. Of course there's always the Depression; however, I understand that business in general, just at the moment, seems to be growing better. Harry Aldrich was elatedly telling everybody so at the table this very evening; but I happened to glance at your father just then and he looked as though such optimism made him sick. Of course it's a strain to be fighting off insolvency year after year and—"

"Bankruptcy?" Hatcher said. "Oh, well! Everybody's in the same boat. I suppose we'd manage to live somehow; they all seem to. Father'd mortgage the house or—"

"No, I believe that was done as long ago as 'Thirty-three, Hatcher, when almost all of Butternut Lane fell very much indeed into the same boat. I'm afraid your father's house is like most of the others—already mortgaged for more than it'd sell for, because nobody'll buy such houses nowadays. About this recent apprehension of his, don't you think your mother might have more than an inkling of—"

"Yes, I do."

"So do I," Mr. Linley said. "Have you asked her what—"

"Asked her?" Hatcher echoed impatiently. "She couldn't answer me. Says nothing's the matter and cries. I'm to run and play with my toys. Everybody treats me as if I were about four years old!" He looked angrily at his uncle, turned on his heel and strode to the other end of the room. "Yes, and that's about how old I feel right now, too, if you care to know!"

Mr. Linley didn't seem aware of the outburst but stood apparently lost in thought, his preoccupied gaze upon the illumined green cloth of the billiard table. "Your youth may not be the reason why she doesn't answer," he said; though Hatcher, muttering profanely to himself, didn't hear him. "Some things sometimes daren't be told to anybody, young or old."

"What?"

"I was just thinking," his uncle said musingly. "They're very dear to me, your father and your mother; no man ever had a better brother-in-law. The Aldriches, too. I was Harry's Best Man, and Eleanor's lovely as a flower —and as fragile. Odd contradiction. How can anything be that wrong with the business when Harry and Eleanor are so exuberant? And yet—there it is!" He looked up, met his nephew's staring eyes absently. "It's significant that you should have noticed it, too. Yes, very significant. I'm glad you've spoken of it to me. I—" Abruptly these ruminations came to an end; Mr. Linley took a flat watch from the pocket of his white waistcoat, glanced at it and spoke briskly. "Ha! I believe I can say goodnight to Eleanor now without being accused of not having enjoyed myself. Locksie has a clock in his system and knows to the minute what time to expect his final evening stroll on Sheridan Avenue. He's expecting it now and might disturb the other boarders if his demands become sonorous. I can just comfortably catch the half-hourly trolley. Going my way, Hatcher?"

"No, I'm not. I'm going; but I'm going my own way," Hatcher said, and he added, as his uncle left the room ahead of him, "And the hell with it!"

. . . The moon, high and bright over the frosted earth, made a smooth slim path down Mr. Linley's silk hat as nephew and uncle said goodnight to each other outside Harry Aldrich's driveway gates and went their separate ways. Hatcher walked slowly, came to a halt and looked up at the moon. From down the street the light tap of Mr. Linley's walking-stick upon the pavement was becoming inaudible; the tom-tom beat of Lansor's orchestra thumped faintly through the cold air, and Hatcher's urge to follow an impulse was strong. He wanted to go back; he wanted to stand for just one more long moment looking through an open doorway at the back of a beautiful head and the sculpturing of shoulders envied by a pair of poisonous stringy girls whose own shoulders were always on the jerk.

After first finding it impossible to leave that house, he had become unable to remain within it. Now it seemed impossible to continue to move away from it. Time and again, since his infancy, he'd thought he must be really in love; but he'd never felt anything comparable to the racking that now possessed him. Never, indeed, for Dorcy! Maybe at times he'd been almost in love with her; maybe some day he might have drifted into being more so, if he'd never seen Sarah Florian. What he felt for Sarah Florian was measurelessly deeper than the utmost emotion any girl of his own age, or younger, could have caused within him, he was certain. Only a woman superbly matured could inspire such a passion; and so he didn't wish Sarah Florian younger—he only wished himself older. Then neither could be smirched. Where on earth was there a more agonizing position than that of a man all upset like this about a woman who had once been on the point, people said, of marrying his uncle? Of course anybody'd call such a man an infatuated little damn fool.

Hatcher thought of his father and mother and of the worrying he'd done about the anxiety they couldn't conceal. Only a business trouble! He still pitied them; but how really petty any mere business trouble was, even a bankruptcy, compared to the tragic condition in which he found himself to-night! He knew that he'd have thought his position comedy if another had occupied it; might even have laughed at the sufferings of a penniless young man horribly talked about for being in love with a beautiful millionaire woman probably at least twelve years his senior. Yes, of course people were laughing at him—giggling, stringing him, trying to make him feel guilty—even a grand girl like Mary Gilpin trying to do that and despising him—everybody trying to destroy the finest experience he'd ever known, something that was now the very life of him.

Hatcher looked up at the inscrutable moon and had one of the oldest thoughts that it inspires; poets long before the Renaissance worked embroideries all through Hatcher's question: How could that moon look down now, and thousands of years ago and thousands of years hence, and not weep for the anguishes among the children of earth it beheld from its icy height?

The moon remained emotionless, as cool as Uncle Victor Linley himself. Hatcher walked on. How long could he bear the state of things—and the state of his own feelings—without doing something? Doing what? He hadn't known how to make himself ask his own uncle a simple direct personal question; what could he say to Sarah Florian? Well, he could say the truth to her, the crazy truth—and he'd go to her and do it. The words he'd use began to come into his mind: "Do you remember that first evening you gave me? Do you remember our little ceremony of friendship? Do you remember all the freighted moments we've had together since then? Now you see what they've done to me! Everybody in this town's laughing at me. Old spite-cats are calling me your gigolo. Well, let 'em! I don't care. To me not a damn thing on this earth matters except one—and that's you. Yes; here I am. I've got an education that's no use to me and thirty-one dollars in the bank. They tell me you were once engaged to my uncle. Well, if that's true it can't be helped now. It makes me just that much more ridiculous; but you've utterly fascinated me. I only know that my life's yours to do what you will with it because, damn it, I love you! I love you! I love you! What are you going to do about it?"

Hatcher considered saying this to her to-night; he thought of going into the "Lash place", sitting on the cold stone steps until Sarah Florian came home, when he'd rise before her, pale and stern in the moonlight, and begin with, "It's I! Yes, half frozen but—"

Then rose in his mind the picture of her as she sat composedly at the bridge table with her fine motionless back to him; and, for reasons he didn't try to explore, he postponed his climax to the morrow.

XVI

WHEN the morrow came something appeared to stand in the way, preventing him; and this was the technique that had been evolved by Mrs. Florian to regulate, so to speak, their meetings. All of these had been upon her initiative. Just before he left her she'd say, "To-morrow?" or perhaps, if he'd been driving with her, "To-night?" Sometimes she'd telephone, "Would you care to come to me—immediately?" or "Would you like to spare time for a drive and tea to-morrow?" Now at their last parting she'd said nothing, and five whole days passed without word from her. He suffered, his heart burned with urgencies; but her method upon him had been so effective that in spite of everything he couldn't bring himself to go to her door and ask for her. She'd delicately implanted within him an awareness that he was to come to her when she signalled and not otherwise—or something might be spoiled!

Before he knew Mrs. Florian he couldn't have imagined himself in such a coil—to be in love with somebody next door and incapable of moving an inch toward her unless she happened to send for him! Love, it appeared, was crazy nowadays, like everything else: business and politics and the wars in Europe and Asia. Youth was as helplessly baffled by love as by the insanity of the general world;—and how had it lucklessly befallen him that he hadn't been born at least twelve or fourteen years earlier? If he were that old, he thought, he'd not only be safely beyond the reach of ridicule, but he'd surely know how to ring a lady's door-bell. She was avowedly his dearest friend, and he was afraid even to telephone her!

In other fields than love he did better than he knew, and the days that passed without summons from next door might well have pleased him as portents of a business career. The house with the freshly painted doorway and window frames and interior refurbishment was leased by a solvent tenant. "Snapped at it!" Mr. Barley said. Then, on the strength of this plain testimony to the worth of Hatcher's idea, Mr. Barley assumed the responsibility for allowing him to extend his other renovations and to double the number of his renovators. "I haven't been able to gain your father's attention," the old man said, "but on the strength of this rental I think we may dare go that far without undue risk."

One squad, for exteriors, Hatcher put under Mr. Floatus, the one-armed painter, and the other, for interiors, under Gilpin Murray, who was proud of his subordinates, though they consisted of the two out-and-downers and the two colored widows. Gilpin's exhortations kept the out-and-downers sober, and the widows, though elderly, were diligent. Hatcher, setting-to with this group, himself, proved that he was a thorough hands-clothes-and-face-painter. One of the colored women helped to clean him with turpentine, and gave him kind advice: "Some people got the brains to work with their han's an' brains, bofe," she said, "an' some only got the brains to work with their brains. You jes' keep you' han's in you' pockets, honey."

Mr. Barley, visiting the scene of experiment, said the "new generation" was going to take hold the right way, nobody need be uneasy any more about that; and Hatcher should have been delighted so to stir this dried old man. Perhaps there was a slight elevation of spirits after the tribute, before its recipient remembered that really he was suffering all the time. He worked harder and walked faster on his collecting rounds in order to come home earlier in the afternoons with a good conscience, hoping that Mrs. Florian would telephone him; but she maintained her unfathomable silence.

As twilight on the fifth lorn day began to dim the living-room where he did most of his waiting and hoping, his manner disturbed his little sister. "I'd hate to *haf* to go to my own room without even Mother making me do my home work there, Hatch," she said plaintively, from the fireside. "Couldn't you sit down?"

"Yes, do, please!" Aunt Ada, the other occupant of the room, looked up from an embroidery that engaged her.

"Young people seem to feel they can't live unless they're restless nowadays."

"No, we don't, Aunt Ada," Frances said. "Look at me; I'm just sitting here quietly. Why didn't you come home to lunch to-day, Hatch? You oughtn't to work so hard, especially not on Saturday. I've seen Mrs. Florian six times now altogether, Hatch; she dresses well. Polly Wilson that used to be my most intimate friend at school said this morning her mother says she bets you want to get married to Mrs. Florian, Hatch, and must be a simple idiot; so I've stopped speaking to her."

"Frances!" Aunt Ada's tone of reproof was mild; she looked amused. "Don't talk so absurdly!"

"I wasn't the one," Frances explained. "It was Polly Wilson's mother. I wouldn't like Hatch to get married to Mrs. Florian because then he'd have to go and live at her house. Aunt Ada, what was it old George wanted Father to do about Mrs. Florian?"

"Never mind," the aunt said. "Little pitchers needn't have such big—"

"Mine aren't and he did, Aunt Ada. Poor old George was crying when he came in the kitchen, and I heard him, and he asked if he couldn't see Father, and Father came and talked to him and I heard them saying 'Mrs. Florian' any number of times. I—"

Hatcher turned sharply from the bay window. "What is all this? What are you talking about now? What do you mean about old George crying and wanting to see Father?"

"Never mind!" Aunt Ada used one of her formulas. "It's nothing that concerns you, Hatcher, and it isn't this family's affair. Young people don't need to know every—"

"Damn it!" Hatcher broke out, and he continued to speak harshly in spite of Aunt Ada's pointing eloquently at Frances to remind him that there was an innocent child in the room. "I'm sick and tired of all the hush-hush business always going on in this house as if I were still a schoolboy and had no right to know anything about anything or—"

"It happened at lunch-time, Hatch," Frances interposed eagerly. "I like it when you swear, Hatch. I've heard lots and lots all over everywhere, Aunt Ada. Father was home at lunch-time and that's why old George came to see him; and another thing I heard him tell Father was he'd been to the Aldriches but Mr. Harry Aldrich said he couldn't do anything to help him. Old George was in a great deal of trouble, Hatch, and you could see Father felt sorry for him; and so did I and so did Lora and our old Berry, because Berry came in the kitchen, too—he came in with George—and Aunt Ada and Mother heard them and came out there, and I thought Mother was almost going to cry on George's account before they noticed I was there and told me I had to go out. Do you remember those Great Danes Mrs. Florian had when she first came, Hatch?"

"No, I don't. What have they got to do with old George?"

"Nothing except he said she treated them better than him. She wanted 'em to trail around after her in the garden and everywhere, one on each side, and when they wouldn't and didn't pay much attention to her, she had 'em sent where they came from and got her money back; but George said they'd be happy compared to him. I wish you'd swear some more, Hatch; it makes your voice sound so nice."

"I will!" Hatcher said. "I'll swear plenty if I don't find out—"

"Very well!" Aunt Ada really wanted to talk about what had happened. "Since you *must* know, then, old George came here because he'd just been discharged. He came to beg your father to intervene for him with Mrs. Florian."

"What?"

"Yes. It seemed he'd been discharged just for leaving a door open somewhere last night—discharged and told to move his things out of that little cottage he's lived in on the rear of the Lash place so many years. She ordered him to go immediately and declined to listen to him. He told us he supposed maybe he was growing forgetful in his old age because it was true he did leave the door open; but it had never happened before and never would again, if your father would only persuade her to take him back."

"Go on!" Hatcher spoke sharply. "What'd Father say?"

"He told George he'd try to help him along till he could find another place—but at George's age who'd hire him, and for what? George said he'd rather die than give up his cottage, he's so used to it—and the little garden he's made for himself there so many years!—but your father told him he didn't feel at liberty to speak to Mrs. Florian about it. Naturally Frederic knew it wouldn't be the slightest use."

"Why not?" Hatcher's voice was loud. "*Why* wouldn't it be of use? If she understood—"

"You think she doesn't?" Aunt Ada laughed.

"Certainly she doesn't!"

"You think not, Hatcher? I suppose because she's rather taken you up lately—an old habit of hers, by the way, so look out!—you think you understand her better than we do who knew her from A to Z when she was the worst spoiled brat and afterwards the worst spoiled flapper that ever—"

"See here!" Hatcher said. "See here!"

Aunt Ada laughed again. "Ask anybody that knew her! She was ingrowing enough on her own account; but her grandfather spoiled her, just the way he'd spoiled her father, who all his life thought everybody on earth had to get out of his way and finally thought so once too often! That was when he and his giddy little wife were driving at eighty miles an hour on Jefferson Boulevard and a milk-wagon didn't get out of the way because it couldn't. After that, her grandfather only had Sarah to spoil, and I must say she took to it! If there ever was a worse self-centered, more affected do-whatever-she-pleased hard-as-nails show-off young girl that didn't care for anything on earth except to be a sensation and make people talk about her, and pose and have her own way willy-nilly over anybody's dead body, and do any wild thing that came into her head—and so no wonder when that Spaniard came along she—"

"That's enough!" Hatcher shouted. "You seem to forget that you're speaking of a lady of whom I have the honor to be a friend!"

"Is she, Hatcher?" little Frances asked. "I'm glad that's all, because Polly Wilson's mother told her—"

"Damn!" Hatcher said fiercely. "Damn and damn!" he added, strode from the room and out of the house.

He blamed himself as well as Aunt Ada. His intuition had told him from the first not to speak of Sarah Florian to anybody, not to listen to a word spoken of her if he could possibly help it, and now he'd just let himself be betrayed into something like a discussion of her. What had happened, in consequence, were these fresh wounds. Was love, after all, as many poets complained, nothing but torment? No; other young men fell in love and everybody was pleasant about it, seemed delighted, said nothing that wasn't agreeable. Why was he singled out to be rolled in thorns and showered with darts—even in his own home? There was only one house, it seemed, where slander wasn't spoken and indignity couldn't reach him.

In the darkness that had fallen he pressed through the widely bordering shrubberies and looked at that substantial house, intending only to look at it. No stained-glass pattern shone through the night from the nearer wing; but there were faintly lighted windows farther on, both upstairs and down. Hatcher went forward, slowly crossing Mrs. Florian's wide dim lawn; then he halted, looking up at a figure vaguely seen between the curtains at one of the windows of the second floor. He couldn't be sure, but had a catch in his breath as he thought he recognized the figure as hers and that perhaps she saw him standing out there, a lonely shape in the cold darkness. The curtains closed; and, at that, he went on,

ascended stone steps and dared to push the button beside
the door above them. He waited long enough to regret
the desperate impulse and to decide upon retreat; then a
Filipino suddenly opened the door, and Hatcher heard
her piano.

The Filipino said, "Walk inside. I go see." Hatcher
went into the Louis XV room; the Filipino retired and
didn't reappear; the piano continued to be heard. Its
music was disturbingly elegiac. There were passages re-
sembling the Death March in the "Eroica", though
Hatcher didn't identify them; and other mournfulness
was heard, sometimes borrowed, sometimes improvised,
while the caller waited and waited and waited. At last, at
the end of half an hour perhaps, an almost too poignantly
familiar melody succeeded the funerary demonstration.
The strains of "Liebestraum" caressed his ear with an
infinite tenderness, speaking of love ineffable—then a
third of the keyboard crashed as if struck by a passionate
arm. There was a moment's silence and Sarah Florian
swept into the room, sank swiftly into a chair in a beautiful posture of pain, her head thrown back, her eyes
closed and her extended arms resting listlessly upon the
arms of the chair.

"How did you know?" she asked; and her richly
hushed voice expressed emotional exhaustion. "How did
you know that I wanted you to come just now? I sent
a message through the ether; you must have caught it.
The first time I saw you—as you stood above the crowd
on the stairway there in your house—I knew that we
could do things like this together. I'd have telephoned
you; but you *felt* my call and came."

XVII

Yᴇꜱ—I think so—I believe I did." The lovely exhausted voice convinced Hatcher that maybe he'd obeyed something like a mystic urge. "Yes, I wouldn't have come if I hadn't felt—hadn't felt I don't know just what. It's mysterious but—"

"Yet I kept you waiting." She opened her eyes languidly and repeated, "I kept you waiting."

"Yes. Five whole days."

"No; I mean just now." Mrs. Florian disposed of the five whole days by ignoring them. "I went on playing, trying to get myself out of a desperate mood before I could see even you."

"Desperate?" The word shocked Hatcher; it was unthinkable that this proud splendid woman should speak so strickenly. "You say you've been feeling desperate? I do hope you haven't—haven't been hearing—"

"Hearing?" Mrs. Florian looked at him with quickly widened eyes. "Hearing what?"

"Nothing. I didn't mean—"

"Oh, yes, you did!" she said. "You mean there's talk—talk about me. Frogs' chorusing in this little pond! Of course there is; there always was. As if I ever cared or could care now for *that!* Do you suppose I'd change any slightest thing in my life because of gabble? No, I don't yield to froth. What plays dirges upon me is this futility —this vacuity—in my life!"

"Vacuity?" Hatcher wasn't resentful; he only felt overlooked. "You mean there isn't much that appeals to you—hardly anything at all? You mean—"

"No, I don't. Some things appeal too much entirely. I mean that I'm getting nowhere, not achieving what I want—and isn't that dust and ashes in the mouth? What a life; what an emptiness! What have I? Nothing!"

"You?" Hatcher said plaintively. "Nothing?"

It was on the edge of his lips to insist that she had one possession at least. He wanted to say: "You have *me,* Sarah Florian. I own nothing but my life to give you; but that's yours. Even if it's true that you got tough with old George and once fell for my uncle and then threw him off the boat, I offer my life to you. Take it and do what you will with it. It's not much; but couldn't it be anyhow something?" Hatcher was so near saying this that probably the reason he didn't was that he hadn't the time. Mrs. Florian's listlessness was gone; she sat straight, made a protestive gesture with both hands and uttered an exclamation that sounded like anger.

"*Uh!*" she cried. "These damnable days, and this one worst of all! It began wrong—the most sordid episode this morning. I think you once said you knew that petti-fogging old George who's been living on my place all these years."

"Yes." Hatcher was greatly troubled. "I—I thought I'd ask you— It seems he came over to our house all upset and—"

"How exactly like him!" Sarah Florian's face flushed with indignation. "Whining all over the neighborhood for sympathy! I'm furious with myself for standing the old hypocrite as long as I have. He wasn't telling any-body what he'd *done*, I'll swear. *Why* did he say he was discharged?"

"I believe there was something about a door and—"

"Yes, there certainly was; but I'll be bound he didn't say which door, or what he murdered! It was the door to my hothouse. He'd let my greenhouses all go to rack and ruin; but I've been having them restored, and only yesterday I had my florist begin to fill one of them with plants and flowers. George has been pretending to be a night watchman so he could put it over on me he's doing something useful. He poked around in the hothouse; then went out and left the door open for·pipes to freeze in the bitter cold. This morning there was hardly a plant or flower he hadn't killed. He brought death to my flowers! Can anything excuse that?"

"Oh, I didn't know," Hatcher said feebly. "I didn't—"

"That's murder!" she interrupted. "It may be worth it to get rid of him. Nobody could know the boredom I've suffered from him and his airs of being the old family retainer, his never-ending garrulity—to show how devoted and useful he is, so that he could go on sponging on me the rest of his life! All this time he's had his cottage and the same wages from me that my grandfather was foolish enough to give him, a hundred dollars a month! I've paid it year after year because Harry Aldrich wrote me that the place had to be looked after and George was honest. Honest! Living on me, doing less than nothing, drawing all that money from me, and then finishing by murdering my flowers that had a better right to live than *he* had! Do you think I should bear that?"

"N—no—" Hatcher said. He was still sorry for George; he couldn't help but be so. Yet it seemed to him that in this passion for her flowers she showed a poetic kind of chivalry. "Of course I understand. I know how you feel. You went in there and saw everything all frozen and withered and—"

"It was criminal!" she cried. "So was his neglect of my house. Workmen told me the dust and cobwebs in my garrets and cellars were dreadful. What did *he* care, so he had his wages for nothing?" Mrs. Florian's indignation became even sharper; her voice had lost the rich hushedness she usually put upon it and was loud and determined. "Cheating! He cheated me for twelve years—because I'm a woman! Well, so I am; but that's one thing I'll not let anybody on earth do to me and get away with it. I'll not be cheated!"

Her militancy astonished Hatcher; for heretofore he'd seen but gentle aspects of her. She'd been elusively moody sometimes but always sweetly so; now she was flashingly in arms, a beautiful strong woman who could

and would give alms, he thought—would give tremen-
dously if she chose—but knew her rights, would fight for
them at the drop of a hat and couldn't be beaten down,
much less cajoled. She could be as sternly just as she
could be divinely tender, and this showed the opulent
variety of her nature: What could be more stirringly ad-
mirable? Still there lingered within Hatcher a faintly felt
sting of sympathy for old George;—but it certainly had
been a pretty bad thing to kill all those flowers, and Sarah
Florian was magnificent. Hatcher said so, in a voice as
hushed as hers usually was.

"I think you're magnificent," he said.

Again she proved how various she could be. She
jumped up and in two strides reached him where he sat
facing her. She sank upon one knee before him, in the
loveliest of all her postures. She took both of his hands
in hers and looked at him dizzyingly. "You don't mean
that!"

"Mean it?" the whirling Hatcher whispered, almost
voiceless. "Oh, my darl—"

Then she was more various than ever. Before he knew
it she was on her feet again, had caressed his cheek with
a light hand and had turned away. "You're wrong of
course," she said quickly, and laughed with a little pathos.
"Only sometimes I like to hear someone say it!"

"Sarah—" Hatcher rose and he stood at her shoulder.
"Sarah, I—"

"You're sweet, Hatcher." She turned to face him, smiling wistfully. "Of course I know that I'm anything but
magnificent. I'm just a woman who won't be battered
about." Then her smile vanished; she looked at him with

sharpest inquiry. "Before I told you just now that George had murdered my flowers, were you inclined to be critical of me?"

"Why—no. No, I—"

"I'm glad you weren't," she said. "It would have been the end of this friendship. That's one thing I never could endure, criticism from a friend. The rest can say what they please of me; but not my friends. My friends must accept me wholly or not at all." She began to speak with great vigor, frowning, and more as if she declared herself to the world than merely to one rapt caller. "I don't ask them to understand me; I do ask them to take me as I am, and I'll not have them pecking at me. I won't endure it! If whole belief in me's too much, then they're not my friends; they're my enemies. Understanding's more than I expect from either friends or enemies; I've never had it from a soul upon this earth."

"Are you sure?" Hatcher said. "Don't you think—"

"No, you couldn't," she interrupted, not abating her intensity. "In my whole life nobody ever did, no matter how I've tried to reveal myself. Yet how simple I am! I'm just a huntress for happiness; that's all. How long and how hard I've sought it—and how often I've thought, for a moment, that I was almost on the verge of finding it! Then—collapses, treacheries I couldn't even avenge, peckings, flaws found in me, emptiness where I thought there'd be perfect beauty. Yet still I'm a huntress. How bitter! I was put into this life to find happiness and there isn't any. I hunt for a thing that has no existence anywhere."

"No; you're wrong," Hatcher said, in a voice as faint
as his words were brave. "I have it when I—when I'm
here with you."

At this, suddenly, her mood once more changed entirely. She looked delighted with him, was all smiles and
pleasure. "You dear boy!" she said. "You really *do* know
how to be my friend. There!" She took his hand and retained it. "See what you've done: so quickly I'm all
soothed out! I mustn't keep you any longer because I've
got to fly to dress and dine with those Wilsons and go
to a concert with them. It's the symphony orchestra.
You're going, perhaps?"

"No, I believe we don't subscribe any more. I—"

"Nor any of your family?" she asked, still keeping his
hand. "Your Aunt Ada—or any of them?"

"No, I don't think so."

She looked disappointed. "I only thought if I happened
to see one of them it'd be a little—well, almost like seeing
you. A rather far-fetched pleasure, perhaps!" Her fingers
increased their pressure upon his own strongly; then released them. "There. You darling boy!" She set her hand
upon his breast, gave him a light push toward the door.
"Run!"

Hatcher, as lightfooted now as lightheaded, was out
of the house and across the great space of starlit lawn
almost as swiftly as if he did actually run. An unbelievable triumph was in his heart, and his physical eyes saw
little of what they looked upon. At home, he thought of
going to the concert where from the gallery he could perhaps look down upon a lovely head of symphonically
arranged black hair; but he couldn't afford a ticket and

really didn't need to do anything like that. His exhilaration required no such feeding.

He was in great spirits, teased his little sister gayly, scarce knowing what he said; and so, until more than an hour after dinner, wasn't aware of what an extremity of gloom his parents had reached. He'd consented to backgammon with Frances before she went to bed and was playing the game hilariously with her in the living-room when they were interrupted by the chattering summons of the telephone bell in the hall; Frances jumped up, dropping her dice-box upon the table.

Hatcher caught her by the arm. "Sit down, you squirrel. What's the matter? It's your move."

"Let me go, Hatch. Didn't you hear the bell? Father and Mother both promised I could be the telephone-answerer for this house." She called to her parents for corroboration. They sat together at the other end of the long room, Frederic Ide with a magazine and his wife with a book, though they were not reading but talking in lowered voices. "Didn't you promise I could be telephone-answerer, both of you?"

Preoccupied, they paid no heed, and Hatcher still detained the little girl. "What on earth do you want to be telephone-answerer for?"

"Please let go, Hatch! It's because that way a person gets to know a good deal of what's going on and I like to."

"Just a natural-born gossip!" Hatcher laughed loudly. "I never saw it come out earlier on anybody. You ought to be ashamed of what you're going to grow up to be, Francine!"

"Stop calling me 'Francine' and let me go! It's ringing again and if I don't get there Aunt Ada'll hear it in her room upstairs and beat me to it the way she did that last time Mrs. Florian called you, because Aunt Ada loves to just as much as I do—so please, Hatch!"

He released her. "Scram!"

She ran out lightly; and then, as the room became quieter after the noise she and Hatcher had been making, the voices of his father and mother unfortunately became audible to him. "It was grasping at a straw," he heard his father saying. "The crazy hope that these years might have made a change in—"

"Yes, all thrown away!" Mrs. Ide said, lamentant. "I might have known nothing could change such a woman. If she can be that hard-hearted to poor old George—"

Hatcher jumped up and strode the length of the room. "What's this?" he said. "I'm getting pretty tired of hearing such things! Mother, if you don't like Mrs. Florian what'd you break your neck to give her that Tea for?"

His mother looked up at him. "I didn't know you could hear. You weren't supposed to—"

"Yes, I know!" he said bitterly. "I'm never supposed to hear anything or be told anything. I'm too young, of course. I'll repeat my question: Mother, if you don't like Mrs. Florian what'd you spend all that money and energy giving that Tea for her for?"

Mrs. Ide put her hand in her husband's and hung her head. "We hoped it would please her."

Hatcher remained stern. "If you don't like her, why did you want to please her?"

"That'll do, Hatcher." Frederic Ide looked up with

eyes too dulled to be commanding. "Your mother and I
are having a private talk."

"It's too late for that," Hatcher said. "You've both got
to be made to understand I'm no longer a minor, and if
your private talks include the name of Sarah Florian I
demand—"

He was interrupted. Little Frances appeared in the
doorway. "Hatcher, it's for you; but don't let her keep
you long or we won't get to finish our game unless
Mother'll let me stay up. It's still my move."

"Who wants to speak to me?"

"Dorcy."

"Oh, all right!" Hatcher said roughly, and went to the
telephone.

Dorcy's voice sounded tense and queer; there were
quavers in it. "Hatch, can you come here—I mean to our
house? Would you come right away? Will you, please?
Will you?"

"Well, I—"

"Please, Hatch! Oh, please!"

Hatcher, sickeningly afraid that he was going to have
to tell her as gently as he could that he'd never really
cared for her in that way, said, "Yes, certainly," and went
forth.

XVIII

He needn't have feared that he'd have to tell Dorcy how sure she could always be of his true friendship for her, though unhappily not of more; she was already counting upon the friendship. She was waiting at the door for him, opened it before he rang, and he saw that under a white fur wrap she wore a pretty pink evening dress familiar to him, but that her eyes were frightened and her lips twitchy.

"Come in just for a minute," she said. "I want you to go somewhere with me, if you can."

"I can. I will." Hatcher spoke promptly. "What's the matter?"

"It's about Father. I want you to go with me to bring him home, if we can find him."

"Your father?" Hatcher, who'd stepped in and closed

the door, couldn't imagine what she meant. "Find your
father?"

"Oh, Hatch!" Dorcy was shaking; she leaned against
him, her cheek upon his shoulder, and he put an arm
about her. "Hatch, it's awful! Mother and I didn't know
what to do or who to send for to help us. Your father's
looked so ill lately Mother thought— And besides we'd
rather he didn't know. You won't tell him. Your Uncle
Victor was out, the telephone at his boarding-house told
us. We haven't any right to call on you, of course; but—
but you've always been so good and kind and such a—a
dependable neighbor and friend that I—" She looked up
at him then, as he held her, and for a moment it seemed to
him that his apprehension was realized; that her wet eyes
were really asking him if he wasn't, in spite of everything,
more than a dependable neighbor and friend—or if he
wouldn't some time care to be—but, if such a question
was indeed in that instant asked of him, Dorcy must have
seen the answer quickly. She stepped away from him.
"We don't know where Father is, Hatch. He's—he's—"

"He's what?" Hatcher was incredulous. Big, hearty,
jolly Harry Aldrich was the last man in the world anybody'd ever be worried or distressed about, he thought.
"What's the matter with your father?"

"He's drunk," Dorcy whispered.

"What! Why, I never heard of—"

"No, nor did we, Hatch—Mother and I. He never in
the world before to-night—"

"Oh, see here!" Hatcher, relieved, patted her shoulder.
"Why, Dorcy, that can happen to anybody. With a man
like your father it'd be just an accident—a little more than

he realized he was pouring in, that's all. Good heavens, old girl, don't take such a thing seriously! What's got into you? Your mother certainly knows better than to worry about it, doesn't she?"

"She's sunk, Hatch; completely. We're both scared."

"But why? Almost every man—at least once or twice in a lifetime—"

"No, no!" Dorcy said. "It wasn't like that. Mother and he were going to the Symphony and so was I. It was seven o'clock and I was just starting for the Wilsons' to dine there and go with their party—when Father came in. I never saw anything like the way he looked—it just wasn't the same man. He frightened us both."

"What? But that's nonsense, Dorcy. Anybody when he's oiled up a bit doesn't look—"

"No, no!" Dorcy put both her hands over her heart. "You just couldn't understand unless you'd seen him, Hatch. I've seen plenty of people badly off, but not like that. He hadn't been here a minute before Mother got just weak and I ran to telephone the Wilsons I had a sick headache. He was tragic, Hatch. He said the most terrible things."

"What sort of things?"

"He kept saying there was going to be nothing but war in the world and God was going to strike it down. It was more as if he'd lost his mind than as if he'd been drinking; but of course he had—and he said he was going to stay drunk forever. Then he got to sobbing and laughing together and telling Mother over and over she mustn't mind anything he said because everything would be all right to-morrow. Of course we didn't want the servants to hear him, and I ran to close the doors to that part of the house; but I heard Mother call me and ran back. They were at the front door here and she was trying to hold him; but he tore himself loose from her and shouted he was never coming home again and ran out. He had a taxi outside and was gone before I could get to it."

"I see," Hatcher said thoughtfully. "Maybe you're right; maybe we'd better go look for him. Where—"

"We don't know. We telephoned and telephoned—even to all the hotels, getting him paged, and waiting and waiting and waiting. Then, when it was all of no use, I thought of you, and Mother said yes, you'd be the one. I've got her lying down in yonder, and I thought if you'd come, you and I could take her big car and we'd go the round of the bars and I'd sit outside and wait while you went into the different places alone, because if I went in with you I think the mood he's in would make him break away again or start up another scene like the one that went on here. He likes you, and if we find him and you could persuade him to come out to the car and get in, why, then I'm pretty sure I could handle him while you'd drive us home. It's all I can think of. I don't know what else to try."

"I do," Hatcher said. "There's not the slightest use of your going, Dorcy. All I need's the car. I'll go through every rum hole in the town till I find him and I'll bring him home and put him to bed, myself. Just you and your mother keep out of the way when I get him here and I'll—"

Dorcy shook her head determinedly. "No; you don't know the state he's in. It'll need both of us."

"No, it won't." Hatcher held up a hand, and laughed. He'd just heard wheels on the driveway. "It won't need anybody. There's a car right now and I'll bet anything you like it's your father. He's come home himself, probably a good deal sobered up. You'll see."

Dorcy uttered a great sigh. "Oh, if it only is!"

They listened and heard laughter outside, Harry Aldrich's laughter, and his voice calling something indistinguishable but cheerful to the departing driver. Dorcy threw open the door, and Harry walked in, still laughing but not steady upon his feet.

He took Dorcy in his arms effusively. "Only child I ever had," he said. "Best one, too! Hello, Hatcher-young-fellow-me-lad! Where's your mother, Dorcy? Got to swear myself—I mean square myself—for being downtown so late, keeping dinner waiting and everything all this time. Must be after seven o'clock and she'll give me fits because we're going to the Sylph—Symphony and she loves to be on time to music and I've still got to dress. Can't help it. Unfinished business kept me at the office; simply had to be 'tended to. Been at my desk every minute since lunch, hours and hours and hours!" He released Dorcy and leaned against the wall. "Wasn't I asking you where's your mother, or not?"

Mrs. Aldrich, with tears just swept from her pretty face, appeared from the living-room, stared unbelievingly and then, with a sharp cry of relief, rushed to her husband and flung her arms about him. "Oh, Harry!" she cried. "Thank heaven! Thank heaven! Dear heart, you frightened me so!"

"Me!" He was deeply puzzled. "Wouldn't frighten a

pigeon! When'd I ever frighten my own baby, my own sweet love Eleanor? What makes you tell such stories, honey?"

She clung to him; then took a step backward and tried to be severe with him. "Harry Aldrich, where on earth did you get such a binge?"

"That's incorrect, beloved." He folded his arms upon his chest, evidently hoping to look more dignified. "One doesn't get a binge; one gets on one." His eyes, not focusing easily, again became aware of Hatcher. "Well, well; isn't this Fred Ide's boy, young Hatcher? Hatch, you're too young. That's the only trouble; you're too young."

Hatcher laughed. "No, I'm not, sir—not too young to help you up to bed."

Mrs. Aldrich laughed too, and thanked him. "No, dear boy," she added. "I'll do that easily."

"You will not! Never!" her husband said; but his gaze remained waveringly upon Hatcher. "Nobody will. Hatch boy, I've always loved your father. It was your grandfather took me into the firm; but Fred got him to. I love Fred Ide dearly and I always will, no matter what he does. We all of us make mistakes and they get us into big trouble. If your poor father—" Harry paused; his arms slipped, spoiling the dignified posture, and he tried fumblingly to put his hands in his trousers pockets. "Well, anyway, I love Fred Ide. Whatever he does, or's done, or's going to do, I'm still *for* him; remember that! Stay to dinner with us, Hatch. Eleanor Aldrich, you little skeezix, what you laughing at?"

"At you, because you're just babbling—and because I'm so glad you're home," she explained, as she put an arm about him. "Come on; you're going to bed."

"I'm going to play the piano. Bed, no! I wouldn't for—I wouldn't for the last twenty-two thousand dollars in the world. I won't!" He continued to protest, seemingly unaware that all the time he was yielding to his wife's pressure and moving with her down the hall toward the stairway. "I decline! Four of us here, aren't they? That's exactly a quartet; so we're all going to sing. Sing as long as we live! Sing anyhow that long. I won't go to bed! Hate bed."

"Lift your foot and step up," his wife instructed him, as they reached the stairway; and they began to ascend, with Harry insisting at every step that he wouldn't take the next one.

In her great relief Eleanor Aldrich continued to laugh fondly, radiant because he had come safely home to her. Nothing was more evident than that she loved him as much when he was drunk as when he was sober, and that Harry, drunk or sober, adored her. So, with a pang of envy in his heart, the young man gazing up at them thought that here was a picture of triumphant love, another example of love that wasn't baffling and painful. From the landing Eleanor looked back over her shoulder.

"Don't come, Dorcy," she called. "Thank you again and again, Hatch—you were so kind. But everything's all right, bless heaven!"

"Yes, of course it is," Hatcher said, and turned to Dorcy. "I'll be trotting along."

She was staring toward the upper flight of the stairway. "It's so strange—his forgetting he'd been here before and all that terrible—"

"Nonsense! Didn't you ever hear of anybody's drawing a blank before?"

"Yes, of course; but not like— Oh, well!" She extended her hand, withdrew it as soon as he'd clasped it. "Thank you. You've been kind. Goodnight."

"Goodnight, Dorcy. You'd be foolish to worry any more about nothing. You and your mother are all right now."

"Are—we?" she said, as he stepped out into the darkness; and the slight hesitation before she added the second of the two words held the disturbing implication that although everything was now probably all right for her mother it mightn't be quite so all right for herself.

The involuntarily conveyed slight hint of pathos remained with Hatcher botheringly, bringing upon him the same unwarranted sense of guiltiness that cool Mary Gilpin and spiteful Lennie Aldrich had incited, on the night of the Aldriches' great dinner for Sarah Florian. *Why* should he feel guiltiness when he was guilty of nothing? Dorcy, in trouble, had sent for him and he'd been glad to come—he'd always do anything on earth for her— but why hadn't she and her mother sent for Pinkie Wilson, instead? Because Pinkie's parents were giving a party and might have objected to his leaving it? No, that didn't seem to be the answer. Hatcher knew that in her moment of need Dorcy's heart had still turned to him and not to Erdvynn Wilson; this was what caused the sense of guilt. Once, he and Dorcy had both rather expected to be engaged some day, he supposed; but it hadn't happened and now it never could. That it couldn't wasn't his fault; yet here he was bedevilled for it! What were people made of? What was he himself made of, that he had to suffer for what he couldn't help?

Not rid of bafflements brought upon him by Dorcy's pathetic "Are—we?" he found others to oppress him. Castaway imaginings again began to land upon the shores of his mind, though no longer was any absurd old scandal concerning Mrs. Florian brought with them. Before his first sight of her, Hatcher had been able to imagine that even his good father might be penalized for an ancient amorous dalliance; but the very air the son breathed throughout his whole boyhood at home had precluded any thought that financial dishonor could ever by any possibility taint the name of Frederic Ide or that of the firm of Ide and Aldrich. To-night he hadn't paid serious attention to Harry Aldrich's liquored maunderings in the moments of their utterance; but afterward some of them seemed to repeat themselves, becoming significant.

Was the gist of them that no matter what his partner had done, Harry'd loyally stand by him? In wine there is sometimes too much truth: Did Harry mean that worse than insolvency was hovering, that there might be—some sort of scrape? Once more, Hatcher began to be frightened about his father; but the amorphous fear was only a malicious squeak from one of the harpies that again flew to harry him.

The exultant mood of a few hours ago was gone. A statistician's chart of Hatcher's feelings during this one evening would have carried a line from a point far down on the page to the upper margin, then dropped it all the way to the lower, not omitting some wobbles on both the upward and downward side of the acute angle. These

deflections would mark the jolts in the young man's emotions, in particular an almost submerged yet hurting
doubt concerned with Sarah Florian. People didn't like
her because of course they didn't understand her, and she
was all the more perfect because she was so far above
them that they couldn't. She'd been absolutely right
about poor old George, certainly; but—but, after all,
Hatcher found that he couldn't think of the old man
without adding the compassionate adjective. "Poor" old
George! What had happened to him was just, of course,
but maybe a bit tough if you thought of poor old
George's way of looking at it.

In childhood and first youth, troubles usually seem to
come one at a time because one is enough to fill the young
heart. To be able to suffer from several simultaneously
is sometimes a sign that the youth has begun his advance
toward maturity. Not six months ago young Hatcher Ide,
a grave old Senior, had stood with his Class for the evening music on the campus, and had loudly sung, with but
the airiest sense of the words:

> "When the cares of life o'er-take us,
> Mingling fast our locks with gray,
> Should our dearest hopes betray us,
> False Fortune fall away—"

To-night Hatcher began to know a little about this.
He almost began, in fact, to be his age.

XIX

POOR OLD GEORGE, who'd been more or less in the compassionate thoughts of several of Hatcher's relatives most of that day, put himself bodily into the sight of one of them the next morning. Mr. Victor Linley, in this commercially idle and less fortunate period of his life, had developed a routine; and a feature of it was that on one of his daily walks with his golden spaniel he passed his sole possession in the way of real estate and gave it first a shiver and then a meditative glance. He kept always to the opposite side of the street. That abominable-looking big relic, the old Linley house, was a little the more bearable for the distance and the additional intervention of smoke-thickened air. Mr. Linley's habit was to give the house only the one brief melancholy look as he passed; but, on this cold and therefore more than usually smoky Sunday morning, that look was lengthened, as it had been upon the afternoon early in the autumn when he'd seen his nephew trying to collect rent from the verbose landlady, Mrs. Schapp. Again, as on that afternoon, he paused across the street, and Locksie sat down.

Old George came out from the marble vestibule; and soot-streaked Mrs. Schapp, a half-eaten link of sausage in her hand, called cacklingly after him before she closed the door. Old George, stooping and slow, descended the steps and crossed the street to the waiting gentleman.

"I was setting at the window looking for you," George said. "She told me you 'most always come by, Sunday mornings, about this time. Hollering after me just now I got to pay my room rent in advance next Saturday same as yesterday. She needn't worry."

"No, George," Linley assented. "Neither need you. The fact is, I suggested your taking a room there because I thought you could chalk up anything you might come to owe Mrs. Schapp against what she owes me. It wasn't my idea that you'd pay anything at all."

"Yes, sir, I know. It was kind of you; but I can handle the three dollars and a half a week for the room all right. That leaves me about four to eat and dress on, and, as I've got a little kerosene sort of stove, I can do it. My stomach don't relish much but coffee anyhow, and my great-nephew's invited me to have supper with him and his family whenever I get a mind to. Oh, I'll do, sir; I'll do well enough except for missing what I been used to. That hits me kind of hard."

"Yes. Too bad!" Linley said. "Don't forget, though,

that when you want to spend that three dollars and a half a week on yourself instead of paying Mrs. Schapp, you have a right to do it. If she makes a fuss, just refer her to me."

"Thank you, sir; but the financial part of my trouble isn't worrying me much. You see, after my family died I was able to save some; and last year Mr. Aldrich told me to put it into the Heat and Light Company and I did, and it's been picking up; so I figure it'll bring me in as much as four hundred dollars a year. You see, a man like me can figure out to live on that, sir." George glanced over his shoulder and shook his head. "My, my! It seems pretty strange to me, and must seem more so to you, to think I'm living in the grand old Linley house. Why, my heavens, I remember when—"

"Yes, George; so do I."

"I bet you do, sir," George said. "I guess I'll get used to always hearing that squalling voice of hers whatever part of the house she's in. It seems wrong to hear such sounds and think of what goes on in all the fine big rooms with the beautiful walnut wood-trim and parquetry floors—and everything all so dirty and smoky and noisy! My room's up in the Mansard roof where she's got it all subdivided with wallboard partitions to make the rooms smaller and get more lodgers in. I guess, though, you know better about how she's got the place fixed than I do and—"

"No." Mr. Linley's smooth brow was shadowed for a moment; his imperturbability flickered. "No, I—I haven't been in the house for some years. I don't—"

"No, sir." The sympathetic George spoke quickly. "You wouldn't like it, and I guess the more you don't see what's inside there the better you'll feel. On the other hand, sir, I just wanted to tell you I'm all right. She keeps the house pretty cold; but I own a couple of quilts and I can get nice and warm cheap whenever I choose to go to bed. Well, sir, I just wanted to thank you and apologize for having bothered you with my troubles."

"Not at all," Linley said. "Every man must go to his friends sometimes, and, since you insist on paying Mrs. Schapp for your room, I'm afraid you're thanking me for nothing."

"No, I'm not, sir. You see, I've got your idea about not paying to fall back on, if ever I get pinched or sick or anything, and that's a big comfort. Besides, I been thinking over one or two things you says to me yesterday and it give me quite a brace." George laughed a little ruefully. "In particular, there's what you says about when a man's in hard luck, what a comfort he can get out of his vanity if he learns he's got the backbone to stand up and say, 'Go ahead, Trouble, get worse. You can't squeeze a yip out o' me!' Guess that might be the last and only satisfaction some of us'll get out of our life, speaking of myself. I got one yip left, though; can't help it. Leaving that door open didn't do all she claims it done; not by no means!"

"No," Victor Linley said slowly. "No, I was sure of that, George."

"No, sir. Guess *you* know her all right! Them pipes didn't freeze and it only damaged one or two plants near the door. Of course I ought to've shut it tighter so the

wind couldn't blowed it open; but it looks to me like just
an excuse. Yes, she's been wanting to get rid of me all
along. Everybody but her's been mighty kind. What a
woman! Well, sir, good-bye for the time being. I didn't
mean to intafere with your walk this long."

The interference had been a pleasure, Victor said; and,
to the spaniel's delight, resumed the walk northward. A
few minutes later master and dog were in their quarters
in the brick boarding-house and both began to enjoy a
luxury reserved for Sundays. Linley lighted a fire in the
grate under the "fumed oak" mantelpiece in his sitting-
room; the kindling crackled encouragingly, and a drift
of early snowflakes outside the grimed windows completed a picture of philosophic coziness.

"There, Locksie," Linley said, placing a cushion near
the hearth for him. "Excuse my dissipation." He took the
dissipation from an upper waistcoat pocket, a cigar of
the one type he enjoyed. For economic reasons he smoked
on Sundays only; then he allowed himself two of these
rewarding cigars, and presented the first to himself as
a complement to the morning walk. "Snug enough,
Locksie, what?" he said.

He was, in fact, as his nephew had discontentedly ob-
served, by no means a discontented man; and he'd made
his lodgings pleasanter than the exterior of the house suggested as possible. The bedroom was not uncomfortable,
and in the sitting-room he'd himself neatly built the book
shelves that supported the well-bound remaining items
of his once elaborate library. Across the front of the
room, beneath two windows that looked down upon the
street, a long table extended, displaying unfinished archi-

tectural designs, drawings in experimental stages and
light sketches of details.

True, everything in the place was slightly grimy to
both touch and sight despite Mr. Linley's own incessant
tidiness and the struggles of a stout housemaid who'd
become romantically devoted to this boarder; the air was
tinged with a repulsive blue-gray, for the city smoke
crept everywhere and could not be excluded. The fine
cigar had lost no more than a third of its length when the
fastidious bachelor, sighing, rose from his chair beside
the fire to resume his war upon the creeping smudge. He
brought a clean bit of soft cloth from a drawer of the
long table and began to wipe carefully the framed photographs he kept upon the mantelpiece.

These, five in number, were "amateur shots"; but his
expression as he cleaned them was token that he treasured
them. All but one were of "family groups". The first that
he cleaned was new; it showed his handsome sister Alice,
Mrs. Upham, her handsome husband and their two
homely little boys who'd arrived late to the Uphams and
were approximately contemporaneous with their small
cousin, Frances Ide. The second photograph was of Victor's sister Harriet, Mrs. Ide, her stalwart husband, Frederic, and their three good-looking children, Hatcher,
Janey and little Frances. The third was of his friend
Harry Aldrich and Harry's pretty wife, Eleanor, and
their pretty daughter, Dorcy, taken when Dorcy was a
child.

Victor Linley looked fondly at one after another of
these little pictures, though his gaze dwelt longest on the
third—that of the young Aldrich family; it seemed to

bring upon him a solicitous perplexity. The fourth of the photographs he touched lightly indeed, for it showed three people laughing together on the front steps of the old Linley house—his father and his mother and a young girl, delicate and fair, his sister Nancy. His moment of communion with the three figures was brief, as if a longer one couldn't be borne; and the movement of his hand, when he set the picture back upon the mantelpiece, was as gently careful as if he feared its slightest fluctuation might jar the dead themselves.

The last of the framed "shots" was of half a dozen youthful officers in khaki seated about a sidewalk table before a French café; and the soft cloth had but touched it when there was a knock upon the door and one of Mr. Linley's fellow-boarders walked in—a thick-haired, hollow-eyed young man whose scarlet tie was the more noticeable for its background of dark blue shirt. His facial contours expressed amused superiority, projecting upon the world the continuous self-congratulation of an intellect convinced that its capacity for deep thinking isn't likely to be matched anywhere.

"Hi!" he said amiably. "I was walkin' up the Avenue a ways behind you, and I got onto something about you that handed me a laugh, Linley: you limp worse when you don't think anybody's lookin' at you."

"Do I, Mr. Boerl? Won't you sit down?"

"Nope; I just come in to see if you don't agree we boarders better fix up a Round Robin against all this mashed turnip at table. If she won't listen, might picket her—'Unfair to boarders' stomachs', what?" He looked over Linley's shoulder at the photographed group of

officers. "Guess that's when you got your limp, huh?
Guess you feel like a sucker when you remember you
fought in *that* war, huh? 'Make the world safe for democracy'. That's a hot one! Gives you a laugh now to
think you thought you were makin' the world safe for
democracy when you went over the top, don't it?"

"No," Victor Linley said reflectively. "That was just
a civilian's oratorical slogan, a mistaken afterthought. The
army didn't go for that reason, you see. I don't recall
ever hearing it mentioned among us then."

"You don't?" Boerl looked surprised; but recovered
himself immediately and became informative. "Then you
must been like a lot the others—just let drums and bands
and the old star-spangled banner shot-in-the-arm drag
you into an imper'alist war without the slightest real idea
what you were fightin' for. Just sucked in to be cannon-
fodder, the same as these boobs right now in the phony
war that's on, over in Europe. Maginot line, Siegfried
line, phooey!—British Tories and American airplane and
steel plutocrats gettin' rich, and all it amounts to is a sit-
down strike. But you wait till the cap't'list foreign gov-
er'ments try to demobilize! I'll give you a tip: when they
try to demobilize, look out!—because right then the
phony angle might be over. Certain parties on the inside
track might decide it's the psychological moment for sort
of a *class* war—and, boy! will that be a real one!"

"I'm afraid this one is," Mr. Linley said. "I'm afraid
this period you call 'phony' can't last much longer. I
fear—"

"Listen, Linley. Don't kid yourself. Both sides, it's
only a couple gangsters walkin' around each other and

both afraid to use their guns, while good old Soviet Russia's just lookin' on laughin' because Uncle Joe Stalin knows if them two ever *did* begin shootin' each other up, why, *his* Big Day's come! Don't trouble your head, Linley, because them two gangsters know it, too; they won't fight." Boerl glanced at the drawings on the long table and became approving. "Pretty good. First rate. Somebody hand you a building job at last?"

"No. Just keeping my hand in."

"I see," Boerl said. "Trouble with you, Linley, the way I size you up, it's you don't know how to push yourself. As long as we keep this crackpot cap't'list system a man's got to plug for himself or he can't succeed, and you don't know how to do that. Building's beginning to show life again, some, and there's several firms of architects in this city already up to real business right now. Well, you're as good as any of 'em; so why aren't you—"

"No, I'm not." Mr. Linley looked ruefully amused. "It's friendly of you to think so; but I never was a really important architect, I'm afraid, and now I doubt if my ideas would do at all. I'm too crotchety and traditional, you see, Mr. Boerl. I'm not up with these times; I never could bear to design flimsy houses and I don't like purely functional buildings, either. No." He shook his head. "I'm afraid there's no hope for me at all."

"None at all?" Boerl asked, and laughed. "Well, you used to make a pretty good income out of architecture, didn't you?"

"No; not very. Fair, but—"

"I see," Boerl said. "But they say you used to live pretty high, even sweller than this. If it wasn't out of your profession, you must have had big outside resources. Depression hit your dividends, did it?"

"Yes; it seems so."

"Seems so? That's cool!" Mr. Linley's fellow-boarder looked at him with a condescending indulgence. "You're a queer bird, Linley. Fact is, I think you're one of the oddest guys I ever met. Everybody in the house likes you, and I guess they all of 'em think they know you; but I happen to have just a few more brains than the rest of 'em, so I see that we none of us do. I don't really get you at all. For instance, you're the star boarder and you got a swell place here, perfectly elegant—but not a radio nor current literature, and you don't go to movies; yet you always seem interested in everything. Some people might say you're sort of haywire, kind of an innocent foolish guy." Boerl laughed. "Not me. I think you're deeper than that. I expect maybe the truth is you're what might be called a good deal of a philosopher."

"I?" Linley looked surprised. "No. I believe philosophers are usually supposed to take a much less personal interest in things than I do."

"That so, Linley? Well, then, maybe we'll just have to classify you as sort of general good fella. That teacher across the table from me, though, claims you're what they call a socialite. Guess she's right. Take these swell dames, now, that drive up and send their chauffeurs in to get you to come down and—"

"I'm watched, then?" Linley laughed. "The few times that's happened, Mr. Boerl, I think the ladies were probably relatives of mine or—"

"Oh, of course! All of 'em just his sisters and his

cousins and his aunts. Foxy guy!" Boerl became humor-
ously insinuating. "How about the dark brunette in the
platinum-plated town-car? Saw you out in front on the
curbstone talkin' through the window to her, myself, day
before yesterday—you bare-headed and serious as hell,
and the slick mulatto chauffeur wise enough to act like
he was interested in his radiator. Some baby, pal! I took
a good gander at her and she's some baby, believe you
me. Boy! I sure yearned. You *bet* you're watched, Linley,
when you're talkin' to tricks like that. Don't try to tell
me that black-haired, black-eyed babe was just one of
your relations! For that matter, I guess some of *them* are
pretty high-flyers, too."

"I'm afraid not," Linley said. "I'm afraid they fly
rather low nowadays, Mr. Boerl."

"That so? Well, anyhow, that teacher says they always
been big bugs in the city, because you belong to one of
the old original cap't'list families that used to run this part
the country." He laughed genially. "Well, since Hitler
and Uncle Joe Stalin jolted us with their pact, some of
us aren't talkin' so loud; but our crowd still kind of ex-
pects to take over this old U.S.A. some day not so far
off maybe, and run it scientifically on our own lines. I
guess, though, you're one of the few of the old oppressors
we won't send to the guillotine. No, sir, you live in a
good deal of style here; but anybody can tell by lookin'
at you that you wouldn't harm a flea, and so we'll go
easier on you than on—"

He was interrupted by a tapping upon the hall door.
Victor Linley said, "Excuse me, Mr. Boerl. This is very
interesting and I hope to hear more of it; but I—" Then,

as explanation of the unfinished sentence, he opened the
door and beheld the stout housemaid who tried her best
to keep his rooms clean.

"It's a lady caller, Mr. Linley," she announced deferentially. "It's Mrs. Frederic Ide, sir."

"I'll get out," Boerl said, stepping toward the door.
"No high society for me, thanks! I'll—"

"Not at all," Victor interrupted, as Mrs. Ide came in.
"Won't you stay? I'd like you to meet my sister. Harriet, this is Mr. Boerl, one of my friends here and—"

"Glad to made your 'quaintance," Boerl said to her,
obviously intimidated and in hasty departure, though her
nod and glance were not discourteous. "Be seein' you,
Linley."

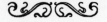

XX

W HAT an unpleasant type!" Harriet Ide sat down sadly. "I can't tell you, Victor, how it makes me feel to see you living in such a place and with such people about you!"

"Dear girl, I can only tell you again how wrong you are." He took a chair opposite her, beside the fireplace; the golden spaniel jumped upon his lap and disposed himself there for renewed slumbers. "These rooms are comfortable and the people are interesting."

"Oh, Victor!"

"They are," he insisted. "They lead as interesting lives as anybody does and have as interesting thoughts. My fellow-boarders are anything but commonplace, though I admit nothing's commonplace if you really take time to look at it. It's absorbing to see how perfectly my

198

friends here fit into the pattern of all human life—just as
the rest of us compulsorily do, of course, every man in
his own way. I don't know anything more dramatically a
cross-section of the world than what's narrow-mindedly
called a 'second-rate boarding-house'. It's always fascinating."

"Fascinating? Oh, Victor, what a word for this
dingy—"

"It's a beautiful example of a microcosm!" he protested, with unusual animation. "By the pattern of all
human life I mean the variegated shapes produced by the
single force that moves us—the force that's sometimes
called good and's sometimes called evil but is always the
same thing, the root of all human action, the thing that
makes progress and decadence, and war and peace, and
generosity and greed—and booms and depressions—and
capitalism and communism and—"

"Victor!" His sister's sad voice was a little impatient.
"I really don't know what you're talking about."

"Why, about human egoism of course, Harriet." His
eagerness increased. "Every meal here is a treat, and I
like my associates at table all the better for the openness
with which they show how natural-born universal egoism
controls the stuff they're made of—a substance about as
good as you'll find at most tables. I can't tell you how
much I enjoy—"

"Oh, Victor!" Mrs. Ide softly cried again. "You think
I don't *know* what this impoverishment and the dreadful change in your living mean to you?"

"Impoverishment, no!" he exclaimed. "I used to live in
buzz and bustle—a dozen different kinds of activity.

What you call impoverishment gives me time for meditation; and how does anybody get at realities without it? We don't know at all what we're doing so long as we live busily in action, or in emotion, or by stimulants from our five senses. A man *can* live, instead, in his mind; and for me this has been a happy discovery because I've learned that I possess some mental resources—not important ones of course, except to me; but they suffice. For most people these lean years have been hard and for some they've been killing. Thinking of what they've done for just my inconsequent self, though, Harriet, I could easily find it in my heart to thank God for the Depression!"

"What?" she murmured vaguely, and, perceiving that she wasn't listening, he lost his animation, laughed briefly at himself, and, having thrown the remains of his cigar into the fire, stroked Locksie reflectively.

"You're on your way home from church, Harriet?"

"Yes, I—I thought I'd stop in and see you for a moment."

"Just for a moment? Something you'd like to talk about?"

"No, not in particular, Victor. That is, I—"

"Yes, there is." Victor's hand, about to move caressively upon the spaniel's golden coat, paused and was still. "I'm afraid I know there's something in particular you'd like to talk to me about, Harriet."

"No, there isn't, Victor," she said stoutly; but the firelight into which she gazed showed him the sudden moisture upon her lower eyelids.

"No?" He began to stroke the dog again. "I seem to gather from Hatcher that he's perceived in you and Fred a considerable uneasiness. I think he said he'd been asking you about it and—"

"I'd rather not speak of it." Her voice had a little sharpness. "There's one thing, though, I think perhaps I'd better tell you. I haven't mentioned it to you before, because what's the use of adding to your distresses, especially if it mightn't happen? Now, though, I'm afraid it's going to. When Ada came home from visiting Alice out west she was worried. Things were going pretty badly with Jack Upham, and Ada was afraid there was going to be a crash. Well, it's happened. That utility corporation had to make an economy drive, and Jack's been dropped. I had a letter from Alice day before yesterday. She said that if he couldn't find a new position quickly—and there wasn't anything in sight—she was afraid she'd have to ask if she couldn't bring the children and the three of them visit us—she spoke of it as a visit, poor thing!—until Jack could get into something else. It's going to be a problem to arrange proper room in the house for them, especially if Janey comes home for the holidays, and with only the cook—no maids to do the rooms— Oh, well, I suppose we can manage somehow. If it only hadn't had to come upon us just now!"

Victor put Locksie down on the rug, and rose. "Well, Alice is my sister, too," he said.

Mrs. Ide jumped up. "You don't think I've told you about it in the hope that you could do anything for them, Victor! Good heavens, don't you suppose we all know you can't? When you're down to living like this—"

He was troubled. "I ought to be able—"

"No—no, please!" She put a hand on his arm. "I oughtn't to've told you. We can manage. We'll find room in the house and food for them somehow, and that's all they'll need. Jack's a capable man and he'll get into something. Ordinarily Fred and I'd be able to handle it if it weren't—"

"Yes?" Victor said quickly. "If it weren't for what?"

"Nothing."

He took both of her hands. "Harriet, this bad luck of the Upham family *isn't* what's on your mind. You can't look me in the eye and maintain it. Won't you tell me?"

"No; I can't tell anybody," she said desolately, released her hands from his and moved slowly toward the door. "I can't, even though it mayn't be long before everybody'll know it."

"It's that bad, Harriet—and that close?"

"Yes." For a moment she said no more; then she turned toward him with the air of one who absent-mindedly introduces a negligible subject. "Oh—I suppose you haven't happened to call on Sarah yet?"

"No, I haven't."

"I suppose you're going to, though, aren't you?" In response he only looked at her; and, at that, she made a remonstrance. "Oh, but don't you think you really ought to, Victor? She's asked you, hasn't she? Hasn't she done more? Hasn't she telephoned? Hasn't she even written to—"

"Yes, I believe so."

"More than once, Victor?" He was silent, and Mrs. Ide

spoke impulsively. "Yes, I see she has! That's a good deal
—from Sarah Lash—don't you think?"

"Is it, Harriet? Well—let's not go into that."

"Others might envy you," Mrs. Ide said. "Your own
nephew, for instance."

"My nephew?" Victor, after the briefest moment of
surprise, spoke musingly. "Yes, I see. A good-looking
young man only next door. Oh, yes, of course!"

"Yes," Mrs. Ide said. "Poor Hatcher! She's quite taken
him up; so I'm afraid he'd rather begrudge the invitations you've had. Poor boy, I'm afraid he's in quite a
state."

"You mean he believes he is, Harriet."

"No; I mean he is."

"Dear me!" Victor said. "I'd rather taken it for
granted that he and Dorcy Aldrich—"

"No; not any more, Victor—at least, not any more for
Hatcher. I don't know about Dorcy. I'm afraid the
gorgeous Sarah's overwhelmed him. Preposterous, isn't
it?"

"No." Her brother seemed to ponder. "I shouldn't call
it preposterous. He's not much like the boy in the old
jokes, falling in love with the schoolteacher twice his age.
Sarah'd most easily capture a good young imagination.
It'd be natural, under the circumstances."

"Perhaps," the sister assented. "I don't know why I've
mentioned it; I didn't mean to, and I don't really take it
seriously. At Hatcher's age—"

"It's highly sensitive," Victor interrupted. "People
usually feel pretty sharply at Hatcher's age."

"Yes—but briefly, Victor."

"If they're sound," he said, "and of course Hatcher's—"

"Victor!" Mrs. Ide stepped toward him. "Couldn't you —couldn't you bring yourself to be nice to her? I mean couldn't you at least go to see her and be friendly and— and—"

"And what, Harriet?"

"Oh, dear!" she said, and the words were a moan of confession—confession that she was desperately asking a great deal of him. "Couldn't you?"

"No, I could not," he answered.

Her right hand, lifted to add eloquence to the appeal she'd just made to him, dropped to her side. "I must get myself home," she said in a dead voice. "You'll come out to us to-night for Sunday evening supper as usual, won't you?"

"Yes, dear."

Without any more to say she again turned to the door, which he silently opened for her. He went downstairs with her and out to the curb. She stepped into her car and drove away, not having spoken to him, or looked at him, again.

He returned to his room and sat before his disappearing fire, regardless of the summons of a gong downstairs. Ignoring the sound's more clamorous repetition, to warn him that his mid-day meal would be both chilled and sparse if he didn't bestir himself, he became so deeply preoccupied that he had even no ear for his spaniel's repeatedly expressed wish to return to his lap. This meditation, by no means the abstract thought of a detached philosopher, was informing Victor Linley that the people he most loved in the world were facing imminent peril.

They stood close to calamity, a hint of the nature of which began to be dimly revealed to him by what his sister had just pitiably implored him to do. He knew that it wasn't on Hatcher's account that she had begged him to marry Sarah Florian.

XXI

ON SUNDAY EVENINGS the Ides had supper, not dinner; and, when Janey or Hatcher, or both, were at home, Mrs. Ide sometimes asked four or five of their young friends to join the family party at the table and enliven mild "parlor games" afterward. This evening when Mr. Linley arrived, a little while before the time set for the meal, he was clamorously welcomed by his niece, Frances, as he removed his overcoat in the hall. She came running from the living-room and threw her arms about him.

"Thank goodness you've come, Uncle Victor!" she cried. "There's a whole crowd in there and I been trying to entertain 'em; but Hatcher told me we didn't need anybody to be the life of the party. Hatcher's acting terrible for a person a party's for. Uncle Victor, would you like to know a secret?"

"Yes, indeed, Frances! Always."

"It's about Hatcher," Frances whispered. "Mother asked all these people of his to supper on his account; but she didn't think to tell him they were coming till late this afternoon and he said he didn't want 'em, she better telephone 'em not to come; but she said it was too late and he said all right, he might decide to go out somewhere any minute right in the middle of it and they'd be on her hands and she deserved it. He stayed mad about it till they commenced coming and I think he still is, Uncle Victor, and that's why he was so rude to me about my being the life of the party that certainly needs one. Don't tell him I told you."

"I won't, Frances."

"Thank you, Uncle Victor." Frances again spoke aloud. "It's stupid in there. There's only one I can get to do anything and she isn't enough to make it a good game."

"Game?" her uncle inquired. "What game?"

"Animal-Mineral-or-Vegetable, Uncle Victor. There's Hatcher and Dorcy and Mary Gilpin and Mr. Wilson, the one they call Pinkie, and Gilpin Murray and Amy from across the street; and only one of 'em's willing to play. It's Mary Gilpin, because most of the rest of 'em act like they just want to sit around and say 'What?' like Hatcher; so I bet they're in love or've had their feelings hurt or something. Anyhow, it's the way they act and it gets in my hair! Uncle Victor, will you play Animal-Mineral-or-Vegetable with me and Mary Gilpin?"

"Glad to," Mr. Linley said. "Just a minute first,

though, if you don't mind." With Frances beside him, he stepped into the living-room to exchange greetings with the young guests, whom he at once perceived to be as subdued in manner as his small niece had said. An uneasiness seemed to prevail, perhaps an emanation from the acting host, Hatcher. Standing with his back to the room, and apparently unaware of any hospitable duties, he was gazing out of the bow window.

Mr. Linley made the customary inquiries in regard to the health of parents, coming to Dorcy last; and, as he took her hand, he looked at her somewhat attentively. His expressions of solicitude were a little stressed.

"Mother's fine, thanks," Dorcy said languidly. "Father walked over with me. He's here, though he isn't staying for supper and's got to go home to take her to a party somewhere. He's in the library talking to Mr. Ide if you'd like to see him."

"Yes—yes, I should." Linley turned to Frances, who was insisting upon her game. "I will, I will," he assented. "Just give me time to say hello to somebody my own age and I'll be back."

"I bet you won't!" Frances protested. "If you go in the lib'ary with Father and Uncle Harry Aldrich you'll get started into old people's talking and you won't come. You'll—"

"Yes, I will!" Linley laughed, touched her cheek, went out into the hall and took a dozen steps toward the closed door of the library. Having gone this far, he heard voices suddenly become loud within that enclosure. He walked more slowly, and then, five feet from the door, stopped short.

Two outcries, both harshly passionate and almost simultaneous, yet distinct in his ears, were what halted him. "You damned fool, haven't I told you how to save yourself?" This was the voice of Harry Aldrich, altered but recognizable; and almost at the same time Victor heard the answering fierce shout of Frederic Ide: "Never, by God! I won't do it!"

There was an abrupt silence, one that projected a picture of the interior behind the baleful door: two hard-breathing men staring at each other with inflamed eyes. In the hall Victor Linley heard a light gasp just behind him, and he whirled about to find that little Frances had thoughtfully followed him and stood there, awed.

"We better not go in," she whispered. "Are Father and Uncle Harry having a fight?"

"No. What an idea!" He contrived to laugh. "They're just arguing. Didn't you ever hear anybody talking politics before?"

"Yes; but I never heard—"

"Yes, you have—lots of times. People get excited when they talk politics nowadays; but it doesn't mean anything." He took her hand. "Let's go back now. We won't tell anybody, because pretty soon you'll see; when your father and your Uncle Harry come out of there, they'll be just as good friends as ever."

"You think so?" As they moved away, she pulled him toward an open double doorway on their right. "I'd like to be sure, though, myself, Uncle Victor, if they're going to be friends again or not. Let's go into the drawing-room instead of back where the others are; then we can look into the hall and watch them if Father comes, the way he usually does, to let Uncle Harry out the front door, because I heard Uncle Harry say when he came that he had to go home right soon. We can kind of sit in the drawing-room because there aren't any lights lit in there, and then we can tell if they're going to be friends again by how they act. Don't you think they sounded awful mad at each other, Uncle Victor?"

"No, of course not. Not really." He laughed again, reassuringly; but let her have her way, and they went into the dark drawing-room, where they sat together on a sofa that let them see, through the open double doorway, the forward part of the hall.

Frances sat close to her uncle. "They kind of scared me," she said in a small voice.

"Nonsense, dear! They were only—"

"*Sh!*" she whispered. "They're coming already."

Footsteps were what she'd heard, not voices. The two men came quickly into view, Harry Aldrich a step or two in advance. His face deeply flushed and his chin up, Harry strode to the front door and opened it with a jerk, as in headlong departure; but he stopped abruptly and turned to face his tall partner. Frederic stood before him with head bowed and shoulders stooped in gaunt dejection. Harry was breathing hard; but he spoke in a quiet voice.

"I just didn't want to leave any last stone unturned, Fred," he said. "I really knew it couldn't be done. You understand, don't you?"

"Yes." The answer was just audible. "Yes, I do. I'll see you there at ten to-morrow morning."

"If—" Harry hesitated. "If I'm a little late don't worry; it won't matter."

"No—it won't matter, Harry."

"Well—" Harry hesitated again, smiled uncertainly; then suddenly extended an arm and put a friendly hand on his partner's shoulder. "Goodnight, old man."

"Goodnight, Harry."

The door closed; Harry Aldrich was gone. Frederic Ide, walking slowly, returned across the oblong of the drawing-room doorway, and his steps began to be heard ascending the stairs. To the mind of his brother-in-law those ascending steps, pausing at intervals, suggested exhaustion—and a worn-out, distracted man who had to lean heavily upon the stairway railing in order to complete his ascent.

"Was Uncle Harry going to cry?" little Frances whispered. "His face was pretty funny and the way his mouth was moving it looked like he was going to. I guess you were right, though."

"Right?" Her uncle's question was merely murmured; he sat in a profound cogitation. "What was I right about?"

"Why, about how they'd turn out to be friends even after they were yelling that way over politics."

"Yes, of course! Of course they're friends." He patted her hand and rose. "We won't tell anybody about it."

"Why not?"

"Well—just to have another secret between us. Won't that do?"

"Yes—if—" Frances said. "I'd enjoy to have it be another secret with you, Uncle Victor, if you'll come and play Animal-Mineral-or-Vegetable with Mary Gilpin and me right now."

"Animal-Mineral-or-Vegetable? Hurrah!" Victor was boisterous, hoping to make her forget. "Brilliant you and clever Mary Gilpin and stupid I, we'll play Animal-Mineral-or-Vegetable for hours and hours and we'll not let anybody stop us!" He took her hand, and, in spite of his limp, began to prance.

Frances, shouting, capered beside him; hand in hand they danced across the wide hall and into the living-room. There, however, the small niece was again disappointed; for they'd no more than sat down with Mary Gilpin to play their game when Aunt Ada appeared dismally in the doorway and summoned everybody to the dining-room for supper. They'd have to put up with her at the head of the table, she said, as Mrs. Ide had a headache and Mr. Ide didn't care for anything to eat. Then Aunt Ada added, to Victor, "Harriet sent you her love and asked me to tell you not to come up to see her, because she's going to try to get to sleep."

"I see," he said. "No, I'll not disturb either of them."

At the table he joined Frances and Mary Gilpin in a struggle to breathe some gayety into a too-obviously disheartened little party. Aunt Ada, silent, was like an open sepulcher of half-buried forebodings. The habitual cheerfulness of Amy and Gilpin Murray, already defeated by the preoccupation of Gilpin's employer, surrendered the last flag to Aunt Ada. Dorcy, almost talkless, carefully looked anywhere except at Hatcher; and the young Wilson, at first insistently possessive in his manner toward her, became sulky, for he didn't wholly lack powers of observation. He ate doggedly, not speaking to anybody, or caring how visible he made his jealousy. Hatcher, paying as slight attention to his food as to his guests, appeared to be listening and waiting for a sound from without that would be a signal; and this was, in fact, his impatient state of mind.

He'd thought all day that such a parting as he'd had with Sarah Florian last evening must surely, surely be followed quickly by a summons from her; but it hadn't come —not yet. He'd meant what he said to his mother about leaving the party on her hands if he should "decide to go out". Well, he'd have to leave it on Aunt Ada's hands, instead, heaven help it! but he'd go just the same—if and when the call sounded—and he sat in suspense. Toward the close of the meal he was needlessly infuriated by a special solicitude of Aunt Ada's.

"Can't you eat anything at all, Hatcher?"

"Can't I what?"

"Eat," said Aunt Ada. "You haven't touched your spaghetti or your sweetbread salad. Usually you devour them. Only last Sunday you hardly left enough for the rest of us. Dorcy'll be wondering what's the matter with you, Hatcher. Can't you—"

"Eat your own!" Hatcher thus became primitive. "What's on my plate's put there to do what I like with, isn't it? It's mine, not my relatives', isn't it? If people attended strictly to their own food this world might be a better—" Interrupted by the sound of the telephone bell ringing in the hall, he sprang to his feet and strode to the door. In the same instant Frances, squealing, was also out of her chair and running to intercept him.

"Hatch, you sit down!" she cried. "Mother and Father both appointed me telephone answerer for this house. They gave me the rights and you *haf* to let me! You stop, Hatcher!"

Clamoring as she ran, she followed him into the hall; then, within a few moments, both Hatcher and Frances reappeared in the dining-room and resumed their seats, Frances arriving first and looking pleased.

"Just a wrong number, Aunt Ada," she said demurely, as she sat down. "Hatcher told 'em so impolitely and hung up; but when I answer people with the wrong number I always laugh nicely and say they needn't excuse themselves or anything because I don't mind."

"Junior does, though." Erdvynn Wilson laughed artificially. "Junior minds. Anyhow, he did this time; didn't you, Junior?"

" 'Junior'?" Hatcher said indifferently. "What do you mean, 'Junior'? My father's name's Frederic and mine is Hatcher."

"Yes." Young Wilson laughed again. "What I mean is Hitler, Junior."

"What?"

"Yes," Pinkie Wilson said. "Seems to be a rumor going round—among all these other rumors about you—that you're quite the juvenile Hitler, the way you slave-drive one-armed painters and poor old colored women, fixing up those hovels you're doing over that ought to be pulled down for slum clearance." Falsely waggish, he looked about the table for encouragement. "Yes, indeed; they tell me that as a business man this young feller Ide's a typical little dictator—eh, Gilp?"

"Terrible," good-natured Gilpin Murray responded. "I'll say this for him, though: he gets results."

"Yes," Pinkie said. "We *hear* he does! Particularly along certain lines touched upon by all the talk going round about his recent spectacular private life!"

Hatcher, straightening suddenly out of a slump, looked at him across the table. "What do you mean by that?"

"Oh, nothing. Just trying to get a rise out of you —and it rather appears that I have! What makes you so jumpy when you hear the telephone?"

"He isn't!" Frances loyally defended her brother. "I mean he isn't always. It's only sometimes."

"I'll *bet!*" Erdvynn burst into loud triumphant laughter. " 'Only sometimes'! Right you are, young lady!"

Aunt Ada rose. "I think we'll have to give up waiting for Hatcher to eat, since he hasn't even begun. Perhaps he'll show more interest in bridge, if Dorcy'll kindly be his partner."

At the card table in the living-room, however, Hatcher's manner was still discouraging, though Dorcy was his partner. They played against Aunt Ada and the young Wilson, while at the other end of the room Frances had succeeded in adding Amy and Gilpin Murray to Mr. Linley and Miss Gilpin for the postponed game of Animal-Mineral-or-Vegetable. The adult participants in this latter contest, striving to lighten the gloom and please the little girl, made themselves at times too noisy; and, when this happened, Aunt Ada looked palely at them over her shoulder. Thereupon they would chide themselves for their thoughtlessness and be quieter; but finally Aunt Ada did more than merely look at them.

"Frances, really!" she said. "Can't you subdue your voice a little? How can anybody play contract with all that whooping and squealing going on? Anyhow, it's your bedtime."

Victor spoke up briskly. "I'm afraid she means the rest of us, too—me in particular!"

His sidelong observation of the card table had suggested that something decisive ought to be done. Hatcher, almost oblivious of his cards, sat gazing into vacant distances like a longing, troubled lover; and Dorcy, still never looking at him and with her eyes downcast, seemed to be bearing about as much as she could. Erdvynn Wilson, sullenly boiling, appeared upon the point of saying something openly destructive. It was for Dorcy's sake that Victor made his diversion; he thought she badly needed an excuse to go home and be alone. "Yes, I'm sure your Aunt Ada means me in particular, Frances," he said, and rose. "I was squealing worse than anybody. I don't see, though, how she knew it's my bedtime, too."

Frances made a despairing uproar; but, at the bridge table, Dorcy at once put down her cards, said flutteringly that she must be getting home, and the unfortunate game dissolved to no one's regret. Perfunctorily, Hatcher saw the evening's guests to the front door and called drearily after them his manufactured objections to their leaving so early; then, sighing, he sought his own room, his ears pelted by a shower of reproaches from his small sister. She was ascending the stairway a step or two in advance of him.

"It's all your fault the party broke up, Hatch!" she cried, repeating herself; but lowered her voice in response to Aunt Ada's warning that she'd wake her mother. "Anyways it's your fault and Aunt Ada's together. Aunt Ada made the fuss about noise that disgusted everybody; but you were the skull at the feast the whole time, Hatch."

"I was what?"

"You were a skull," Frances explained crossly. "It's Greek. The way they took their meals. We've been having it in school this week. You either kept looking at the wall or else you pulled your chin down long with your mouth kind of open, and frowning so that even Uncle Victor himself couldn't brighten anything up much. You acted like that all evening!"

"Did I?" Hatcher muttered, and he added, not for her ears, "Well, I guess I've got enough to make me."

He felt that the "cares of life" had overtaken him indeed; and, alone in his room, pondered long upon the new one that by this time had become the most pressing of them. Last night he'd come from Sarah Florian's house ecstatic because that superbly matured woman had implied beautiful, unbelievable things. She'd knelt before him, glowing, seized his hands in hers; she'd spoken marvelous words to him, putting a spell of caressive togetherness about them both. She'd admitted him to her inmost being, revealing her very self to him. He'd thought: What did anything in the world count against this glory? He was hers, a thousand times utterly hers; and she—hadn't she virtually told him that she could and might be his?

If that effulgence had been renewed to-day he wouldn't have been troubling himself about any old "cares of life"; he could have sent them all to the devil—including even the one set upon him by the probability that she'd formerly been engaged to his uncle. When he'd left her, a rosy glow of love had seemed to spring upward like sunrise on the horizon of the morrow. But to-day had been the morrow and she'd made it blank. Why? Surely she must know in what suspense he'd be waiting, all of to-day, after such a parting. Had she let some mood of hers get in the way? Wasn't he of more weight with her than just one of her moods? She didn't—didn't merely play with him, did she, leading him a while, then checking him at will? No, it couldn't be, because a perfect woman wouldn't do that; and, with this thought, Hatcher was happier—happy enough, in fact, to believe that she'd surely send for him to-morrow.

So, in the end, youth's celebrated elasticity brought his spirits up again, made him more fit to meet what was coming upon him. Like an army in a long battle needing fresh troops to come up singing from the rear, man's spirit must summon reserves of hopefulness and bright interpretations to bear what shall befall; and in youth these reserves are readier to the summons, else the progress of the generations would be down hill. The intricate interplay of human destinies—that is, the simple working of causes and effects—was bringing tragedy toward Hatcher Ide, that night, as he moved restlessly about his room, or sat, chin in hand, trying to cheer his thoughts of Sarah Florian.

Across the hall his father was not asleep; and, elsewhere

along Butternut Lane and all through the town, men of
business and the professions, whether awake or in slumber, were harried by their own condition and that of
the country. Not even the luckiest of them yet saw an
end to the Depression; but worse moved in the world.
Upon the narrowed ocean and beyond it, bombs were
crashing into flesh; eastward of armed France, eastward
of the Maginot line and the Siegfried line, airplanes and
steel tanks rolled underground in endless mass produc-
tion. A few miles from Hatcher, old George slept sadly
in the despoiled Linley mansion; while a little farther
northward on that same smoky street Victor Linley sat
before his drawing-table, not designing a house but busy
with arithmetic, anxiously scribbling figures in a notebook. Nearer to Hatcher, much nearer—just beyond the
dark lawns of the "Lash place", in fact—big-shouldered,
fair Harry Aldrich tenderly kissed his adoring wife goodnight after a jolly party.

. . . Reality sometimes mingles with the end of a
dream, so that for the half-waking sleeper what's actual
is indistinguishable from what's fantasy. Hatcher woke in
the morning with the impression that he'd been dreaming
about his mother and that he'd just heard her scream. He
couldn't remember what fantastic thing in his dream had
caused the scream, and the sound in his ears seemed real
—almost enough so to be alarming. Sunshine was strong
outside his open window; drowsily he looked at the little
clock on the table beside his bed, and, comprehending
that he'd overslept again, bestirred himself. He was getting into his bathrobe when he heard someone running

in the hall outside his door—someone with a heavier step than his little sister's. Running. That was queer. What was anybody running through the upstairs hall for? He went to the door, stepped out and saw that the speeding person was his Aunt Ada.

"What's the matter?" he called, as she reached the head of the stairway to descend. "Is anything wrong with Mother? Where is she?"

"Your mother?" she called back, letting him see her startled face for an instant. "She's gone to the Aldriches'. They just telephoned your father and they've both gone. I'm going, too."

He advanced farther into the hall. "To the Aldriches'? What for, this early? What—"

"Harry Aldrich is dead."

Hatcher didn't know what she meant. "What did you say? What about Harry Aldrich?"

Aunt Ada was half way down the stairs; but her voice came back like a blow in his face.

"He's dead."

XXII

SEVEN or eight cars stood in the Aldriches' driveway when Hatcher arrived, breathless and still dressing himself; and when he went into the house it seemed full of silent or whispering people. He didn't see his father or his mother or his Aunt Ada but caught a glimpse of his little enemy, Dorcy's cousin Lennie Aldrich; she was sitting on the stairway half way up to the landing and crying so hard into a blue handkerchief that although he hated her he felt sorry for her. Mary Gilpin, who'd just descended the stairs, saw him and hurried forward to speak to him.

"Come with me, please," she whispered quickly, and took him to a rear hallway, where there was only a small table with a telephone upon it and a chair beside it. She closed the door. "I've got a tedious job for you," she told him. "Your mother said you weren't up, and I was just

221

going to send for you. I'll have some breakfast brought to you here and I hope you'll get a chance to eat it. I'll relieve you myself for half an hour at noon and you can get some lunch in the dining-room. We'd like you to take charge of the telephoning."

"Mary!" he said. "I don't believe it's happened. What was it? What—"

"It was in his sleep, Hatcher. That's what you're to tell people when they ask. You're just to say that it must have been his heart, because when they went to call him this morning they found he'd died peacefully in his sleep. The funeral will be at three o'clock Wednesday afternoon. You'll have a great many calls because he was the most popular man in town. Just tell everybody what I've told you. That's all, except that your uncle, Mr. Linley, is going to see any reporters who come to the house; but if newspapers telephone ask them to wait a minute, and go into the living-room where your uncle will be and tell him. He'll come and answer them. He knows what to say and will attend to the papers if you'll take care of the rest."

Hatcher sat down at the table. "Of course I will. But, Mary, please—"

The bell of the telephone was already ringing; she paused for a final injunction. "Your mother and father are upstairs with Dorcy and Mrs. Aldrich; but of course you'll say none of them can talk to anybody. Don't forget to call your uncle when any of the papers—"

The voice already speaking into Hatcher's ear came from a newspaper office; he told Mary so, and, as she was at the door, it was she who hurried to send his uncle.

Victor came quickly and, standing, took the instrument from Hatcher.

"Yes? . . . This is Victor Linley, at Mr. Aldrich's house . . . Oh, it's you, is it, Bewley? . . . Yes, of course, any questions you like . . . Very sudden indeed . . . No, I haven't heard anybody speak of his having been depressed lately; I should say he's consistently been the most cheerful and optimistic business man in town . . . No, I don't see why you should infer any such thing, Bewley . . . Oh, very possibly, very possibly; but for the past six or seven years hasn't almost everybody been raising every cent he could at the banks and elsewhere? I don't see anything exceptional in that . . . No, Fred Ide can't talk to anybody; he's too much overcome . . . Yes, you can send a man up here if you like; I'll see him, certainly. Tell him to ask at the door for me . . . Yes, as soon as you like. Good morning."

"Uncle Victor—" Hatcher began huskily, as Mr. Linley set down the instrument. "I wish you'd—I don't— How long have you been here?"

"About an hour. Eleanor sent her car for me."

"Well, then? Do you know—"

Hatcher'd risen, and his uncle took the vacant chair with an effect of dropping upon it. "Harry was the best of men!" he said. "The best of men—the kindest— No one could have foreseen—"

"I just don't get it. I—I—" Hatcher stammered. "Why, he— Wasn't he in robust health? He's always looked so husky and—"

"I think I'll have to tell you, Hatcher. It seems—it seems to have been an accident."

"Accident!" Hatcher cried; then choked down his voice. "Accident?"

"Yes. He and Eleanor got home a little after twelve last night. He'd been as jolly as usual and still seemed so when he told her goodnight. At some time after that he appears to have done a thing he'd never done before. He wrote a message on a slip of paper and fastened it with a thumbtack on the outside of his door. It said that he'd taken something to make him sleep and he didn't wish to be called in the morning because he wanted to get all the rest he could before an important business engagement he had to-day. When Dorcy got up and saw the paper on his door it frightened her because she'd never known him to do such a thing and he'd always been violently opposed to any kind of sleeping potions—so she opened the door and looked in. Dr. Loffen says that by then Harry'd been gone several hours."

"But, Uncle Victor, that looks—it looks—"

"Yes, Hatcher. Loffen says it was morphine. Nobody knows where Harry got it. Probably now nobody ever will know; but that isn't important. He may have had it for some time. It's got to be an accident, Hatcher."

"But, my God, Uncle Victor—" Hatcher clapped his hand over his mouth, apparently knowing no other means to check his outcry.

"It's got to be an accident," his uncle repeated doggedly. "What's left of Eleanor's mind is trying to believe it and we're doing all we can to get Dorcy to see it that way, too. What helps us most is the fact that Harry hadn't locked his door."

"He hadn't?" Hatcher said. "He even thought of that —to make it look like an accident?"

"Keep your mind on the one necessity, Hatcher: that it's *got* to be an accident. Dr. Loffen was one of Harry's closest friends and he's going the limit that the overdose was just a tired man's mistake. All the insurance Harry had was hypothecated long ago; so that isn't in it."

"Then what is?" Hatcher's voice was so thick, and yet so broken, that the question wasn't distinct.

"What?"

Hatcher drew a long breath and made himself understood. "Then what *is* in it? Why did he do it?"

Victor looked at the shaking boy compassionately. "Why does anybody do anything? Is there ever a human action into which an almost infinite number of motives haven't—"

"Damn!" Hatcher said. "I didn't ask you for one of your philosophical disquisitions. I asked you why my father's partner has killed himself!"

"I can't tell you."

The telephone rang again, and Victor rose quickly. "There; sit down and take that call. Mary says she gave you your instructions. You're only to answer all inquiries by saying it happened in his sleep and must have been his heart. That's true, and is enough. You'll have to help us see it through, Hatcher."

"I'll try," Hatcher said, and took up his task.

The telephonic calls came steadily, with scarce time between for his mind to repeat to itself the shrieking question that beset it. Not until near midnight did the telephone abate enough for him to lie down on the cot Mary Gilpin sent to the small hallway for him; and by seven in the morning the insistent little bell was ringing again. He was busier throughout this second day than on the first; but by evening there was a slackening.

He'd had a peculiar disappointment, one he was able to feel in spite of an overwhelming weariness: Sarah Florian's voice hadn't been of the multitude he'd heard. He'd hoped for the reward of a few tense words with her, but they'd not been spoken; so probably she had come herself to condole, rich-voiced and gentle—had been in the same house with him and he hadn't even known it! "No luck," he sighed, and wasn't aware that his thought was incongruous.

At eleven o'clock Mary came to tell him to go home; henceforth she could easily take care of the lessened pressure, herself. Hatcher went out limply, and, on his way to the front door, passed through the room where stood Harry Aldrich's piano. It was closed, and a tip-toeing tired sister of Eleanor Aldrich's was arranging flowers in vases upon it. Hatcher had no memory of ever seeing that piano closed; the lid should never be lifted again, he thought—as if the black shining case contained the dead relic of a merry and manly voice to be heard no more, forever.

At the other end of the room Victor Linley sat flaccidly in a big chair, and Hatcher stopped to speak to him, in a voice appropriately hushed. "I guess those damn calls are about through, because everybody in the city directory's rung up at least twice. I'm gone in the head." He looked about the room, the air of which was daunting

with the smell of flowers that already were everywhere
and rose high against the walls. "Lord, isn't this horrible! Aren't you going to get any sleep?"

"Yes—later. I had quite a rest to-day; I was downtown all afternoon."

Hatcher was drooping; but he lingered. "Is it always
like this—always people murmuring or whispering in the
next room or in the hall, and you don't know what goes
on upstairs but keep thinking about it—and all these
ghastly-smelling flowers? Is it always the same?"

"Yes; pretty much," his uncle answered gently. "I
don't find that I get very used to it, though."

" 'Very'? My God!" Hatcher said. "Me, I've got a
million voices in my ears, all squeaking, 'I can't believe
it! This is the greatest shock to me!' and 'Why, I saw him
downtown only last Saturday and he was looking so
well!' Ninety-nine out of a hundred all saying the same
thing, and do I wish I could get 'em out of my hair! Mary
says I'm to be one of the 'active pallbearers' to-morrow
afternoon; I suppose you and Father are 'honorary'. Pleasant job for all of us. Of course I've been present at—at
things like this—two or three times during my life; but
I don't think I ever realized before that people really do
die. I almost wish they didn't. Listen to me—talking
waggish! I'd better be getting home before I go crazy;
I'm all in. See you to-morrow at the— Oh, damn! Goodnight."

. . . His own words, "See you to-morrow at the—"
recurred to Hatcher as he and seven other young men,
"friends of the family", carried what was left of Harry

Aldrich out of the room where was Harry's beflowered closed piano and through the lily-scented dim hall toward the flaring light of the opened front door. They moved solemnly between two lines of middle-aged men who stood with heads bowed, and Hatcher was aware of his father and his uncle, members of this formally stricken assembly. For a moment his glance met Victor's and seemed to say, "Yes; well, here we are at the—" as if it made things easier to avoid the word "funeral" in connection with jovial Harry Aldrich.

Hatcher realized that his uncle wouldn't omit the word; middle-aged people, it seemed, could bear such words and what they meant. Middle-aged people could say terrible things and do them; they could go about everywhere, laughing and being hail-fellow-well-met with everybody, and then without warning they could shut themselves up in a room and kill themselves. Young people, too, could kill themselves sometimes, of course; but Hatcher'd never known any young person who'd done it. Middle-aged people could do it almost as if it were all in the day's work; and then their middle-aged most intimate friends could stand up in two decorous files and, not weeping, see them carried out to be slid into a horrible hearse. Hatcher bitterly thought he hoped that he'd never live to be middle-aged; it seemed to him that probably he was the only person except Mrs. Aldrich and Dorcy—and that spitfire little Lennie—who'd ever really cared about Harry Aldrich.

During this dismal passage he had other thoughts, too, without realizing that they were inconsistent. The rooms on both sides of the hall were filled with people so motionless that no faintest rustling was heard from them; but, passing the open doorways in their view, Hatcher felt a certain distinction in his present position. He couldn't help feeling a little pride that he had been chosen for it, and he became slightly self-conscious. Sarah Florian, he thought, was certainly among the mourning throng, since she was a next-door neighbor and the Aldriches had so recently given a dinner for her. Though propriety didn't permit him to turn his eyes to look for her, it was gratifying, in a way, to know that she must be seeing him and that the sad office he was performing might be to a certain extent impressive. He was sure he felt her dark and glowing gaze upon him and that she understood all about his being the one who was suffering the most for Harry Aldrich, in spite of the stoic face that had to be worn.

On the way to the cemetery, disappointingly, he was forced to abandon this illusion of his. Looking forth from the window of his car in the funeral procession, he saw Sarah Florian. Behind her mulatto chauffeur, she was coming rapidly from the opposite direction, unquestionably not from the ceremony Hatcher'd been undergoing; and his fleeting glimpse of her made him hope that she wasn't thinking of him just then. Never more beautiful, she was looking straight ahead; his swift impression was of a lovely face set in a determination that carried with it, vividly, an air of resentment. Hatcher, badly let down, had the plaintive idea that during her drive this afternoon she'd happened to see poor old George somewhere and was brooding upon him, the murderer of her flowers.

Even Sarah Florian was swept from Hatcher's thoughts, however, a few minutes later; and, when his final duties for the day had been performed, and the pallbearers' car had set him down at his own gate, his mind's eye could see nothing but the racked black figures of Eleanor Aldrich and Dorcy clinging together above a sinking coffin. He'd had to turn his head from them—and he'd kept his eyes upon the frostbitten sod upon which he walked as the funerary party left the grave. He was aware that Erdvynn Wilson moved from his place among the pallbearers and went to Dorcy, and that Erdvynn helped her into the car that bore her and her mother away; but, at the time, this didn't seem to mean anything. Now, at home, Hatcher shambled into the house, coughing, and, relieved to find the others not yet returned from the cemetery, went upstairs and washed his face in cold water. Then, not freed of a smarting of the eyes, he moved aimlessly about in the upper hallway, waiting— waiting for something unknown that was coming. He'd often asked for it; but, now that he knew it was coming, he was afraid he couldn't stand it.

He heard the front door closing, heard his mother and Aunt Ada begging his father to go to his room and lie down, heard his father sharply refusing.

"*Now* it's coming," Hatcher thought.

He was near the head of the stairway; he stood there, listening, and for a while heard nothing more. When his mother called him from below, her voice wasn't loud; but he started.

"Hatcher, are you there?"

"Yes, Mother."

"Come down, please, dear. Your father wants to talk to you."

"Does he? All right."

Hatcher descended as slowly as he could without pausing on every step. He thought of Sarah Florian—what did anything else matter so long as her beauty was in the world?—and yet he felt that he moved toward the sheerly unbearable.

XXIII

In the small library, as he entered, his father stood looking out of a window. Mrs. Ide was beside him with her hand upon his shoulder, and Aunt Ada, in an old brown leather armchair, seemed to have treated herself to a condition of pale collapse. The light through the windows was failing, and, when Frederic Ide turned to speak to Hatcher, the son couldn't see the father's face distinctly.

"You—you want to talk to me, Father?"

"No, I don't want to. I've got to."

Hatcher had a slight sense of relief. His father's tone was crisp, unexpectedly steady, not weakened or desperate. It was, in fact, the tone of a man of affairs who meets a crisis practically when it finally arrives, no matter how shattering its approach has been.

"Well, I'm here to be talked to," the son said. "I think it's about time, probably. You and Mother have seemed to think everything tough had to be kept from—" Hatcher's voice trembled, though he tried to hearten himself with a little bumptious sarcasm "—from Frances and me, on account of our tender years."

"No." Frederic Ide shook his head. "I wish it had been on account of your youth, Hatcher. It wasn't. If Harry and I could have raised enough money in the short time we had to do it in, I think we could have kept our difficulty to ourselves permanently. I had to tell your mother some time ago because she began to guess it; but if Harry and I'd had a little better luck nobody but the three of us —your mother and he and I—need ever have known. Now, of course, all that's blown up. I mean it's just about to."

"Yes, sir; I think I get you. You mean this family's on the skids and got to take it, don't you?"

"We've got to face a painful adjustment, Hatcher; and I'm afraid that means you too, Ada, and that poor Alice won't be able to come here with her children. Harriet, she'll have to be written to and—"

"I see," Hatcher interrupted, and tried to speak roughly. "Janey's got to quit college and we're practically on our way to Uncle Victor's boarding-house. Well, what's going to happen to Dorcy Aldrich and her mother? I suppose the whole town's practically certain by now that Harry didn't pass out with any heart failure."

"If it isn't certain, it ought to be!" Aunt Ada spoke suddenly and shrilly. "Everybody ought to know it.

When a man brings ruin on his best friends and then takes his own life because he can't stand up and face what he's done, I think the whole world ought to know it! For my part, I blame Eleanor as much as I do Harry. She's gone on all this time living like a perfect sultana, leading him into every extravagance and crazy—"

"Ada, that's cruel!" Harriet Ide said. "Eleanor's light-hearted and loved the easy life they led; but she didn't know. I don't think he ever spoke a word of business to her in his life. Eleanor's no more to be blamed than a—"

"Blame?" Frederic interposed. "What's the use of blaming? If you've got to pin the blame upon anything, it would be upon something usually thought good—a man's love for his wife and their happiness together. Harry just couldn't bear to let Eleanor down. She'd got used to living in a kind of whirl of gayety and luxury— oh, they both had—and he didn't know how to stop it. It's harder to stop than most people understand, and for such a man as Harry it was impossible. It sounds crazy; but only a month ago he signed for his usual big subscription to the Community Chest. He kept up their way of living on somebody else's money, Hatcher. He used securities we held in trust."

"Yes, sir." Hatcher's hands were trembling; so he put them in his pockets. "You see things like that in the newspapers right along; but you—you hardly think they'd ever happen in connection with—with a firm like Ide and Aldrich. I think I know when you began to suspect it, sir; that day you were sick—"

"No; I never did suspect it, Hatcher. Harry's spending bothered me at times; but he often laughed to me about

what a show they were making on practically nothing and
he said Eleanor was a wonderful manager. I didn't quite
see it; but he was probably the most convincing man in
the world; I just went on bothering vaguely to myself
and didn't press it. Then Harry found he'd got himself
into such a jam he had to tell me the truth. What made
me sick was getting that in the face without having suspected." Frederic Ide sat down, sickened anew. "Harry
saw the day coming on him suddenly when we'd have to
account for the securities he'd used."

"Yes, sir." Hatcher trembled more. "Whose—whose
securities were they, sir? A number of people's?"

"Sarah Florian's."

"Sarah's!" Ada spoke suddenly and shrilly again. "Yes,
they'd have to be hers! Of all people!"

"They'd come to her from her grandfather," Frederic
said. "Old Sheffley Lash thought a great deal of Harry,
and Harry got him to let Ide and Aldrich handle about a
sixth of the Lash investments. That's what it amounts to
—something like a sixth of Sarah's holdings. Harry'd
brought in the Lash account and from the first he had the
managing of it; so it came to be our habit that though
he'd usually consult me he had charge of it pretty completely. She got the income from it regularly and let it
stay; but the war made her decide to come back here to
live, and she notified Harry from Paris that when she
arrived she'd expect him to have the whole account in
shape to go over with her. That was when Harry woke
up to find himself living in hell and had to tell me what
danger we—"

"Poor Harry!" Mrs. Ide had begun to cry. "Ah—and poor you!"

"Poor all of us!" her husband said; then showed a pathetic flicker of business vanity. "I don't believe any other two men could have come nearer doing an impossible thing than Harry and I did, trying to raise that money. He was only sixty-five thousand dollars short— about a tenth of what Sarah had with us—and, if it hadn't been for the Depression and our already having had to scrape and borrow our damndest, we could have done it. Up to the year 'Thirty-three, of course, it would have been a trifle. As things are, it's been just twenty-two thousand dollars too much for us. That's all—twenty-two thousand!—because by working miracles during these few weeks since Harry told me, we did raise forty-three thousand; but that was the utmost possible limit to what we could get. It's this last twenty-two thousand dollars that's finished Harry and sunk us."

His wife sat beside him, caught his hand in hers; but his sister was inspired with a desperate hope. "Fred!" she cried. "If that's all, couldn't you even yet—"

"No, Ada. Time's up and we squeezed every single last thing so dry the dust choked us. The one expensive thing Eleanor'd never cared for was real jewelry—she likes stage necklaces and gewgaws—and Harry was even two installments behind on the new car he got her this year. He owed everybody. He'd been putting Sarah off from the day she got here; and those parties we gave to placate her a little—well, they didn't get very far with *her!* Oh, yes, she thanked us nicely—but precisely when did we propose to have the Lash accounts for her inspec-

tion? Poor Harry kept his nerve and talked his jolliest to
her; but last Saturday morning when I was out, George
Clise called at the office and notified him he was acting as
Sarah's attorney, and at ten o'clock Monday morning
he'd bring her downtown to see exactly what we held for
her—or else!"

" 'Or else'!" Ada jumped up, and her echo of the phrase
was a sharp outcry. "You needn't think I've been completely in the dark all this time; I've known more than
you and Harriet think I did. If you care to learn the
truth, I was half way down the stairs when you and
Harry came out of this room on Sunday, and I was absolutely certain you'd had a terrible quarrel. You can try to
defend Harry all you please; but you can't deny that just
then you'd been telling him what you really thought of
him and—"

"No, no!" Ide said. "He knew what he'd done; he
thought worse of himself than I did. On Sunday he asked
me to do something I couldn't do; but he didn't really
expect it. I see now it was just a despairing, automatic
gesture to relieve the pressure in those last few hours. If
I'd known his life hung upon it—"

"No, you couldn't!" His wife clung more tightly to
his hand. "One thing I can't bear, Fred, is any more re-
proaching of yourself." She spoke angrily to her sister-
in-law. "Sit down, Ada, and stop making it worse. It
wasn't a quarrel; they were both just suffering. Harry
told Fred that legally they'd go down together, the one
just as much as the other—as if Fred didn't know it and
as if poor Harry didn't know Fred knew it!—and he said
Fred would have to join him in juggling some of their

other clients' securities to get that last twenty-two thousand dollars so that Sarah'd be satisfied. Of course Fred couldn't do that and—Ada, won't you please sit down!"

"No, I won't!" Ada cried, and she stamped her foot. "I've been suspecting something ever since that woman came home because she'd have to pay too much taxes in France. I knew something was wrong and I was sure she had to do with it; but I didn't know just what. Now that I do know, I'll thank you not to tell me to sit down!"

"Please do!" her brother groaned. "I wish to God you would, Ada. Haven't we got enough other—"

"I'll not!" Ada said fiercely. "I'll not sit down for anybody! So it was all 'so that *Sarah'd* be satisfied', was it? This family's to go to the poorhouse, and the Aldrich family with 'em, and our father's and grandfather's firm wiped out, and you'll be tried in a court of law, Fred, and Harry Aldrich killed himself—all 'so that Sarah'd be satisfied'! My God!"

"Ada—for heaven's sake!" her brother begged.

"No; you can't stop me! She gets everything back that you and Harry had of hers—all but this bit of money that means just nothing to her, not a hundredth of what she owns—and we're all to die for it. What'd you waste your time and money on giving her those crazy teas and dinners for? Why didn't you ask *me?* I could have told you she'd sick her lawyers on you just the same. Oh, yes, by the time she kicked old George out, you *all* began to understand she hadn't changed or softened one whit; but *I* could have told you so before then. I know that woman like a book! I know—"

"Ada!" Her sister-in-law put forth this useless effort.

"Ada, *please* have a little self-control. Fred's trying to tell us—"

"What's that to *me?*" Ada cried. Beside herself, she didn't care, this once in her life, what Hatcher heard. "I guess you and Fred remember Foster Early, Harriet. When I was twenty-nine and she was twenty-one she noticed that Foster Early was taking me about a little; and she got him over there to her disgusting Gothic oratory and candlelight, and kissed him—and thank God I had too much pride to bear the sight of him when he came back and wanted to tell me all about it after she'd thrown him over for Victor! Oh, yes, Harriet, you needn't think I haven't seen what you've been hoping Victor'd do since she came home! You needn't think—"

"Ada! Ada!" Frederic begged. "Please—"

"What do I care?" Ada was not to be silenced. "If you'd asked me, Harriet, I could have told you Victor's got too much sense. You thought that woman had come back here just to get Victor, and so you depended—"

"I did not!" Mrs. Ide protested lamentably. "I didn't think she'd come back for any such reason; but—but after she was here and saw him again I thought— Yes, I *did* think that her old feeling about him returned, and it did. You could see it. I was right. I—"

Ada was scornful. "Yes; you hoped he'd marry her—I know you did! You hoped so because you thought if he did you could go crawling to her and even *she* wouldn't send her new husband's brother-in-law to the penitentiary. Harriet, I believe on my soul you're still hoping that when Victor understands he's the only life-saver left he'll leap in and deliver us by selling his soul to Sarah

Lash. For my part, I'd rather die in disgrace than see her get him. She's the—"

"She is not!" This was the best that poor Hatcher could do. Speechless during the tumult of his aunt's fury, he now found part of his voice, though all of his mind failed him. "She is not!"

Ada turned upon him. "You defend her? Why, you poor little softie, don't you know yet that your mother's right and Sarah's been after your uncle again ever since she got home? Can't you see she's let you play around her just to keep tabs on him and because she never could let any male idiot alone that's over sixteen? *You* standing up for her! Harry Aldrich'd be alive this minute if it wasn't for her. Don't you know what she'll have her lawyers do to your own father?"

"Nothing! She wouldn't dream of—"

"Oh, wouldn't she!" Ada said. "Ask him!"

"I will! Father, do you believe—"

"Hatcher!" Mrs. Ide was feebly indignant. "You'll have to begin to try to be a little older. George Clise called your father up this morning to notify him to be ready with all the Lash Estate accounts to-night at Sarah's."

"There!" Ada cried. "*To-night*—because all the effect on her of what Harry did was that she turned more suspicious she might lose a dime. She could hardly wait till he was buried. There's the truth for you, my fine young man!"

"Let the boy alone, Ada," Hatcher's father said. "It's Sarah's money. She's got a right to it."

"Yes—if it kills all the rest of us!" Ada still faced

Hatcher. "*Now* you see, don't you? She'll have the last drop of blood out of—"

"You shan't say it!" The disordered hair over Hatcher's pallid brow was damp; he shook from head to foot. "It's all false. She's been slandered and slandered and slandered, and I'm going to stop it. She wouldn't do a damn thing that wouldn't be—wouldn't be from the highest motives. I'm going to prove it!"

"Prove it!" His aunt uttered a scream of laughter. "Prove it, you poor thing? Oh, dear me!"

"I will!" he shouted. "You insult her; you try to put everything on her, every falsity and cruelty and meanness there is! Do you think I'll stand for it? Do you think I'll let *her* stand for it?" He swung to the door and jerked it open. "You stay here, by God, till I bring her answer to you!"

With that, disregarding his mother's cries of entreaty and the protestive commands called after him by his father, Hatcher ran out of the door, through the hall and out of the house.

In the library Frederic Ide put his hand on his wife's shoulder. "Let him go. What's it matter? She'll only know it an hour or so earlier. It's all up anyhow, Harriet."

Ada laughed again. "Harriet doesn't think so. She's still counting on Victor's saving us. But she's wrong; she doesn't know her own brother. Victor'd die a thousand deaths before he'd marry that woman!"

XXIV

Lost in thought, a pale slight gentleman in black was approaching the front door as Hatcher plunged out of it. Victor Linley beheld without any evidence of surprise the impetuous rush of his nephew; but, pausing, inquired mildly: "Can I be of use to you, Hatcher?"

"*You?*" Hatcher shouted, passing him at a run. "Hell, no!"

Mr. Linley remarked the contemptuous implication of this violence; but his expression showed no resentment. The direction of Hatcher's flight, however, increased the avuncular thoughtfulness. Hatcher ran across the lawn and disappeared among the leafless thick shrubberies that separated it from the "Lash place". His uncle, staring after him, hesitated, seemed to debate with an impulse to follow—then dismissed the idea and entered the house somewhat hurriedly. Hatcher, by that time, was ringing at Sarah Florian's door.

As upon the other occasion when he'd come unbidden she kept him waiting; but this time she did not prepare him with a distant musical expression of her mood: there was no piano prelude to her appearance in the Louis XV room. The big house seemed all silent except for Hatcher's footsteps as he paced the parquetry floor; his breathing, too, was noisy enough to sound as a disturbance in that still apartment where the long rose-gray curtains, closed, softly repudiated what was left of the light of day.

Crystal, porcelain, gilt cabriole legs, *petit point* and Aubusson weavery intruded upon him as a background unfit for this interval. The delicate shapes and tints, though but faintly revealed by newly lighted candles, seemed unendurably artificial presences in a scene of such suspense and preparation; for he was strugglingly preparing himself to speak up roughly and say what his anguish pressed him to say. Her delay by no means gave him time to cool off; but did permit a particular realization—that in emotional moments with older people he'd seldom said what he meant. He hadn't been man enough to ask even his uncle a vitally important question; he'd never come anywhere near saying to Sarah Florian what he'd burned to say. Every time—every single time!—he'd fumbled it.

With Dorcy or Mary Gilpin, or with other contemporaries, he could be in almost any kind of a stew, yet could and did speak out freely in their own and his own language. He made them understand him; he was not to be manipulated or verbally baffled—but with a grown

woman, thirty-four years old, he'd made a flop of everything he'd ever tried to say to her. That appeared to be
one of the disadvantages of being young; but youthful-
ness wasn't going to balk him now. No, and he wasn't
so darned young any more; he'd lived enough lately—
yes, and suffered enough!—to add youth-destroying years
to twenty-two, and *this* time he'd say his say!

He looked at himself in the dim mirror over the suave
marble mantelpiece and swore he'd say his say. As he
swore it, he saw how his hair looked; did hurried brushy
work upon it with one hand and adjusted his tie with the
other.

"Yes?"

Sarah Florian spoke from the other end of the room.
She hadn't come through the doorway he'd kept in view
in the mirror.

"Oh, *gosh!*" Hatcher said despairingly as he dropped
his hands and turned to her. She seemed more beautiful
than he'd ever seen her, and, at the same time, taller and
colder; her face, non-committal unencouragingly, expressed nothing divinable. "Yes, you *would* come just
then!" he cried. "I've *always* got to look a fool to you—
even now when I'm going insane."

"Are you really?" she asked, but didn't seem interested
to hear details. "I'm sorry to've kept you waiting; but
I've quite a lot of things to attend to to-day. I'd have
told them to say I wasn't at home, except that I want a
word with you. It's only this: I'm afraid that something's
going to happen so that presently we mayn't be as good
friends as we have been; but I'd like you to bear in mind
that it's not my fault."

"Your fault?" Hatcher stepped toward her. "I came here to tell you that you haven't any faults—that you're perfect!—and that you never did anything they say you did and that you never will."

"Oh?" she said. "So that's why you came?"

"Yes, it is." He began to speak loudly, sometimes brokenly; but he felt that at least he was speaking out at last. "You're—you're a *grand* woman! You're everything that's brave and strong and—and generous and—and loyal —and they lie about you! Well, I don't intend to let them lie about you any longer; but you've got to help me. You've got to hear what they say and give me the—the authority—to show them it's all lies."

"I'm afraid just now I haven't much time," she said, and might less painfully have dashed a little vitriol upon him.

"You—you haven't *time?* Not after what I've just said to you?"

"I fear I haven't."

"You're too busy! Oh, my God!" He struck his forehead with his clenched right hand, and immediately disavowed the gesture. "There I go! I try to speak my feelings and right away begin to act like a screen idol! I don't do that with other people and I don't believe I've often done it with you; but as soon as I make up my mind to tell you what I've got to, that's the way I do it! I'm a mess— I'm a terrible mess and I know it—but I'm going ahead and you'll have to listen whether you've got time or not. I want to talk to you calmly. Let me get my thoughts together. You see I'm in torture, don't you?"

"Torture?" She seemed indulgent, though her air of

being pressed for time wasn't relinquished. "Rather a pushed word, isn't it? At your age—"

"Now for both our sakes," he begged, "don't start me making theater gestures again. My age! Don't you suppose I've stood enough about that already? I didn't come here to talk about my age. I came here to get your answer to questions that are killing me. I came here to—"

"*Hush!*" she said; and at that, and her imperative gesture, he stopped short.

One of her Philippine Islanders stood in the corridor doorway. "Mista Lidley," he announced.

Sarah Florian's eyes dilated; her mouth opened, and she stared at the man as widely as Hatcher was staring at her. "Who?" she asked, with a break in her voice that made two syllables of the word. Then she repeated it sharply. "Who?"

Victor Linley appeared from behind the Islander and came in apologetically.

"If you'll forgive me—" he began; but got no further.

"Forgive you?" Sarah Florian spoke loudly and haughtily. She wholly disregarded Hatcher; the unfortunate young man, gasping, perceived that so far as she was concerned—and right in the midst of his utmost tragedy—he was no longer even present. "Forgive you?" she said. "You condescend to come into my house at last to ask me that, do you?"

Mr. Linley's face flushed a little; but he smiled politely. "Yes, indeed! I mean that if you'll forgive me I've taken the liberty of looking in for a moment to tell my nephew he's rather pressingly wanted at home. His mother thought that if I'd just step over and bring him—"

"Bring him?" she said. "You're on a hurried errand? You've come for him and are going with him? That's why you came?"

"Why, yes."

"How damnable!" She reached Victor in one of her graceful long strides, and with her open right hand struck him hard upon his unflinching chin. "How hateful!" she cried. "It's you that ought to have killed yourself. Whatever Harry Aldrich has done to me, you've done a thousand times worse. You keep me waiting, waiting, waiting, and then when you do deign to step into my house, at last, it's to tell a boy his mother wants him!"

"I'm extremely sorry," Victor began. "I most deeply regret—"

"Most deeply!" She mocked him. "Is that tone a continuance of the condoling you've been doing with the bereaved Aldrich family? Don't bring it around here. I don't care for it."

"Yes," Victor said gently. "I'll take it away. Hatcher, if you'll come now I think we'd better—"

"No, you don't!" As he turned to the door, Sarah caught his arm and swung him round. Her voice had lost its accustomed deep richness; had suddenly become high-pitched, raw and genuine. "I'll have it out with you now! You won't slide away from it. No man ever treated a girl as you did me. No, and no man's ever treated me as you have since I came back here. You don't get away with it so easily, my friend. You're going to listen!"

"Indeed, yes," he said. "That is—if Hatcher doesn't mind returning home ahead of me. Hatcher, your mother said—"

"I won't!" Hatcher spoke fiercely. "I'm over five years old, damn it, thank you! I'm going to say what I came here to, whether *you* stay and listen or not. I came here to—"

"I know, I know," his uncle said soothingly. "Another time may be better, though. If you—"

Sarah laughed aloud. "Do you think I'd be more tractable if he weren't here, Victor?" Hatcher perceived that she was again aware that he lived. "What do I care?" she cried. "Indeed I'm quite willing to have one of your family here to listen!"

"I don't want to," Hatcher said. "I didn't come here to listen to this. I came here to say—"

"Look at him!" Sarah swept to Hatcher, apparently to use him as a rostrum, for she pointed and looked at his deprecatory uncle. "See that man! I'll tell you a little about him, my boy, and how he treats women who trust him! When he first made love to me I was a girl—I was a devoted little idiot—and wasn't he a maiden's dream, though!" She laughed again; then sobbed, but without interrupting herself. "Oh, but he was a sweet thing with his hero limp and exquisitely adult calm—and all the girls keeping dead flowers from him in their desks—"

"Sarah!" Victor said in mild remonstrance. "I don't recall that any such testimonials—"

"The same old pretended modesty!" she cried. "Still working the same old affectation? Do the ladies find it as fascinating as of yore?"

"I'm afraid not as of anything, Sarah. I'm afraid they never did."

"Poseur! You *are!* You've *always* been one; there was

never a natural or impulsive drop of blood in your body
—and think of what you dared to call *me!*" She appealed
passionately to Hatcher, as if, for an instant, he repre-
sented Justice. "He did! He called me horrible things—
and just before we were going to announce our engagement! Would anybody believe it of him, seeing him stand
there so smugly? Almost in so many words he called me
a self-indulgent egoist, a man-collector, spoiled, and he
said I wasn't even truthful with myself. That wasn't the
worst: he said I was stingy—except with myself! Yes,
stingy! I! At first I thought he was joking—" She sobbed
again.

"Hatcher, really!" Mr. Linley sent an urgently suggestive glance from his nephew to the door. "Don't you
think you might—"

"I won't!" Hatcher said. "I'm staying."

Sarah ignored this hasty clash of ideas. "He *meant* it?"
she cried. "There we were—going to be married—and
that's what he said to me! I told him if he didn't take it
back I was through with him, and he said he was sorry—
'sorry'!—but that was what he thought. So I showed
him what *I* thought of *him*—what I thought of the kind
of lover he was! There were others, I let him discover."

"Discover? No," Victor said, with neither reproach nor
satire. "Dear Sarah, it was always apparent that there were
others, naturally."

"Do you hear him?" She appealed tragically to
Hatcher. "He didn't *mind* the others! That was flattering,
wasn't it? I didn't stay to see how much he minded my
marrying one of them; I let him think *that* out at his
leisure."

"I didn't need the leisure, Sarah. I understood immediately."

"You didn't!" she cried. "You probably thought I was 'repenting at leisure'!"

"No, no. I never—"

"You did! That's just what you were thinking in your infernal, insufferable self-conceit. You were never more mistaken, Victor Linley! I forgot you. I lived a full life and there were whole years when you weren't twice in my thoughts."

"Of course, Sarah. I had no idea you'd—"

"Stop interrupting me! I forgot you, I tell you; but when I came back here and saw you again I thought you'd at least have the grace to try to make up to me for the old insults and—"

"Insults? Indeed they weren't meant to be. You asked me for the honest truth and I merely—"

"Shame!" She seemed about to strike him again. "Shame on you for your—for everything that you are! Do you think that any woman—any such woman as I!— would *let* herself be treated so? You didn't come to see me; you didn't let yourself be caught alone with me. If I wanted to talk to you I had to drag you from your villainous boarding-house and out to the public street! That was nice for a woman of any pride, wasn't it? You hide away in a third-rate *pension*—"

"No, I don't," Victor said; and he smiled suddenly. "I moved early this morning."

"What?"

"I've taken a room in the old Linley house."

Upon that, it was as if she'd had physical blow for blow

from him; she wavered back from him. "You— You're as poverty-stricken as that?"

He smiled again, amiably. "I'm afraid so."

Sarah Florian stood straight and her breath came fast. "Then I've received the worst of all your insults, and let me tell you it'll be the last!"

"You mustn't see it so," he protested. "I needn't be uncomfortable there. After all, the old house is solid and rather—"

"Now damn you!" she said. "You've made it clear enough, I think. I'm through with you, this time for good and all—through with you and your whole hateful family. This boy's made it pretty plain to me how some of your relatives talk about me!"

"Ah, Hatcher!" the uncle murmured. "What have you done?"

"Not half!" the desperate Hatcher said. "Not half what I came here to do. I—"

"Plain indeed!" Sarah Florian, now, in voice and look, was bitter with more than Victor. A natural vindictiveness, most human, distorted the features habitually held calm for the preservation of their beauty. "This boy's come straight from home before this, filled up with lies and poison and scandal about me—straight from your malevolent female relatives, Victor Linley. I know that, though I don't know in what *other* way your sanctimonious family has been despoiling me—with Harry Aldrich's help. But I intend to know—yes, this very night!"

Hatcher uttered indistinguishable sounds, strange ones, in his throat, before he became coherent. "You—you warn us?" he asked, and with both hands undid the arrangement of his hair he'd accomplished before the mirror. "I can't stand this. I got so I didn't care if you'd been engaged to my uncle; but if you're still in love with him—or again in love with him—"

"I? *Now?*" Sarah strode away from him, laughing. "You little utter fool!"

"I am not," poor Hatcher said. "I have been; but I'm not. You talk at him as if I weren't here. When he comes in, you don't pay any attention to me at all except to use me to get an effect on him. Well—all right—but from what you say it sounds as if you'd like to be even with him because he isn't falling for you. That'd be pretty unworthy, I think. One of the things I came here to say was that I knew you were too high-minded to do what they said you would. I told 'em I knew you better; you wouldn't do such a thing."

"What 'such a thing'?" she said.

"To my fa—" Hatcher began; but paused abruptly. His uncle had stepped between him and Sarah Florian. A whisper reached Hatcher's ears, but not hers—a whisper so commanding, so poignant that it was paralyzingly effective.

"*Shut up!*"

Hatcher was silent. His uncle turned about with a gesture of apologetic explanation. "He's naturally a little confused and we've interrupted you long enough, Sarah. His mother really does want him rather urgently. If you—" He made a little bow. "If you don't mind, I think we'll be—"

"Go on!" she said passionately. "I'm sick of you! Be off with you! Both of you!"

She didn't stay to see them out of the room, but turned to the door by which she'd entered, passed through, and closed it clashingly behind her.

XXV

OUTDOORS, the compassionate uncle limped as fast as he could, to keep up with the striding nephew. There was still a little daylight sieved through the woody groves west of Butternut Lane; the scrambled tips of old forest trees didn't merge with the sky but rose against it as if scrawled in brown ink with a haphazard pen. This effect went unseen by the younger of the two hurrying across Sarah Florian's frozen lawn; but the elder remarked it with a melancholy eye and the thought that it was being repeated above a sylvan enclosure of marble shapes where to-day he'd left forever the semblance of an old friend.

Hatcher stopped suddenly in the shrubbery of the boundary. The bow window of the living-room at home had just become visible, and its springing into shape with a flare of warm light was what checked him. "I don't want to go in there." As he spoke he turned his back upon his uncle, and his utterance was impeded as by a cold in the head. "You go ahead. I'm not coming."

"You wouldn't rather I'd wait with you, Hatcher?"

"No, I wouldn't." Hatcher used his handkerchief as furtively as he could and tried not to speak huskily. "You —you're one hell of an old bird, it seems to me. You certainly must have had your own way of being engaged to a woman. If you didn't care for her, what'd you ever tell her you did for?"

"What for?" his uncle said. "I was in love with her."

"What?"

"Why, naturally, Hatcher. Overwhelmingly in love with her."

"Then in God's name what did you say those things to her for?"

"Why, she asked me," Victor Linley said in his mild way. "I hadn't expected to be happy with her, of course, because I knew no one could be that; and, though I was so deeply in love with her, I can't say that I ever admired her or liked her, Hatcher. You know it's sometimes possible to be in love with a person you dislike, don't you? When she asked me for my honest opinion of her I thought she had a right to it. At least it would put our relationship on a firmer base for the future—and, fortunately for us both, it did."

"But—" Hatcher was still turned away. "But she—she's been after you ever since she came home. She wanted you back—up to just now. Up till you practically told her you'd rather live in that old ruin downtown than—than with her, it looks as if she's been wanting to—to actually marry you."

"Oh, perhaps, perhaps," his uncle said lightly. "Some such thing may have been in her mind since her return. She may have felt that it was due to herself. I dare say. Nothing to do with me, of course."

At this, Hatcher faced him. "Nothing to do with *you!* What on earth do you think you're telling me?"

"Why, that she's had no feeling *for* me, Hatcher—one rather against me, in fact. You see, when she came home and found me still wobbling about, an old half-buried protest against me must have flared up. She couldn't endure that I shouldn't at last be so dependently in her possession—at least for a time—that I'd be sorry I was ever critical of her. She felt she had to make me feel that; she had to reduce me. In what I am, except in relation to her, she hasn't had the slightest interest—never did have."

"What! Why, when you came in that room she was like somebody I'd never seen before. Me—she treated me as if I'd been part of the wall. No interest in you? That's a hot one!"

"No," Victor said. "She isn't capable of any, Hatcher. One doesn't blame her for it because she was born so, and, what intensified it, she was helped to grow up that way. She isn't interested in anything except in its relation to herself, and she never will be. Most of us are more or less like that, even in our love affairs; so there have to be some extreme cases, of course. She's one of 'em; that's all. You'll understand it better when you're a little older, Hatcher."

Hatcher fell back upon mere profanity as the expression of his weariness of this eternal repetition. When he more controlled himself he made a bitter gesture. "How old do you have to *be* before all the damn gray-haired naggers on earth stop telling you that?"

"I don't know," Mr. Linley answered. "I'm still telling it pretty often to myself."

"Well—" Hatcher paused, sunk in miserable thought. Then he asked faintly, "What do you think life is?"

"I haven't an idea."

"You haven't? Not at your age? Then what do you think we get from it? What's the use of it? Old enough to have an idea about that?"

"Yes—a vague one," the uncle answered slowly. "So far as I can gather, the thing to learn is how to gain some slight bits of information on your subject—'life'—from adversity."

"How nice! A pleasant prospect to dangle before an infant of twenty-two! The best we can look forward to is tough times, then; and the tougher they are the more we'll know about something that nobody can know anything about. Thanks, Uncle. Wait!" Hatcher held up a forbidding hand. "Don't tell me I'll understand all these advantages better when I'm older! I want to ask you something that maybe you can answer more practically. When I was going to tell her I hadn't believed she'd set her damn lawyer on my father, why did you yell 'Shut up!' at me?"

"I only whispered it, Hatcher. I was careful that she shouldn't hear."

"I asked you why—"

"Yes, I know." Mr. Linley's manner had once more

become apologetic. "I don't wish to increase your feeling that I take a somewhat uncharitable view of her; but the truth is, Hatcher, she's rather sharp in her own interest."

"Yes; so you once told her, I believe! Go ahead."

"Yes, Hatcher. She's possibly almost too sharp where her money's concerned. The way she got rid of old George, for instance. I've been a little uneasy for some time; and last Sunday your mother came to see me in the morning and—well, I needn't go into it; but she might as well have told me she was in fear of Sarah. I heard your father and Harry being pretty strenuous later in the day, and when poor Harry took himself off that night the whole thing was only too suddenly clear to me. Of course for anybody who knows Sarah it's plain what suspicions Harry's death would intensify in her and what she'd do about them. She's always been rather too ready to think somebody's cheating her. Apparently that goes with such a nature as hers, Hatcher."

"Does it? I suppose when you were telling her the other things you told her that, too?"

"No, I'd said enough, I thought. I'm explaining why I had to tell you to cut the reference to your father, Hatcher. You see, she's always been a bit inclined to even up scores with people, and she seemed to have gathered from you that your mother and aunt weren't in the habit of admiring her—"

"Thanks for keeping me reminded!"

"I'm sorry," Victor said; "but it's unfortunately pertinent to your inquiry. You see, she had that injury—the unfavorable opinion held of her in our family—and also the fancied old and new slights from myself to brood upon. If you'd come out with it that there'd been a shortage in her account with your father and Harry—"

"If I what?" Hatcher half-choked. "Why, my God, it wouldn't have been telling her anything she hasn't already practically guessed! She's had her lawyer notify Father he's got to bring the account to her house tonight. She'll know it *then*, won't she?"

"No," Victor said. "I don't want to be hard on her; but I'm afraid she's in a mood to damage your father and all of us in any way she can. Well, we're all safe from her; but if you'd given it away to her that there's been a shortage she'd at least have told it all over town pretty ruinously. Since you didn't say what you intended, she can't."

"*Why* can't she?"

"Because there isn't any shortage, Hatcher. She's in for a pleasant surprise, or an unpleasant one—depending upon which view of her you take. Another reason I was so rude to you: I thought your father might as well continue to have the benefit of her account. I know her pretty well, and I believe she may see advantages to herself in leaving it with him. Investments are difficult nowadays, and the old firm—"

"I think you're stark crazy," Hatcher said. "Or else you just don't know! I tell you they raised everything they could with their last heart's blood but there's—"

"Yes, I know. Twenty-two thousand, three hundred and sixty-two dollars. It's all right, Hatcher. Your father has it."

"He has not!"

"Yes. Go in and see."

"I don't—" Hatcher began; but broke off and pressed through the crackling bushes, moving toward the house.

His mother was standing outside the front door, peering into the dusk. When she saw the two figures, the taller one ahead and the slighter limping behind, she came running. It was not to her son that she ran; she swerved round him, and, weeping, threw her arms about her brother.

XXVI

Hatcher went into the house and met Frances in the hall. "I had to go to my friend Bettina Burney's after school," she said. "I bet they made me on account of Uncle Harry Aldrich's funeral. Mother and everybody seems to be kind of crying or something around here now, and you, Hatch— Why, look at you! You look as if—"

"I do not. Where's Father?"

"If I promise to tell you, will you play backgammon with me first?"

"I will not. Where is he?"

"In the lib'ary. After he tells you please go somewhere else, the way he did me, then will you come and play—" She stared after him, displeased. He was already out of her sight and within the library.

261

His father sat writing at the heavy mahogany table; but set down his pen and looked up at Hatcher anxiously. "Did your uncle get there in time?"

Hatcher dropped floppingly into the chair that stood farthest from the desk lamp. "I get you," he said. "You mean did he get there in time to keep me from blowing the lid off by telling her I refused to believe she wouldn't give you time to try to fix up the last of what Harry Aldrich did to her damned stocks and bonds? Yes. Uncle Victor got there in time to stop me."

The tired man at the desk rubbed his forehead with a thin hand, closed his eyes and uttered a long and heavy sigh. "Well—thank God for that much!"

"Yes, for that much," Hatcher said. "It takes Him to keep me from being an additional curse to everybody. Uncle Victor's haywire; he says you've got the money. Do funny things in his head persuade him he brought it to you, himself? It wouldn't strike me as very likely—not unless he hurried from the cemetery and held up a bank."

"No; he had it, Hatcher."

"How could he? Where'd he get it?" Hatcher sat up, leaned forward, and expressed a strong incredulity. "And if he had it, why in God's name didn't you and Harry Aldrich ask him for it before Harry—"

"Ah, that's hindsight; but wouldn't anybody think it!" Ide said. "One doesn't ask a man out of work for his last cent, Hatcher, not even when he's a close friend or a brother-in-law. That's one reason. Another is that neither Harry nor I had any idea that Victor's last cent would be enough. It's a miracle, you see, that it just covers the hole. Victor's a reticent man and the truth is I had a sneaking idea that maybe Harry was quietly lending him a bit from time to time—just to keep him going. I haven't a doubt now that Harry thought I was putting up the little that Victor needed. Another reason is that it was sheer instinctive self-preservation not to speak of the shortage even to Victor. No, as a financial savior Victor just didn't occur to either of us. Pretty horribly ironical to think of, that he's a savior too late for Harry, isn't it?"

"Yes; if it does save us, Father."

"It stops her," his father said, not needing to be more explicit. "When Victor had to give up his old way of living, he appears to have done it just in time to have something under twenty-four thousand dollars left in municipal bonds. They brought him in the taxes he's had to pay on that old nightmare of a house he insists on holding, and just barely enough besides to keep him in his cheap boarding-house." Frederic rubbed his forehead again; his hand drooped to his eyelids, and the tips of his fingers remained upon them. "No, even if we'd known he had it I don't believe either of us could have asked him for it, Hatcher. I think Harry'd have died before he'd do a thing like that—and, as a matter of fact, that's just what he did."

"So he had it in his pocket," Hatcher said. "I mean Uncle Victor. I ran into him as I was starting to— I mean when I started over there. He must have been just bringing that last cent of his to you then. He asked me if he could be of service to me and I said, 'You? Hell, no!' "

"Yes, he was bringing it then, Hatcher. He'd been afraid it wouldn't be enough, of course; and when I told him that by God's own mercy it was, he said it would help us keep the truth from Eleanor and Dorcy, because Sarah'd never know it and so couldn't tell it—and I had to say I was afraid you were—were—"

"Spilling it," Hatcher said. "You had to say I was over there spilling it. So he came on the run to stop me. You must be pleased to have such a serviceable son."

"But apparently you didn't do any harm, Hatcher."

"No, I was prevented."

His father looked at him gently. "I don't think you need reproach yourself for a thing you can't help."

"You think not, sir? Not for being too damned young? I differ with you. I think I need. Being young, I'm naturally likely to be harmful. Doesn't it follow that I'd better begin to be old enough to despise myself?"

"No. Self-reproach isn't much use at any age, Hatcher, and the people who ought to feel it seldom do. If any of us is to be haunted by it, I'm the one. All I needed to do, at the last, was to talk to Victor, and Harry'd be alive. Why didn't I? Well, I've told you—but there it is! You see if I go into the 'if-I-only-hads' I'm lost. If I'd watched Harry more closely and if I'd talked to Eleanor—in time! —and if I'd done this, and if I'd done that! All the 'ifs' slid past me, and Harry's dead and I'm letting my wife's brother go flat broke to save me. No, the older we are, the less we dare dwell on the 'if-I-hads', Hatcher. You have fewer of them, being young."

"They're beginning to be a bit sharp, though," Hatcher said. "It's pretty tough on all of us to think we have to accept—"

"Yes." His father shook his head unhappily. "Victor had one argument I couldn't have resisted even if his others failed with me. He's always cared a great deal for Harry and Harry's little family, as he has for us. I knew what he felt when he spoke of his not having understood in time—in time for Harry, Hatcher—and I couldn't answer him when he said that every suspicion must be met; and this does it. No one can say now that Harry's death wasn't an accident, not even—" Frederic Ide's weary voice stiffened in the moment of bitterness "—not even Sarah Florian."

Hatcher slumped in his chair; but he didn't speak, and his mother came into the room just then. "I tried to keep him," she said. "He wouldn't stay. He'd told old George he'd take him to dinner at a cafeteria."

"Old George?" Hatcher looked up. "What's he—"

"They're fellow-lodgers," Mrs. Ide said. "You know where your uncle's gone to live, don't you?"

"Yes, he spoke of having left his boarding-house. He mentioned—"

"He's where he and I were born, Hatcher—the most dreadful house on this earth."

"It looks it," Hatcher said. "Mrs. Schapp is one of my—"

His mother had begun to weep again, though quietly. "I told and told him we wanted him to live with us here," she murmured through her handkerchief. "I told him we none of us could bear it if he didn't come."

"Why wouldn't he, Mother?"

"I was a fool the other day," she said. "I told him we were going to have to take in Alice and her children and that I didn't know how we'd find room—and I was complaining of having no maids to do the housework! Of

course he wouldn't come after that; but I didn't dream—
If I could have foreseen—"

"But at least he ought to've gone to some better place
than that old mess of a Linley house," Hatcher protested.
"Why didn't he? There are plenty other—"

"He went there because he'll not have to pay anything.
That awful woman owes him so much he says he could
have a room there the rest of his life and just charge it
against her debt to him. Do you know how much money
he has left now?"

"Well, it must be over a thousand dollars, Mother."

"Yes!" Mrs. Ide cried. " 'Enough to take care of an
emergency,' he told me. He meant if he got sick or died.
He meant he wouldn't let anybody else pay his funeral
expenses!"

"Oh, see here, Mother! Don't go piling it on."

"He did mean that! Don't you know him yet, Hatcher?
When I told him we'd all work to pay him back he said
that if we brought Janey home from college he'd never
forgive us, and of course now, after what he's done, we
won't have to write Alice not to come and bring the
children, because the business'll go on and—and—" Harriet
Ide sobbed aloud. "He's saved everything but himself."

"Oh, see here!" Hatcher became practical and began to
remonstrate. "He isn't going to starve. He's asked out a
lot, and naturally he'll come here for meals, anyhow most
of 'em. As for where a person just sleeps, that isn't a
thing to make a fuss about. For my part I'd just as
soon—"

"No, you wouldn't!" his mother cried. "Not in that
house! Not if you'd grown up in it when it was beautiful

and had dear lovely people happy in it! Not if every inch
of it reminded you of their laughter and their singing—
and of how they died. What crueler place could a sensitive man go to—because he had nowhere else on earth to
go? What worse torture for him than to see it every
minute all about him, dirty and bedraggled and insulted,
and with grimy people sprawling and squalling over it—"

"Harriet! Harriet!" her husband groaned. "It's not forever. We'll get him out of it. It's only a loan, you know.
Just give us a little *time*."

"Yes, for God's sake, Mother!" Hatcher said. "In the
first place, Uncle Victor's more philosophic than most
people, and, in the second, Father's right: we'll pay him
back. He's not going to be there forever. Now, for
heaven's sake, stop crying and listen—"

"I can't!"

"Yes, you can." Hatcher continued to plead with her
and to present his uncle's misfortune in its best aspect for
her solacing, and for his father's and also for his own. He
needed some such bracing, himself. The warm and comfortable house where he sat was a little shabby, perhaps;
but he had a sense of meanness in remaining an occupant
of it when he thought of his dainty uncle as one of Mrs.
Schapp's roomers. Victor's boarding-house had been
pretty tough; but that blackened old Linley relic down in
the smog—! Hatcher's voice lost conviction, grew feeble;
he decided that he wasn't bringing much comfort to his
mother or to anybody, and stopped trying.

Before him, floating in the shadows of the lamplit room,
the beautiful hurting face of Sarah Florian began to be
displaced by the pale, neat features of a middle-aged

gentleman whose eyes seemed to regard him reproach-
fully.

. . . It wasn't late in the evening when Frederic Ide
returned from the examination next door. He hadn't
needed much time to prove that Mrs. Florian's account
with Ide and Aldrich was intact and in order, and that
when she and her lawyer would look over her securities
with him at the bank, next day, they'd find nothing
missing.

"She leaves it with me—with the firm—as previously,"
he told his wife and sister and son when he came into the
living-room. He uttered a short sound that was the hint of
a dry laughter. "She was openly surprised—somewhat
invidiously so! We hold about a sixth of her fortune for
her; I got the impression she'd have been almost willing
to find a little of it gone for the sake of seeing justice
done to herself. Her manner was—well, call it annoyed."

Aunt Ada glanced at Hatcher; but he sat expressionless.
"Then why in the world does she leave the account with
you, Fred?"

Ide answered with an increased dryness. "When it
came to us it amounted to about five hundred thousand
dollars. Harry and I did better with it than with any
other—incomparably better than with anything of our
own. We got it up to over six hundred thousand. That's
where it is now."

Ada began to babble. "And she'd have had you indicted
and tried—and Harry died!—for twenty-two thousand!
That woman! She—"

Hatcher was conscious of his aunt's voice as it went into

more elaborate denunciation; but the words carried little meaning to him. He was thinking principally of his uncle, Victor Linley, and engaged in a brief calculation. Six times six hundred thousand equalled thirty-six hundred thousand—something like four million dollars, then.

Hatcher thought of his uncle and old George returning from their dinner at the cafeteria and going upstairs in Mrs. Schapp's rooming-house, through sounds and smells—and Mrs. Schapp probably yelling to know if they'd shut the front door . . . and the mahogany railing of the dirty fine old stairway reminding Uncle Victor of all the delicate hands that had touched it—Victor's mother's hands—his dead sister's hands—

Hatcher rose suddenly from his chair and left the room; something heavy seemed to be heaving upward within him, from his stomach to his throat. It seemed to be not a substance but a. thought—the increasingly weighty realization that Uncle Victor had saved the Ides and the Aldriches, and the firm of Ide and Aldrich, from ruin and disgrace; and that there'd been two ways in which Uncle Victor could have done it. Uncle Victor'd had a choice. He was really a sentimental man, sensitive and highly susceptible to the torture of old memories; and yet, without hesitation, he'd chosen that haunted wreck of the home of his fathers—Mrs. Schapp's rooming-house—in preference to Sarah Florian.

XXVII

WHEN Hatcher came back to the living-room his Aunt Ada was there alone. She was standing at the other end of the room, near the fireplace, but had no difficulty in perceiving his instinctive movement to retire just after he stepped through the doorway.

"No!" she said commandingly. "You'll come all the way in, if you please. I've a thing or two to say to you."

He advanced a hesitant step or two. "I was only looking for something, Aunt Ada, and—"

She came forward. "You haven't apologized to me, Hatcher."

"I haven't what?"

"You haven't apologized for the language you used to me this afternoon."

"When?"

"When you screamed and swore you'd prove that woman next door a traduced saint and me a slanderer. Just before you galloped off, raving, to tell her what your mother and father and I thought of her. Have you forgotten the terms you used to me? I should think that under the circumstances the least you'd feel is that as a gentleman you owe me an apology."

"Do I?" Hatcher hung his head. Of the scene to which his aunt referred, his memory now brought him only semblances of explosion and concussion, fireworks in his head. He had indeed forgotten the terms he'd used to her, and also the worse ones she'd used to him. "Well—all right. I'm afraid I was excited. I apologize. I beg your pardon, Aunt Ada, if it does you any good."

Ada's severity wasn't eased. After long suppressions, old wrongs and new burned within her; and, once this heat had burst into expression, she couldn't turn the damper upon it. Hatcher had been a partisan of the enemy, and, even though he now stood helpless, he could still be punished for having been of the wrong party. "There are one or two things I want to tell you, young man," Ada said. "I imagine you remember I once informed you that your uncle was never in love with that woman, and you probably think, now, you have reason to believe that once he was. You'd be very much mistaken. Nobody was ever in love with her—nobody! For a while they just got caught; but it never lasted long, because they couldn't help seeing what she was—and that's all that happened to your uncle. Nobody with any sense would call it being in love. I told you the truth. Do you understand?"

"I'd rather not talk about it, Aunt Ada."

"No!" she returned shrewishly. "I guess not; I should think you wouldn't! Not when you think things over and look about you and see what you've done."

He was humble. "What I've done?"

"Yes! What you've done to yourself, for one thing." Aunt Ada was never much given to relenting, and her emotions were now well out on an unlimited spree. "At the supper table last Sunday evening you may recall I warned you what might happen to you, Mr. Hatcher!"

"You did?" he asked blankly. "No, I don't—"

"What! You don't remember my telling you that you'd better change your manner or Dorcy'd be wondering what was the matter with you? Well, you didn't change and she did more than wonder. Oh, no; you wouldn't listen to me! Just gave me a black look for my pains! And before that unpleasant evening was over, she knew perfectly *well* what was the matter with you. Breaking your neck to get to that telephone the way you did! You think Dorcy didn't see why? Of course she did! So did everybody else. I suppose you understand that *now*, don't you?"

"I don't even understand what you're talking about, Aunt Ada. You needn't tell me, though."

"Oh, needn't I? I suppose you saw what Erdvynn Wilson did this afternoon, didn't you?"

"I don't care what he did, Aunt Ada."

"That's how it looked then," Aunt Ada said. "It looked as if you didn't care. When Dorcy and her mother were going to leave the cemetery, Erdvynn Wilson left the rest of you and went to Dorcy and talked comfort-ingly to her and helped to put her in her car—while you just stood there. I suppose you were thinking about how soon you could get back to that woman next door. Well, you know better now; but I can tell you—look out! All these things you've done are going to count against you with Dorcy Aldrich; and you needn't expect they won't."

"I don't expect anything, Aunt Ada."

Hatcher's tone was as lifeless as were his attitude and facial expression; Ada, still on her spree, wasn't getting much satisfaction out of him. He might as well have been a piano upon which she had an uncontrollable urge to play a particular tune; but the keys wouldn't sound, so, naturally, she pounded harder.

"Oh, so you don't 'expect anything', Hatcher Ide?" She tried to mimic the flatness with which he'd spoken. "You 'don't expect anything', don't you? You won't put that over on me, young man, so don't waste your breath. You do, too, 'expect'! Your head's probably so full of happy-ending movies you think you can treat a girl like Dorcy as you've treated her and then be taken back. I think you're mistaken! Dorcy wouldn't any more let a man drop her for a creature like Sarah Florian and then come creeping back to be welcomed home and get his bruises all petted up—she wouldn't do it any more than I did, myself! A good many things have changed in these modern days; but I think you'll find that girls haven't entirely lost their pride. No, and there's another thing you may have to take into consideration—"

"You haven't finished, Aunt Ada?"

"Just about!" she said triumphantly. "Dorcy's got to take care not only of herself now but of her mother, too, hasn't she? You've been setting her quite an example, haven't you—showing your preference for driving about town in French limousines?" Hatcher turned abruptly toward the door; but as he left the room his overwrought aunt called after him. "You'd better look out! When you go to pay your call of condolence at the Aldriches' you may find Erdvynn Wilson there before you!"

. . . When Hatcher paid his "call of condolence", the last afternoon of that week, Ada's prophecy was fulfilled. He and Erdvynn Wilson said hello to each other gravely, just outside the front door; then Erdvynn went on toward the car he'd left in the driveway, and Hatcher didn't need to ring the bell, for the door had not quite closed.

Dorcy opened it wider. Her face looked thin; but she was composed and not in black. "Harry always hated mourning clothes," she said, as she took Hatcher through the doorway at the right—not into the room where stood Harry's closed piano. "He wouldn't have wanted us to wear black—he'd have abhorred it for us—but I can't persuade Mother. I'm afraid I'll never get her out of it. You won't mind if I don't go and ask her to come down? She's going to be pretty shot for a long time, I'm afraid. Won't you sit down, Hatcher?"

"Thank you," he said, sat, and felt queer.

She took a chair facing him; and, with her eyes downcast, folded her hands in her lap and sat looking at them. He'd never seen her do anything like this, and felt queerer. "You've been very kind, Hatcher, and Mother told me that when you came I must be sure to thank you for her as well as for myself. We're very grateful to you

for staying so long at the telephone. I'm afraid it was very
tiring for you."

"No, no; not at all, Dorcy. I was only too glad to—
That is, I mean I—"

"Everyone has been so kind," she said. "The whole
town loved Harry, and the letters have been pouring in
—so many from people he'd helped and Mother and I'd
never heard of. It makes us even prouder of him than
we always were."

Hatcher's heart was wrung. "Yes, of course you'd be.
Yes, of course everybody loved him, Dorcy. He—"

"There's something I want to straighten out with
you." Dorcy didn't seem to hear Hatcher's murmurings.
"I'm afraid you may have thought I'd got a wrong idea
about something, partly because of how foolish I was,
being frightened that night I sent for you to help me find
him. I'm afraid that after—after what's happened—you
may have thought that Mother and I were afraid he'd—
that Harry had— I can't say it. In the shock, at first, we—
we were tormented by ideas that maybe something was
terribly wrong downtown and that your father was
keeping something back from us; but since then he's
showed us that the firm isn't even bankrupt, so we know
now that we never needed to have the dreadful thought
about Harry hanging over us."

"No—of course you needn't—"

"No," she said. "I want you to know what a blessing
it's been to be certain it was an accident. I want you to
forget it if you ever thought we might have imagined that
it—that it wasn't."

"Yes, I will. I didn't really think—"

"There's another thing," she said. "I don't want you ever to believe that Mother and I haven't appreciated the kindness that you and all your family have shown us. We've been close neighbors so many years—and when that's changed and we're not here any more in this house, and you naturally won't be seeing us so often, why, Mother and I both hope—"

"Not in this house, Dorcy?"

"No; we can't keep it," she said. "Mother and I are both so happy to think that Harry never dreamed what would happen to us if he should die suddenly. We're grateful that he never had such a thought. There's really almost nothing at all left, you see. Your father's explained it to us several times; and Mother asked your Uncle Victor to go over it with her, too, so that she'd understand better, and he made it as clear as he could. Of course Mother and I neither of us know really much about business—it's so involved and confusing; but one thing at least seems certain: that though the firm's all right what Mother and I'll have coming to us out of Harry's share in it will be just barely enough—now that he isn't there, himself—just barely enough for Mother to take a tiny flat somewhere. Your uncle insisted that your father's figures about our probable income from the firm were right; so of course they are."

"Why, yes." Hatcher felt still queerer. "Of course my father—"

"Yes. Mother and I know, of course," Dorcy said, and her eyes had a strangely distant expression. "We know that your father'd never be anything except fair, even generous; but we'd always had the idea that Harry was the one who brought most of the business into the firm. It's all so mixed up I don't suppose Mother and I'll ever get the details really straight in our heads. We know it's all correct, though, of course." Dorcy paused; then she said, "Still—" and paused again.

" 'Still'?" Hatcher repeated the word. "Still what, Dorcy?"

"Nothing. I just wanted to have you understand that Mother and I appreciate the kindness you've all shown us—and there's one other thing, Hatcher."

"Yes, Dorcy?"

"It's this." She was looking down at her folded hands again. "I've always wanted to have my closest friends like each other—and to bring them closer together. For instance, you and Mary Gilpin for a long time have been my two closest friends, and I've always wanted both of you to like each other as much as—"

"But I do, Dorcy." He was puzzled. "I like Mary top-hole. I think she's a—"

"Yes, I know you do; but there's someone else I want you to like that much, too, Hatcher. He's somebody I don't think any of us ever appreciated enough. I know I really didn't, myself, until—until just lately, when I've begun to appreciate his deeper qualities. He doesn't show them until something brings them to the surface, Hatcher. You know I mean Erdvynn, don't you? I want you to appreciate and like him very much. Will you?"

"Why—if you do, of course, Dorcy."

"I didn't think anybody *could* ever be as loyal and sweet to me as he has," she said, and, looking up for just an instant, let him see eyes liquidly brightened by her thought of Erdvynn. "I never knew that anybody could be so considerate and so understanding and thoughtful as he's been all along, and most of all during this terrible time, Hatcher. The instant he heard about Father he came straight to me. That very morning, that awful morning, he came—and Lennie Aldrich wasn't going to let him upstairs; but he pushed by her and found me, and he said just the right things to help me. I could never forget that, of course."

"No—of course you wouldn't." Hatcher felt not only queer but clumsy. He thought he ought to try to explain something he'd better have let alone. "I—I had the feeling probably you didn't want to see anybody just then, Dorcy. I— Well, the way it happened, Mary grabbed me just after I got into the house and she put me on that telephone job, and after that I really didn't have a chance to do anything else. I— It never occurred to me you'd want me to come up and—"

"No, no, no!" Dorcy separated her hands from each other long enough to lift one of them in a slight gesture. "I didn't mean that you ought to've come, Hatcher. I never thought of it. You were busy every minute being as unselfishly kind as you could be. Please don't think I meant that. Please don't!"

"Well, I hope not, Dorcy. I was trying to be some help. I thought I—"

"But indeed you were," she said. "You couldn't have been more. I just wanted to tell you— You see, nobody knows it yet except Mother and Mary and his father and mother; but I thought I ought to tell anybody that's as old a friend of mine as you are, Hatcher."

"Yes, Dorcy. You want me to know you're going to be married to Pink—to Erdvynn Wilson."

"Yes. It'll be some time toward the end of month after next, Hatcher, and of course very quietly with nobody here but Mother, and his mother and father, and Mary; so don't tell anybody, please."

"No, of course I won't."

She looked up again, this time with a fluttering little shyness, and she smiled. "I know I could never make anybody understand what it's meant to me to find out how dear he is, Hatcher. I know you couldn't believe—"

"Yes, I could, Dorcy. I do."

"No." She shook her head, still smiling. "I want you and Mary to like him terribly much; but there's only one person that'll ever really know how dear he is, and that's me. I like it that way; I think I'd rather be the only one. Do you know when I began to understand how I really felt about him?"

"When you began— No, I don't."

"It was after we'd been to your house to supper last Sunday night, Hatcher. He brought me home and then came in, and we talked until Mother and—and Harry— got back from their party. I don't think Erdvynn and I'd ever had a really serious talk before, Hatcher, and when I saw what depths there were in his nature that I hadn't known were there, why, almost all at once something bright and beautiful seemed to open up before me. It—it all practically happened then, Hatcher."

"Then?" Hatcher said. "Last Sunday night?"

"Yes, practically. Of course all these deeply thoughtful things he's done ever since then have made me all the surer; but, yes, it really happened then, Hatcher, last Sunday night—before our terrible loss came upon Mother and me. I wish I'd told Father that night before he went upstairs; it would have pleased him—he always liked Erdvynn. Next day it was too late, and so now I—" Dorcy rose suddenly and gave Hatcher her hand. "I must stop myself from thinking of all these things I wish I'd done, and stop Mother. I'm afraid I'd better be going up to her now. It was dear of you to come, Hatcher. You won't forget about liking and appreciating Erdvynn the way I want you to, will you?"

Hatcher said that indeed he wouldn't, and, with a humming head, went forth to outdoors.

XXVIII

THROUGH his college years, and here at home, he'd been a rather frequent patron of the movies, as his aunt had intimated; but his interest in them was often skeptical. Ada, trying to sting him, had been mistaken when she'd insisted that his intelligence was so feeble as to be influenced to believe that love in life follows the pattern of love in the cinema. Hatcher hadn't even wished it to do so; he'd spoken the truth when he'd said that he didn't "expect anything", and he knew that he could never have been in love with Dorcy Aldrich. Had she ever been in love with him—really? he asked, as he left her house, putting the inquiry to his recent impressions. Well, if she ever had—a little—she wasn't any more. There'd been a telling difference in her, just now, whenever she'd spoken the name "Erdvynn". She'd worn an

unmistakable look and there'd been a confessional soft-
ness in her voice when she talked of Pinkie Wilson's tender thoughtfulness of her, and of those depths in Pinkie's
nature.

Hatcher knew that she wished him to feel the contrast
between his devotion to the telephone and Pinkie's tactful ardor for herself. In spite of her denials she'd made
it clear that she found Hatcher wanting—derelict in things
he should have done. Evidently she blamed him, her
friend, for not having done what Pinkie, her accepted
lover, did. Yet which was harder: sticking it out at a
telephone for forty hours or trotting upstairs to do a little
soothing and petting now and then? Hatcher didn't find
himself blameworthy in this matter. Why, then, the renewed sense of guiltiness, accompanied ridiculously by
the feeling that injustice was being done him? To feel
guilty and at the same time to be resenting injustice
seemed as inconsistent as it did to be not in love with a
girl and yet finding something lacking in her because she'd
fallen in love with another man. Hatcher had this jumble
of feelings and was sure of only one thing: that he was
as great a failure at love as he was in everything else.

Having once more made this discovery, he began to
mull over other saliences in Dorcy's talk. She'd pressed
the point that she'd become "practically" engaged to
Pinkie last Sunday night—before Harry died. Hatcher
comprehended her insistence;—naturally she wanted it
understood that she'd begun to care for Pinkie before she
knew how useful being in love with him might be.
Eleanor Aldrich wouldn't be long in a "tiny flat", and
Pinkie'd have to be a generous son-in-law; but Hatcher

already knew that Dorcy wasn't a girl who'd marry "just for money", so she needn't have pushed that point about Sunday night so hard—no, nor have shown him so punitively why and how much she really did care for Pinkie. Hatcher'd have believed her without all those comparisons.

A grim thought turned into a grimmer question. Dorcy had become virtually engaged to Pinkie that night when Harry Aldrich came home—came home with what he had in mind to do. Suppose Dorcy *had* told him that she'd just about made up her mind to be the wife of the richest boy in town? Probably girls didn't often tell their parents so promptly as that—but suppose Dorcy had? Evidently, Pinkie was one of the possible salvations Harry'd hoped for—and it was another of the touching things to remember about him that he'd never openly urged it upon his daughter. If Dorcy'd told him that night, would it have saved him—at the eleventh hour? It might have done so, alas! it might. Then there were two things that could have saved Harry's life, if he'd known them. If he'd known that his friend, Victor Linley, had twenty-two thousand dollars, or if he'd known that Dorcy was going to marry Wilson, Hatcher might have been walking away from the Aldriches' house, right now, with the sound of Harry's piano and Harry's hearty baritone following him.

Then Harry was uselessly dead. Worse than that, he was senselessly dead. There was supposed to be some sort of Plan working out the destinies of mankind, wasn't there? Something from on High was supposed to have an eye on people, to be shaping their courses and seeing to it that right and justice and mercy should prevail on earth; so Hatcher'd always understood. He'd understood it a little vaguely, perhaps; but at least he'd taken for granted a kind of symmetry in life, something suggestive of Design and Law and Order. Now here was Harry Aldrich's death directly contradicting any such possibility, making fantastic Hatcher's previous conception of life as something probably governed. He'd long since perceived, even at twenty-two, that expropriation of other people's property doesn't inevitably bring on a punishment. "Thou shalt not steal"—quite right; but Harry hadn't killed himself because he'd stolen; he'd killed himself because he didn't know that Pinkie Wilson would soon be his son-in-law or that Uncle Victor had twenty-two thousand dollars. When you faced such a fact, how could you see any Design? There couldn't be any. There was only senseless scrawl, meaningless tangle; and the old suggestion that Nature disregards the individual didn't untangle it.

No, and blind-ending love affairs and Harry's death weren't the only examples Hatcher saw before him of a meandering purposelessness in life. His cheek began to burn resentfully when he thought of one of Dorcy's implications. Mrs. Aldrich and Dorcy'd "always had the idea that Harry was the one who brought most of the business into the firm"; nevertheless, they had accepted Frederic Ide's explanation of the littleness of their inheritance, so Dorcy said—then she'd paused and added the word "*still*" in a tone that sharpened in significance as it continued to repeat itself in Hatcher's aural memory.

The gist of it seemed to be that the widow and the

daughter, knowing themselves to be inexperienced in business, couldn't help doubting that they were getting an entirely square deal from the dead man's partner. Harry's defalcation was being covered up by Frederic Ide at hard cost to himself—and to Uncle Victor!—and, in addition to this, as Hatcher'd just gathered, his father was going to try to wring from his exhausted resources what would be really a pension for Mrs. Aldrich. It would have to be small, naturally; but under the circumstances the act was one of almost heroic generosity. The reward for it was that the beneficiaries had some doubt of the bene- factor's scrupulousness. They even weren't quite sure of Uncle Victor's! He was living in the old Linley house partly on their account, and yet the two bereft women innocently suspected that Victor, being a man, had en- dorsed his brother-in-law's confusing explanations instead of seeing right done to the defenceless.

What seemed most crazily ironic in this patternless scrawl was that nobody could ever tell Dorcy and her mother the truth. Hatcher didn't believe in fairy god- mothers or the romantic movies, and he no longer even hoped that human affairs grooved neatly toward idealized sequels; but it is of the essence of youth to cling to one lingering tenet of romance: that for even the loneliest deeds of greatness involving self-sacrifice there shall be at last, in the end, at least a little appreciation. The mangled hero, one of thousands, should know in his dying vision that he is to be the Unknown Soldier, and it is inevitable that Jean Valjean should receive in his death scene the remorseful gratitude of Marius and Cosette. Noble deeds done in secret ought to remain secret, of course—but not absolutely forever. In the midst of other disturbances of equilibrium, Hatcher was seriously jolted by his comprehension that Eleanor Aldrich and Dorcy would really never know what his father and his uncle had done for them. Instead, to and through their dying days, the two ladies would think it possible that in their saddest hours they hadn't been treated quite honorably in money matters by Frederic Ide and Victor Linley.

. . . To Hatcher, upon consideration, this seemed particularly hard on Uncle Victor who already began to look as if his new lodging gave him pretty tough going. "His face is so white!" Harriet Ide said to her son and her husband, some hours after Hatcher returned from his call of condolence. Uncle Victor had just departed with a false briskness, having dined with his relatives. "His complexion's always been naturally pale, but not like this —and there's that drawn look about his mouth when he doesn't think anybody's noticing. Oh, it does seem as if we've *got* to do something!"

"Something?" Hatcher rose from an easy chair. "Mother, we'll do plenty."

"How?" she asked, meaning that the best intended answer would be foolish.

"All right," Hatcher said. "I know how it sounds to you. Just the boy's drivel, of course! But before I've half finished the job I'll prove to you and Father that it's simple horse sense."

"What is?" Frederic Ide asked, and looked up at his son.

"Fresh paint!" Hatcher said. He spoke out roundly;

for, as he stood before his parents, with something like defiance in his attitude, his spirit found the vigor that was in him because it had been in the resolute stock from which he sprang. That heritage made some things impossible: he couldn't sit softly and accept the sacrifice an older and better man had made; he could no longer sit softly and accept anything. "Anyhow, for once in my life," he said, "I'm going to say my say."

His mother only sighed; but his father's eyes, fixed upon him, were thoughtful. "Yes; go ahead, Hatcher. What about paint?"

"Yes, sir. When I tried to get Mother cheered up over Uncle Victor, I think the effect on you both was to make you believe I was just too flitter-minded a colt to understand how it would keep hurting him to live down there with everything that's past hitting him in the face with no let-up at all. I told Mother it didn't matter much where a person just .sleeps, and I don't think it does *if* you sleep; but Uncle Victor looks as if he hadn't been doing much of that. Well, we aren't just going to lie down while he takes the rap for us. I bought a used bicycle yesterday for eleven dollars and—"

"You did?" Ide asked. "What about paint?"

"Just this, sir. With a bicycle I can probably do my collecting in a day and a half. That'll give me the rest of my week to put in working at painting and renovating along with the others I've got at it. Father, you still own over thirty vacant houses in this town. Except a couple or so I've had two little squads working on, those houses are all run down and sooty, the color of smoke inside and out; and every one of 'em's mortgaged. They ought to be bringing in at the very least a thousand dollars a month, net; and they could. They can do it pretty soon, at that."

"They couldn't!" Mrs. Ide looked at her husband. "They couldn't, could they, Frederic?"

"I don't know," he said. "Hatcher has ideas about fresh paint. I'd never have thought it worth while trying—against the smoke—but there are some signs that the city's over-housing slack's about taken up, and maybe—"

"Ask old Barley!" Hatcher said. "Ask him how long it took to rent the first of those houses we renovated. I've got *him* convinced, anyhow. Father, if we can put it over, couldn't half the new rents go to paying off the old loans and the other half to Uncle Victor till we've settled with him? Father, if you can possibly stand just the few small bills for paint and a few people's low wages just a few more weeks, why, absolutely I'll prove to you—"

"Prove! That's quite a word, Hatcher."

"Yes, sir; and I'm pretty dumb; but I swear I know at least one small fact in this world. It's that if you show people a bright, clean-looking thing among a lot of horrible dirty ones, they'll go after it."

Ide was serious. "You think so?"

"*Think* so?" Hatcher cried. "Why, we can show this city how that whole dead section could be redeemed! Of course you've got to use the right colors or you'll be repainting all the time; but we've been working that out and I think we've got it, because there's a special kind of brownish gray with a special green trim— But you'd have to see 'em to understand what I mean. If you could just somehow spare the time to go down there with me and take a look at what we've already done—"

"Yes, Hatcher. Monday morning on our way downtown."

"Good boy!" Hatcher exclaimed, and, this point gained, dared to go further. He began to put before his father plans (suggested by the more ingenious of the two colored women) for modernizing kitchens at virtually no expense. Harriet Ide, foreseeing nothing but good money cast after bad, went desolately away, leaving the father and son absorbed.

. . . During the talk with his father Hatcher's concentration upon business was complete; and afterward, for an hour or so, his mind was an orderly arrangement of facts, theoretical figures and computations. He was determined to keep it so, to think of nothing other than his work; but there came the intrusion he couldn't longer exclude: the pursuing vision of Sarah Florian. Sometimes he'd been able to keep Sarah away by thinking of Uncle Victor; but she persistently returned into the air about him, always with an increasing loveliness. In spite of everything he knew of her, her spirit seemed to hover, whispering, "Oh you of little faith!" This was nonsense, he knew; yet found no means to banish it. Her glow— her ineffable glow—fell warmly upon him, and in the darkly shining eyes that glanced from anywhere he saw a strange, beckoning tenderness.

What would he feel when he saw her beautiful actual self again? He didn't know; but his heart beat faster when he thought of a meeting. What would she do, and what would he? Would she only look at him while he'd say, "I'm older now, Sarah Florian. I know you and at last I know myself, too. I think you're rather terrible; but with that glow of yours upon me I know that never, never can I escape!" Or would she, when they met, murmur the one word, "Forgive?" and would he say, "I know you now, Sarah—yes, too thoroughly!—but I'm not like my uncle; I seem to be sap enough to love you, anyhow."

Such was not the outcome. Though Mrs. Florian was close at hand when he next saw her, neither of them said anything at all to the other. She got out of her car, in crowded downtown, to go into a shop, just as Hatcher was passing on his way to take up a providential bargain in paint. When she'd stepped to the pavement she turned her head to speak over her shoulder to a companion, a darkly harmonious young man who remained in the car. "Five minutes at the longest!" she said in her well-remembered voice. The dark young man, protesting "I can't bear it!" leaned toward her with humorous coquetry. He was known to the pedestrian, a contemporary, and in their boyhood had been looked upon as too esthetic. "My gosh!" Hatcher thought. "Sissy Pittinger! Running around with that gigolo already! Oh, my gosh, listen to *me* calling *him* a gigolo!"

Sarah crossed the pavement to the glass doors of the shop, saw Hatcher, gave him an absent nod, and swept gracefully from his sight.

Hatcher had the impression that he'd never before seen her in a really good light. Something seemed to have happened to her face—a little as something had seemed to happen to Dorcy's when he first saw Sarah's, only more seemed now to have happened to Sarah's. There wasn't an ineffable glow; there wasn't any glow at all. It hadn't departed because she was driving now with Sissy Pittinger; it would have been absent had she been alone.

What Hatcher felt was a dismal amazement. Whence had come that glow and where had it gone? If Andrea del Sarto had ever been able to look with a matter-of-fact scrutiny upon his sordid wife, he might have discovered that her loveliness had been all in his paint and his mind's eye. Hatcher, in this mystifying moment, asking himself where Sarah's looks had gone, was like a traveler who returns to view a scene, once an enchantment, and stands wondering why its beauty's lost, since the landscape itself is the same.

Hatcher walked on, startled by the untrustworthiness of sound eyes. If Sarah Florian had actually changed, the alteration was pretty sudden! No, it seemed to be the fact that if she didn't look interested in you, and if you noticed details, especially around under the chin, her face was almost—almost kind of oldish.

Before he'd gone two blocks he found that with the eyes of his imagination he could again see the glowing picture of her that had been in his head, and at the same time he could place beside it the Sarah Florian he'd just passed on the street. The contrast wasn't short of appalling; it proved to him that some tricky picture-painting talent of his own had betrayed him into being in love with the colored glow that it had made at the "you-and-I" bidding of Sarah Florian. She would bid no more; and the illusory enrichment wouldn't clothe her if she did.

Hatcher felt injuredly vacant; the whole world seemed just a vacancy.

He thought of big drinks he seemed to need; and a handsome girl, approaching among the sidewalk crowd, gave him fixedly a responsive gaze. "Sorry!" Hatcher's expression said to her, as she almost stopped and he went on. His pace had slackened after he met Mrs. Florian; now he made it brisker.

"Nothing on earth's any use," he thought. "But I've got to hurry. Somebody else might get hold of that paint."

XXIX

THE alteration in Victor Linley, being actual and not merely the disglamoring of his nephew's eye, caused warrantable apprehension among his kinsfolk and friends. He grew thinner rapidly, began to look a little withered, and he leaned more dependently upon his malacca stick, which he now often found a necessary prop even indoors. When persuaded forth from his grotesque lodging he was as dainty in his dress as ever, listened to ladies, as always, with the same responsive attention he'd shown in his regretted boarding-house when Mr. Boerl or any of the other boarders became animatedly vocal. At his sister's he sometimes made merry. Mrs. Upham had arrived with her two homely little boys, whose unruliness was a trial to the decorous young Frances; and with these three Uncle Victor could become even frolicsome. At such times, his sisters laughed too; but afterward when he'd limped away, waving his stick and calling jocose farewells to small pursuers, the two ladies were all the sadder. They knew his liveliness for braggadocio and heard the mourner's undertone within his laughter.

The ghosts in his old house wore upon him, for he more and more keenly lived with them. "What a dear place it's been!" his dying sister, Nancy, said to him whenever he came up the dirty outer steps, and always, as he climbed the broad stairs within, he heard from below the rippling accompaniment of his mother's piano to the thin sound of a dead 'cello, his father's. Nights in Victor's room at Mrs. Schapp's were long.

. . . Martyrdoms, however, of their own nature cannot last forever: the torture stops or the victim's heart does; and Mr. Linley proved to be a mere transient of three months' tenancy at Mrs. Schapp's. With the end of February he became the lessee of two rooms in an apartment house far out on Sheridan Avenue where the smoke grew a little thinner. Moreover, architecture was feebly alive again. Victor had a country-house to build for the lady who'd given him Locksie—or perhaps this timely idea should be defined as a commission from her husband. In prospect, too, were several smaller possibilities.

"I'm afraid you feel just out of Purgatory," his nephew said to him, the day after the removal to the apartment house. Victor, among packing-cases, was placing old books upon new shelves when Hatcher came in. "You told me once that we learn mainly through misery. If that's true, you must be one of the wisest men in the world."

"No. I've never been miserable enough to become very wise, Hatcher; and there's a paradox to be added. It's that to the mind of an entirely wise person there'd be no such thing as misery."

"Not even when he's in it?" Hatcher said, and with his handkerchief removed some drops of melted snow from his sleeve. "I see. Here's March not bringing us spring but a snow that's just put me in misery because I can't use my bicycle. You mean if I were entirely wise I'd be singing something about it's not snowing snow, it's snowing violets. I don't see it; but I'll snow a cheque on you." He brought forth a notebook and from between two of its pages removed a cheque, which he placed upon his uncle's drawing-table. "Father told me to deliver it on my way home. Don't go buying big cars, though; it's only another soupçon."

Victor put the cheque away. "Your soupçons have begun to come in pretty regularly."

"Yes—begun a bit late," Hatcher said, and, having made a scribble in the notebook, returned it to his pocket and glanced at a blueprint thumbtacked to the drawing-table. "That's your big house for Mrs. Azbrouck—I mean for Mr. and Mrs. Azbrouck—is it?"

"Yes."

"Good job it happened," Hatcher said. "Got you out of Mrs. Schapp's."

"No, it didn't, Hatcher; commissions aren't paid that early in the transaction. I began to see that I'd made a good investment with Ide and Aldrich, not a reckless loan. It's these soupçons from you and your father that got me out."

"From Father, not from me," Hatcher said; nevertheless, he looked pleased. Then his gaze returned to the blueprint, absently. "They like size, all right, don't they? I understand there's to be another château put up out that way—about a mile farther along Silver Creek."

"Yes; so I've heard, Hatcher. A competitor of mine has that job—if you mean the house for the Erdvynn Wilsons. Young Erdvynn likes glass, I'm told; wants windows that 'bring the landscape indoors'."

"Does he?" Hatcher still looked at the blueprint. "I haven't happened to see the bride and groom since they got back from their trip last month; but Amy Murray tells me it's one of these cases of complete bliss that you read about. Almost embarrassing to spectators, Amy reports. I suppose you haven't happened to run into 'em?"

"Yes, I've seen them," Victor said. "Eleanor asked me to dinner and—"

Hatcher's brief laughter interrupted him. "They ask you to dinner, do they?—but not to do their new house for 'em. Who was there?"

"Only the bride and groom and Lennie Aldrich and her mother and Eleanor and I. Amy's right, I should say. I've seldom seen more bridely radiance and devotion."

Hatcher looked up, sardonic. "Radiance? What a mess it all is!"

"Not at all, Hatcher. It's not uncommon for marriage to have that effect upon brides who've previously seemed rather matter-of-fact."

"Radiance!" Hatcher said again. "Was Mrs. Aldrich radiant, too?"

"Eleanor? No, not radiant. She's still looking rather

shattered; but she's able to be pleased with her daughter's happiness, of course."

"That's what I mean," Hatcher explained. "Dorcy radiantly blissful and her mother pleased! Harry Aldrich ruining himself for 'em, then killing himself, and now, no more than a few months later—radiance and pleasure!"

"It doesn't mean heartlessness, Hatcher."

"Oh, I know! It's good Sunday-school to prattle that if we devote our lives to mourning, the business of the world won't go on; but I say it's a mess. One reason is that this 'business of the world' you hear so much about *doesn't* go on. Just look at it! All winter I've had more than half a mind to get to Finland if I could—I ski and I can shoot some—but I didn't dare leave the job here. Then there are the British bombers dropping leaflets over Germany, and a sit-down strike on the Maginot line and the Siegfried line, and this nation all in a stew over who can promise the most money the most economically to the most voters and go on crippling the country and get to be nominated for President! Do you still claim there's any sense to anything, Uncle Victor?"

"Yes." There was a fire in the room, though the day wasn't Sunday, and Mr. Linley took from a packing-case an old cushion, placed it before the hearth for Locksie. The golden spaniel, fatter than when Hatcher'd first met him, accepted this attention complacently. "Yes, I believe there's some sense to things in spite of my suspicion that the 'sit-down strike' along the Maginot line mayn't last much longer, Hatcher. In fact, it may end in explosion and great despairs."

"Fine!" Hatcher said. "Great killings and then peace

filled with great bankruptcies! Mother didn't get me to church much after I was fifteen; but I had a lingering sort of impression that there was direction and shaping to the universe. Of course the last vestiges of *that* notion are all out of me!"

"They are, Nephew? Why?"

"Oh, look at the whole business! War liable to be forced on everybody in the world—and, for a detail, what about Harry Aldrich? Wouldn't the way he died convince anybody that if there are such things as divine shaping and direction, they're entirely too slipshod to consider?"

"No; not anybody," the uncle said. "In a moment of stress you asked me what I thought life is. Of course I still haven't an idea, Hatcher. I suspect, though, that's because I have no understanding of the nature of death. We don't know what's really been happening to Harry Aldrich or to the victims of war. We assume that death is the worst of calamities; but scientifically we don't know, and from the mystic view it may be very pleasant. Combatants inflict it but are unaware of what they inflict. The materialist thought is that the slain—and Harry Aldrich—have finished with pain. So we comfort ourselves without knowledge."

Hatcher stared, surprised. "But that's terrible! Uncle Victor, I thought you thought—"

"Yes; I do," Victor said. "Knowledge of death might give us better comfort or none; that's still beyond us. Another reason for our befuddlement is that the present day is always confusing to the human mind. We can't read the present—not while we're in it—and so of course we're never sure of even the immediate future; but the past is different because we can make at least a stab at reading it. History appears to show a colossal kind of shaping and direction, doesn't it? So we suspect that the shaping's here even now. Probably nothing's haphazard but only seems so."

"Just a good old optimist, after all!" Hatcher regarded him indulgently. "I think the reason you're that way, Uncle Victor, is because, if the dope's right, it's in childhood that we get our lasting impressions, and yours was spent in the Golden Age."

Mr. Linley gave this idea a wistful consideration. "Maybe so. The last of horse-and-buggy days may have been the last of the Golden Age and so my boyhood had the last glimpse of it. No wars to frighten us, no depressions that weren't readily met, no 'ideologies', no slaughter from gas engines, no universal jitters. At least so it seems looking back upon it, and I'm sorry that youth now can't know what it was to live in the kind and easy world that gave me my constitutional hopefulness. Golden Age or not, it's gone like a breath, and yet youth may be all the stronger in these harder times. The upward spiral we infer from the past is discernible. I mean the spiral man ascends as he grows wiser through adversity."

Hatcher's laughter was again brief. "You do stick to it! Tough luck makes wisdom and so, being wiser, we've ascended no matter how rotten we feel! Maybe I oughtn't to cite my individual case against you; but I don't seem to experience any upward spiral under my feet."

"You don't?"

"I do not."

Victor laughed, too. "At least your wisdom's ascended, hasn't it? Don't you think you know more than you did when you came home last September?"

"Ouch!" Color rose in Hatcher's cheeks. "Got me there! I didn't know enough to be let wander about loose. I was one of these boy Hamlets full of cursed spite because somebody else had got the world out of joint. I couldn't see any way to set it right; all I could do was to blame your generation for it. All wrong—it was too great a compliment to pay to any one generation— but why'd I find it necessary to blame you? Why do we always have to blame somebody for whatever goes wrong with us? Just trying to relieve ourselves by kicking the furniture we run into in the dark? Oh, yes; I was a little fool all right."

"No, you weren't."

"I was. I wonder you didn't slap my ears down." Hatcher went to a window and looked out into the whirl of March snow. It fell so thickly that the buildings across the street had no perspective, seemed to be only planes of white-dotted gray. "I was so busy being a sap used by a dame because I was your nephew I didn't know what I was doing. One day I overheard our colored cook saying that some time I'd turn out to be the 'man of the family.' I swelled up like a poisoned toad—and shortly afterward I'd have been the simple ruin of the family if you hadn't stopped me. You say I'm not a little fool? Where do you get your information?"

"To mention two sources only: from your father and from my own acute gratitude."

"Your what?"

"Gratitude," said Uncle Victor. "Your harassed father couldn't pay me these rescuing soupçons if it weren't for an idea of yours, Hatcher—an idea your father tells me that you've made effective with great and persistent energy."

"My fresh paint, you mean?" Hatcher, still at the window, spoke ruefully. "Looks like a case of big-talk-little-do on my part. I bragged about it. Going to net a thousand dollars a month right away quick! I thought by this time it'd be sure to. Gilp Murray's a star econo-mist and better than I am at keeping brightened up houses bright; but it costs money not to take a licking from the smoke. I doubt if the net'll run over six hundred a month by next summer." He sighed. "The firm's look-ing up a bit on its other business, though; and I think Father gets anyhow a glimpse now and then of some faraway time when it might be in the clear again."

"Yes. He tells me you're a great encouragement to him."

"What?" Hatcher turned quickly to stare suspiciously at his uncle. "Always got to have your little joke!"

"No, not this time. It's a good symptom that you think so, though; and it's another that you look upon what you've done—your fresh paint—with discontent. Hatcher, you're all right."

Hatcher couldn't think himself, or anything, "all right". His uncle certainly wasn't. Mr. Linley had re-sumed the work with his books; and, as he now stooped for one, the snowy light from the windows fell reveal-

ingly upon his head, showing it grayer than when he'd
gone to live in the old Linley house. He was shorter of
breath than he had been, and careful not to speak while
he was lifting one of the heavier books. The old Linley
house had thus hurt his uncle, Hatcher thought, because
of a confusion in human movements and emotions that
had sent him there; and the hurt had been forced upon
him by a number of things that were morally good and
ought to have been harmless—and by one thing that was
at least legal. The good things that should have been
harmless were Frederic Ide's complete trust in his partner, the partner's love for his wife, Uncle Victor's self-
lessness and great affection for his relatives and friends;
and the thing that was at least legal was Mrs. Florian's
right to her own property—a right that had created the
necessity to appease her. Looking down at his stooped
uncle's graying head, and hearing him pant a little,
Hatcher thought that all these mixed-up things had produced, among other unprofitable effects, the visible one
of a vengeance. Sarah Florian had avenged herself upon
her old lover; but hadn't the satisfaction of knowing it.
She would never know it. So even that wasn't of any use
to anybody.

The whole business—"this life"—was a rigmarole that
offered no pointers to its meaning because it hadn't any.
The nephew's mind again refused the uncle's "upward
spiral".

"What do you mean, I'm all right?" Hatcher asked.
"Kidding or coddling?"

"Neither," his uncle said. "If you leave it to your father
and your mother and me, I think we'll go further than

your cook did. Hatcher, if you could bear it, I think we'd call you the pride of the family."

Hatcher, red again, was embarrassed—not so much by the compliment as by the genuine view that his uncle might be falling into a dotage. Mr. Linley had spoken quietly, seeming to mean what he said, and, after speaking, bent to take another book from a packing-case. "Is Freddie Upham over his cold yet?" he asked casually.

"Yes, he is, and Mother said to be sure and remind you that you're expected for dinner this evening." Hatcher went to the outer door; but paused beside it. "The children are looking forward to your being there. I have rather a feud with them, and if you don't mind I hope you won't say anything to them about who's the pride of the family."

"No, I won't, Hatcher. I think they already know it."

"Good *night!*" Hatcher said with loud emphasis, and went out, not knowing what to make of such an uncle.

Left alone, Mr. Linley, pausing to rest now and then, slowly completed the filling of his shelves; then he glanced at his watch and at the white tumult whirling against his darkened windows. He decided to allow himself and Locksie a taxicab. It was as well that he did so; otherwise he might not have reached Butternut Lane that evening. What had begun as a quiet last snow of the winter was become a blizzard and the cab floundered threateningly at times; but it finally broke through the drifts in the Ides' driveway and roaringly delivered its passenger.

He was admitted by three shouting children previously

silhouetted against a front window. Frances's voice could be more piercing than that of either of the two Upham boys. "If you'll let me be the first to hold Locksie, Uncle Victor, I'll whisper you what Hatcher said when Mother made him wear Father's goloshes before she let him go out to go to the dinner-dance he's gone to. He told Mother it wasn't a hundred yards away and he wouldn't; but she made him, and he said it while he was putting 'em on. Can I hold Locksie all the time you play Who-Got-Murdered with us? These Uphams always get too rough with him; he barks. After dinner can I take him upstairs with me a while when they make me go to bed?"

After dinner, when bedtime came, all three children made trouble; but Frances had her way and staggeringly carried the fat spaniel up with her, to be surrendered within ten minutes whether she was asleep or not. Mrs. Upham ascended to hear her sons' compelled evening prayers; and Frederic Ide worked in his library. Aunt Ada had not appeared, being confined to her room by the cold little Freddie'd sneezed to her; and Victor was alone for a time with his sister Harriet.

"I'm sorry Hatcher misses this evening, or any evening, with you," she said. "It always brightens him up when you're here and he seems to need that so, poor boy!"

"Does he?" her brother asked. "Why?"

"I'm afraid because—because maybe he takes his feeling about that woman next door more seriously than we thought he would. Sometimes I'm even afraid he still has it."

"Still in love with Sarah, you think, Harriet?"

"No; don't look amused," she said. "Of course we have to admit that he was pretty foolish about her."

"No," Victor said. "I don't think so. He was pretty fine about her."

"You feel so? Chivalrously idealizing her, I suppose you mean. They tell me she's in Mexico, and I hear most people think she won't come back. I'll be glad if she never does."

"But if she does I don't see how it would matter."

"It would to me. I couldn't bear ever to see her again. I—" Mrs. Ide paused. Her color heightened and her voice was small. "I'm afraid you feel that at one time I was willing to sacrifice you—when she wanted you back."

"I doubt if she ever knew what she wanted," Victor said, and added, "Or ever will. My dear sister, don't reproach yourself for that desperate last little hope to save Fred. Simultaneously you can dismiss your imagining that the boy's still in love."

"Then why is he so down?"

"Up and down," Victor explained. "He's only down on himself for a while—at intervals. Thinks he made a public spectacle of himself over poor Sarah; and at his age a young man can't hold that view of his own recent behavior without developing intermittent pessimism. At twenty-two pessimism about yourself includes pessimism about everything else; but Hatcher's gloom isn't so deep-seated as it appears to be."

"What? But, Victor, if you listened as much as I do to what he thinks and—"

"Yes, I'd hear what he often believes he thinks," Victor said. "Hatcher's inner being doesn't reside in that.

Hatcher is what he does; we know him from his acts. He came home to be bewildered by a city in Depression and a half-dead business that had no place for him. There seemed to be no place at all for him anywhere. He's made one for himself out of nothing. He's doing more: he's taking his friend Gilpin Murray up with him and he's already made employment for others—ten, I believe, he has working now. Hatcher and his kind are the best we've got, and our best have always been equal to anything. They still are and ever shall be."

Hatcher's mother, in spite of her persistent worry, couldn't help but be pleased. "If you think so well of him, Victor, why don't you tell him so? He needs—"

"I did," Victor said. "This afternoon I told him all he could stand. I told him he was the pride of the family. If he could have borne it, or could have listened without thinking me insane, I'd have said more. I'd have told him he was the hope of the country. In fact, I'd have told him he's the hope of the world."

"Would you, Victor?" Mrs. Ide was now flushed with pleasure, and yet a distress clung to her. "It's lovely your having such a splendid idea of him; but if it's true, why does he have to go through all this long despondency?"

"Long?" her brother repeated, and smiled. "Did you ever know anything, Harriet, that lasted very long?"

A howl of wind in the chimney made her murmured response inaudible. Mrs. Upham came in to report that the rattling of windows had kept her from hearing her sons' prayers properly; she suspected curtailment, and the blizzard was becoming a fury. Victor said that if

Locksie could now be restored to him they'd best be leaving for home while the way was still passable; but both of his sisters protested determinedly that he was crazy even to dream of such a thing. He must stay the night, they insisted—a little "doubling up" would easily make room for him—and, after trying to telephone for a taxicab and finding that the wires were down, he consented.

. . . With March whimsicality the storm stopped abruptly, soon after midnight; and the cessation of outrageous noise wakened Victor to a stillness in which the gentle snoring of his spaniel, on a cushioned chair, was the only sound. The room, Harriet's, had two front windows and another in the side wall toward the "Lash place". This third window, and its shade, Victor had left partly raised; and through the aperture his opening eyes beheld the sudden peace of clear moonlight. They saw, too, the long stone house next door.

Shapes were all simple in the white of the moonlight on the white of the snow. The elaborate house of Sarah Florian was staringly plain in this clarity but did not stare; for windows and doors were solidly boarded, and the patch of stained glass in the nearer wing hid its colors behind thick wood. The thoroughness of the closure of that house suggested no return to it. "Quoth the raven, 'Nevermore!' " Mr. Linley whispered sleepily to his pillow, sighed faintly to the glittering night, and again slumbered.

When he woke in the morning a regularly intermittent sound of scraping prevented a contemplated renewal of his slumber. It came from outdoors; somebody was diligently shoveling snow from the long path to the front gate, and this was somewhat surprising, as old Berry was surely incapable of energy so brisk or so early. After a time, impelled by curiosity, Mr. Linley got up, went to one of the two windows that faced toward Butternut Lane, and raised the shade. Below him, roughly dressed, two figures rhythmically bowed and straightened as they tossed great shovelfuls of snow from the deeply covered brick path.

"Don't care if they wake up the whole neighborhood," Victor grumbled. "Barely daylight!"

The shovelers were Hatcher and Gilpin Murray, and the watcher at the window accurately comprehended their idea. They'd danced all night; and then, thinking the hour too late for bed and desiring to keep awake till breakfast-time, had devoted themselves to laborious service no matter whom it might inconvenience: mutually helpful, they'd clear their front paths.

They appeared to become dissatisfied with their method; for they stopped work, and consulted. Then, walking side by side, they began to push the shovels powerfully before them, after the manner of snowplows, as they moved toward the distant gate. When they had gone the greater part of the way they stopped again; but not to consult or to rest. What stopped them were two hurled snowballs, one of which skilfully dispersed itself upon Gilpin Murray's chin. Mr. Linley's eye, following the line of flight, discovered lurking in the shrubberies along the street another pair of figures—Amy Murray and Mary Gilpin, dressed as if for skiing and provided with further snowballs held in the crooks of their left arms. They, too, couldn't merely go to bed after dancing all night.

The shovelers didn't waste time making snowballs; they filled their shovels heapingly with snow and strode toward the bushes from which the two snowball-throwers courageously advanced, hurling as they came. In a moment they stood whitened in cascades of white; the shovels were dropped and the snow fight was on.

Instantly disorderly, it was not a struggle between the sexes or between two parties; everyone was for himself. Gilpin Murray put his shoulders into a hard push; Hatcher went over backward into the snow. Gilpin fled; the two girls chased and threw him, and Hatcher, on his feet again, overtook and fought all three of them. Beyond, in Butternut Lane, a fifth person came into view— a fat and ruddy youth in evening black, except for the silk scarf that sheltered his throat and upper linen. With difficulty his dancing-shoes were making their way through the highway drifts, and his recent history was plain: he'd been the last guest at the party, possibly found somewhere and awakened during the closing of the festal house. Disregarding his attire and delighted to find friends still up, he immediately turned from the road and put himself into the midst of the snow fight.

Through the dark trunks of trees across the way a clear day came breaking; long stripes of blazing gold light and vaporous blue shadow appeared upon the snow. Rosy-faced and shouting with laughter, the five young people frolicked fantastically in that jubilant light. They scuffled, fought, leaped, fell, fled and pursued. One, feet in air, tried to walk on his hands, and did till overthrown. Then he rose capering—young Hatcher Ide. The five rolled one another in the snow, or, standing to it, sent fountains of white into the gold air to fall upon the others suffocatingly. Then they'd shout, leap and run again. They were like wild figures in a snow ballet, and they were like children who'd never seen snow before.

To the mind of the pale gentleman at the window they were children—children just now, though they'd begin their day's work when the hour came.

"So it goes," Uncle Victor thought. "For them, there's nothing else in the world but themselves and sunrise."

bYV ·T1745he

WITHDRAWN